D1603515

HOUSE WOMAN

A NOVEL

ADORAH NWORAH

The Unnamed Press
Los Angeles, CA

One afternoon at four o'clock we separated
for a week only ... And then –
that week became forever.
—C.P. Cavafy

To Chika, for all the stories.

HOUSE WOMAN

1

August 2019

Nna let out a faint gasp at the sight of the woman in the kitchen. He took in everything – the small head, the big eyes, the pursed lips, the slender neck, the ankle beads, the measured steps, and the dull thumping of a heart, his heart, against a spindly cage. He rubbed his eyes and licked the bits of peeling skin on his lips. He wiped the soles of his Oxford mules on the welcome mat at the entrance to the brick-red mansion on a quiet street in Sugar Land, Texas.

The house was a four-bedroom single family residence built in the early nineties. His parents, Agbala and Eke, took great pride in it as it was the only house they'd ever owned in America. Over the years, they'd hacked at its vestigial parts like the glass block wall that once stood in the foyer till the house bore the brassy gleam of modernity.

Standing by the entrance to his parents' house, Nna wished he'd listened to his mother, Agbala, who often reminded him to comb his hair. As the dusty black Toyota Camry that dropped him at the house began to pull out of the driveway, Nna fished in his pockets for his handy afro pick.

The woman was clad in a thin beach towel that threatened to fall to the ground. He could make out the outline of her buttocks (small, firm). The dull thumping in his chest increased its volume. She was what Agbala – his hurricane of a mother – would fondly call a yellow pawpaw, to be shielded from the sun at all costs.

But she was more than color, she was melody.

She hummed an old Bright Chimezie number, one Agbala often hummed as she chopped bell peppers in the airy open-concept kitchen of the Nwosu family house. But Agbala did not hum the song like the woman in the kitchen. Agbala was not melody.

Nna opened his mouth to introduce himself. A warm draft of stale air tickled his lips as he lowered his eyes to his torso. The Old Navy flannel shirt hung off his body like it didn't ask to be there. It was not entirely his fault. Fridays were jeans day at his white-shoe law firm in Philadelphia, and the wrinkled shirt was the first thing his eyes, weary from reviewing the organizational structure charts of his clients, had seen that morning.

Nna tore his eyes away from the woman's buttocks and tiptoed up the stairs with his suitcase, past the ledge in the upstairs hallway with a framed photograph of himself and his parents from his college graduation, past the upper-level living room, past the master bedroom, past the room his mother slept in whenever she got into a fight with his father, and into his bedroom.

His bedroom – cornflower-blue walls, fraying posters of Kobe Bryant, thumbprints from years of his mother's egusi dinners – smelled of old spice, teenage angst, and balled socks. He pictured his mother Agbala, her hunched back curved like a sickle as she straightened his pillows and sniffed the air for dust.

His palms dove past the blur of Bob Marley tees and khakis in his closet and reached for a washed black tee with a blown-up image of the Jonas Brothers. A month ago, he'd woken up in his Philadelphia row house to a call from his mother. He'd ignored the headache forming across his temple as she complained that he lived too far from Sugar Land, and didn't he know the long distance was taking a toll on her health? He'd refused to concede to her demand that he leave his corporate job in Philadelphia for a boutique oil and gas law firm in Houston. With his mother, it was important to stand one's ground, trembling knees and all – or risk becoming his father Eke. The poor man sought his wife's stamp of approval for everything, down to the number of fried plantains he could have with his jollof.

Nna ran his fingers through his afro and his mother's disapproving face flashed across his eyes. She eyed his hair, the whites of her eyes butter-yellow from too much melanin, or too much glinting at the sun, or too many sleepless nights. He pictured her in that moment, advising him that young Igbo men like himself must keep neat haircuts, not the *ya-ya-ya* hair of black boys in America, lest they (the ubiquitous powers that be) confuse him for a gangster, or worse, an easy corpse. He would turn the conversation around, announce that his law firm had just adopted a hybrid model that allowed associates to work remotely at their choosing. 'I'll be splitting my time between

Philadelphia and Sugar Land, Mom. You get to have me to yourself,' he would say to her, and for a moment, she would forget about his *ya-ya-ya* hair.

He heard the clinking china. The wooden ladle striking the sides of an aluminum pot. The pretty woman's small feet on the kitchen parquet. Was she a guest? An intruder? Dare he ask? He looked at himself in the cast-iron mirror that leaned against his closet. He nodded approvingly at the big arms, the slim waist, and the toned legs – the result of one too many leg days at the gym a block away from his row house in Philadelphia.

He grabbed a wide-tooth comb from his dresser and ran it through his hair. Then cologne. A breath mint. He wanted to impress, and not just a little.

The woman's back was still turned to Nna when he returned to the kitchen, her towel slipping down her torso to reveal a lacy marigold bra as she bustled around the cooker. She stood in front of one of his mother's aluminum pots, the ladle in her right hand and a mitten in her left. There was a greying birthmark, the shape of a heart, on her upper left arm. He opened his mouth to speak but the words at the tip of his tongue sounded dirty and unfinished.

She raised a slender forearm to her lips and licked stew off her palm. Nna wished he was the stew, or that she would teach him to cook stew. She made it look simple. She was simplicity itself, all florals, and mittens, and diced onions, her tight curls neatly tucked behind her ears.

She reached for a serving bowl and her curious eyes connected with the cusp of his lips. He saw her. He saw the mole to the left of her upper lip, the hardness of her jaw, the crook in her nose and the widening of her eyes. She gasped.

'Ikemefuna,' the woman said, matter-of-fact. Her voice was musical, each syllable stretched thin like an octave.

'Excuse me?'

'That's my name.' She grinned.

Nna stared at the smatter of brown freckles above her cheeks, then at her lips, red and pulsing. She smelled of onions and the first spurt of blood from a gash on skin. Standing before the woman in that kitchen, he was painfully aware of his many imperfections. The penis that sometimes reeked of rancid cheese. The gap teeth. The lisp that slipped into his otherwise impeccable intonation (Bachelors at St. John's, Law school at NYU) when he pronounced words like *sleep*.

'I am Nnaemeka,' Nna announced, extending a hand. 'I don't think we have met.'

'We haven't,' she replied. 'But your parents speak highly of you.'

She ignored the outstretched palm and threw her arms around his neck. He felt the softness of her flesh and inhaled it.

'Our parents were neighbors in Lagos many years ago,' she continued. A smile danced along the edges of her lips. 'Yours were smart enough to move to the United States. Mine are still in the same medium-housing flat on the Lagos mainland.'

'I don't remember anything from my Lagos days,' Nna said apologetically. His parents rarely mentioned Lagos. When they did, it was in the abstract.

'Not surprising,' Ikemefuna murmured, stirring the thick red broth in the pot on the cooker.

'How long are you here for?'

'Who knows,' she replied with a flourish as she scooped spoonfuls of smoldering red porridge and threw it into a serving bowl. 'Your parents have been such gracious hosts.'

It was confirmed then. She was staying with his parents, sleeping in their guest room, traipsing their hallways, always accessible, present. She was *his* present.

'You're smiling.'

'You make me smile,' he replied without thought.

Again, Nna thought of his imperfections as he sat at the kitchen table. He slid his tongue across his gap teeth. He shook off the heavy blanket of his inadequacy and muted his thumping heart.

'Extra spicy porridge yam,' Ikemefuna said with a wink as she slid the serving bowl across the industrial kitchen table and towards him. 'Your mother says it's your favorite. Is that right?'

'My mother is always right.'

He sat down at the table and quickly gulped forkfuls of porridge yam, stealing glances at the woman as she bustled around the kitchen, washing pots, and wiping countertops.

'This is the best porridge yam I've ever had,' he said. 'You must teach me to cook it like you do.'

'If I teach you, I'd have to kill you,' Ikemefuna smiled. Then she shook her head and laughed. 'It's an old family recipe that my grandmother passed to my mother, who in turn passed it to me. I'm a little possessive.'

'Some things are worth dying for.'

'Esau agrees with you.'

'Esau?'

'You know? The biblical glutton.'

Nna shook his head with amusement. He was not a Christian and neither were his parents. Save for a pair of crusty Ala figurines flanking the flat screen TV in the living room, the Sugar Land house bore no signs of organized religion. Through the years, Nna had fallen into a lazy agnosticism, a default contentment with not knowing.

When he raised his head from his empty plate, Ikemefuna was already stretching an arm from behind him to clear the kitchen table. He turned to hold her by her waist and sighed with relief when she threw her arms around his neck and pressed her chest to his torso so that the bulb of her nose rubbed against his clavicle. She was small in his arms, malleable, like playdough.

'You should visit Lagos during the festive months,' she whispered. 'You'd fall in love with your people.'

'Promise?'

'When I was much younger, I spent Christmas as a member of a twelve-person Atilogwu group in Enugu. We'd paint our faces with nzu and wear heavy, glass beads around our necks. We walked from compound to compound, dancing till the soles of our feet bled and our pouches brimmed with naira notes.'

'So, you're quite the free spirit?'

'My mother says I have an impatient *chi*. It's always desiring the next adventure.'

'An impatient *chi*?'

'It's the god in you. We all have one,' she insisted. 'Anyway, I spent last Christmas as one of Fela's wives in a sold-out Lagos musical.'

Nna listened to the beautiful woman's tales about palm-wine-fueled mornings at a shrine in Ketu, all-nighter dress

17

rehearsals, and broken English, a build-your-own English with jagged edges that matched the sharp tongues of Lagosians, those ones Ikemefuna called *his people*. He pictured Ikemefuna amongst those people, his people, dancing with vigor in a tiny rapa, her breasts peeking out the top of a bright red ankara.

He listened some more.

She was the only child of her parents. They'd adopted her when she was a few weeks old.

She had a strictly black nail polish policy, except on first dates (chrome white).

She created a new Spotify playlist on her birthdays – an ode to the preceding year.

And he noticed some more.

Her single dimple was on her left cheek.

She planted her hands on her hips to keep stable when she giggled.

'You're beautiful,' he whispered. There. He'd said the words. 'You must get that a lot.'

'I do, but the mouths that sing my praises are often disappointing.' She chuckled. 'Sweaty vulcanizers, traders with invasive hands, and – do my father's balding friends count?'

'I can't believe your boyfriend doesn't write haikus in your name at the crack of dawn.'

Ikemefuna smiled at him. She cupped his left ear in her palms and pressed her lips to it. He pulled her closer to him. He loved her weight on him, melting into him.

'Nna, I don't think I introduced myself properly,' she whispered in his ear. 'My name is Ikemefuna Nwosu, and I am your wife.'

2

Ikemefuna had hoped to reinvent herself in America. The week before her trip to Houston, Nkemdili, her mother's maid, sat at the edge of her mattress and told her that in America, anyone could be anything.

I see am for TV. Just wait and see.

But the America she met was not the one from opening credits in packed Lagos movie theaters. It was a white-columned brick house with high ceilings and shuttered casement windows. It was Nna, staring at her with those hooded eyes of his as he squinted past layers of her foundation and settled on her wrongness.

She could feel it.

His eyes – dark and hooded – seemed oddly familiar. They roamed around her, lingered on her kneecaps, then her flank, then her cheekbones. They danced around the curve of her belly and the soles of her feet, wolfing her down as ravenously as she was drinking him in. She could have sworn she'd seen them before.

Ikemefuna heard Agbala and Eke before he did.

The five-second honk of a tan Toyota RAV4. The music. Bright Chimezie. 'Life Na Teacher'. Always that tune. Agbala's rubber soles on tar. Eke's hobbling. A puff of snow-white hair. A smoke pipe. Matching Senegalese fabrics. Whites (of eyes, of teeth) a murky yellow. Crow's feet that extended to earlobes. Hunched backs.

When Nna looked to his side, Ikemefuna was gone.

She was already at the door, gathering Agbala, then Eke, in her arms. Carrying their wares (a Michael Kors handbag, an umbrella, bananas, newspapers) into the living room. Dishing their bowls of porridge. Nna marveled at how effortlessly Ikemefuna danced between the two, beckoning, and cajoling, and doting, as his parents took turns running their palms against Nna's skin, unimpressed with its dullness and his weight loss.

'Your mother and I were just checking out the shops,' Eke announced as he pressed Nna to his tapered chest. He smelled of pain ointment and tear rubber. 'Summer is the busiest season, you know.'

Agbala owned three hair salons in the greater Houston area, a business she grew out the living room of a Southwest Houston apartment some twenty-five years ago. When she'd first moved to Houston from Lagos, she braided the hairs of the West African women in her apartment complex to supplement Eke's cab-driving income. Then the booking fees and no-show fees she charged her customers began to add up and she moved her braiding business to the back room of a barber shop on Bissonet Street.

Twenty-five years later and *Agbala's Braiding, Inc.* was three salons deep and the go-to spot in the Greater Houston area for crochet braids and goddess locs.

Agbala pulled Nna against her chest and planted a kiss on his cheek.

'Nna'm, thank you for finding the time to visit us, o! I was starting to wonder if I still had a son,' she teased.

'Come on, Mom! I call you and Dad all the time,' Nna protested.

'The phone calls are not nearly enough,' Eke said. 'We can use your presence around the house.'

'I'll be home for a while, Dad,' Nna announced with a flourish. 'My firm is allowing us to work from anywhere in the country. In fact, I only need to be in Philadelphia for work events.'

'*Ewo!* So you're moving back to Houston?' Agbala cried.

'Slow down, Mom. Consider this a trial run,' he joked.

Agbala squealed with delight, her sunken cheeks rising and falling with every heave.

'We're happy to have you, son,' Eke said, coughing up a dry chuckle and patting Nna's back.

'Nna, I see you have met Ikemefuna,' Agbala crooned, beaming at Ikemefuna as she shoved forkfuls of porridge yam into her mouth.

'Yes, Mom. Forgive me but I don't recall any mention of a guest in the house,' he said, his eyes darting between Agbala and Ikemefuna. 'And certainly not my *wife*,' he continued, a baffled smile gilded to his lips.

Agbala stroked Nna's inner arm in quick short sweeps to keep him calm.

'Ikemefuna, did you tell Nna that we once shared a compound with your parents?' she asked.

Nna threw a sharp look at his mother. It was just like her to change the subject if she wasn't prepared to divulge information. He eyed Ikemefuna. She leaned against a wall in the living room lined with wood carvings carted from a flea market in Katy the previous summer. He wished he could capture the flecks of brown in her eyes and the lumpy bulb of her nose. He imagined her parents, a man and woman with polished oak skin, waving at the lens of a camera like generic African characters in a stock photo.

Ikemefuna started to reply just as Agbala jumped out of her seat. Nna watched Agbala's headscarf fly off her head and land on the shagreen coffee table in the living room. He threw Ikemefuna an apologetic smile. He'd once reserved a similar smile for his American friends in eighth grade each time they visited the house and had to grit their teeth through shaki and ponmo.

Nna leaned closer to Ikemefuna.

'Sorry,' he started to say to Ikemefuna, a shamefaced grin on his face. 'My mother worships Ala, the Igbo goddess of fertility. She breaks into these trances without warning.'

His grin froze in place.

There was a distant look in her eyes. He grabbed her shoulders.

'Ikemefuna, can you hear me?' he called.

Ikemefuna raised her eyes to his face and stared back at him through hard, flinty eyes.

The nausea hit Ikemefuna in waves, rocking her body from side to side. She leaned against the yolk-colored wall to keep from falling to the floor. Something cold and heavy grabbed her by her shoulders. A person. He yelled words at her as she steadied her feet.

Ikemefuna shut her eyes and tried to sift past the loud voice. To practice breathing. She opened her eyes to the living room.

How long had she been standing by the wood carvings?

She scanned the living room. The high stucco walls. The thick vinyl windows with interlocking sashes. Nna was gone, had likely disappeared to his bedroom. But she was not alone. From a corner of her eye, she could make out Agbala and Eke swaying round the shagreen coffee table. Ikemefuna swallowed the lump in her throat. Though she'd been living with the Nwosus for a month, their religious rituals still unnerved her. She made for the kitchen to clear the leftover porridge yam from the kitchen table.

Agbala and Eke stopped swaying and glared at her, their eyes bright with urgency.

'So what do you think?' Agbala asked.

'He's very nice.'

'Did you take off his shoes and massage his feet like I asked you to?' Agbala pressed.

Something scampered across the ceiling. A mouse.

Eke threw a fearful look at the stairway.

'Careful, woman. Keep your voice down,' he chided Agbala.

'I didn't get a chance to. He'd already changed out of his shoes when I saw him,' Ikemefuna confessed. Her throat was dry.

'You should listen to her when she advises you,' Eke said, his steely gaze on Ikemefuna. Though he harbored his private misgivings about Agbala's approach, there was no denying that his wife was a smart woman. Agbala's smarts were his favorite thing about her. He liked that with her, he did not have to be the head of the house. Not in the way other Nigerian husbands clamored for that body part, dogging out their wives like pit bulls in a ring.

'Anyway, you have now met our son,' Agbala said. Somewhere above the living room, something heavy clattered to the floor. Eke threw another sharp look at the stairs. His Adam's apple slid up his throat.

'I think he likes what he sees,' Eke said. His epicene face broke into an impish grin that caused it to contract, then swallowed it whole. 'Nna is a smart boy. He knows that Agbala and I are behind this, err, arrangement.' He paused, deep in thought. 'Nevertheless, he's intrigued by you. Like I said, he likes what he sees.'

'Your job is to erase his doubts about you. Show him you are wife material. Remember all we taught you,' Agbala said.

'Yes ma,' Ikemefuna hummed.

'You must be ladylike. Cross your legs and shine your teeth. But not too much. You are a girl, not a goat.'

'Yes ma.'

'Remember to call him Nna'm. It's our pet name for him. It'll break the ice.'

'Yes ma.'

'*Ehen*. Did you mention that you dance?' Eke added. 'Did you show him some moves? Your mother said you are a very good dancer, and our son loves good dancers.'

'Yes sir, I told him I dance but I didn't get a chance to dance for him.'

'Very well. Make sure you dance for him in the coming days.'

'Yes, o. Dance for him,' Agbala said, waving a palm in the air dismissively. 'But remember the most important thing. You must please him very well.'

'Enough with the innuendos, woman,' Eke interjected. He threw Agbala a furtive look, unsure of how she would react to *woman*. He'd seen his friends hurl *woman* at their wives like cherry bombs, their throats quivering with righteous indignation. He'd wanted to slip that word on, to have it caul his tongue.

'Ikemefuna, you must sleep with Nna tonight. You must sleep with him every night. Show him you're a real woman, you hear me?'

'Yes sir.'

'Remember what we told you?' Agbala asked.

'Ehh. Which one?'

'Is there a single thing you remember?' Agbala hissed. 'We told you that you must prove you are fertile before the wedding. He's our only child and he needs an heir to continue the family name. Your parents are aware that we won't go through with this arrangement until you do your part.'

'I remember, ma.'

'Time is of the essence and wives are like germs, child. They are everywhere. If you can't give him a son within a month, we'll find a woman who can.'

Ikemefuna looked away from Agbala. She bit her nails, a bad habit she'd picked up at ten and never put down. Omoye, her childhood friend who worked as a nail technician in Lagos, would be disappointed if she saw the state of her fingernails, how quickly the shiny shellac had cracked into tiny pieces upon arriving in America.

Houston, eh. I know Houston, Omoye had whispered conspiratorially on the eve of Ikemefuna's departure, her peppery breath falling on Ikemefuna's chest as she painted Ikemefuna's nails. *Abeg, no forget me when you go, oh. Me sef I wan find Naija man for Houston.* Ikemefuna had promised to remember Omoye, to find Omoye her own Nigerian-American husband in Houston. But that was before Ikemefuna clutched the scratchy armrest on her bumpy fifteen-hour flight. Before plastic cups of orange juice and irritable hostesses who glared at dusk-black Nigerian travelers and hated them for their loud chatter. It was before Houston, and Ikemefuna wringing her palms in the back seat of Agbala and Eke's tan Toyota RAV4 as it sped away from the George Bush International Airport. Before she arrived at the brick-red house with wrought-iron banisters that stretched to the second floor. Before Agbala scrubbed the dirt from her nails and taught her to cook porridge yam with just the right amount of bleached palm oil.

'Eke and I have weak stomachs, so we better head to our bedroom,' Agbala said. A thin line of perspiration had formed above her upper lip. 'Now remember, Nna likes massages. Offer to massage him. Lie with him, pull him close to you, till you feel his full length in you . . .'

Ikemefuna looked away from Agbala's bulging eyes and fleshy lips and at the latticed front door of the house. She leaned against a wall to steady her feet. Suddenly, she felt weightless, like she was free-falling through a vertical tunnel. She tried to latch on to the living room's Mesa

Brown upholstery but her attempts only heightened the feeling.

It was exactly a month since she arrived in Houston with two identical cornrows and an airy green ankara jumpsuit that her mother Adina's tailor had stitched together in the rushed hours before her flight. A month since she opened her eyes and mouth to America. The sparkly blue skyscrapers. The lightning-speed metro rail. The weather-beaten cowboy hats. The greasy pepperoni pizza slapped on paper plates.

Everything was different in America.

The movies did not do it justice, could not capture the olive on skin, or the white, or the black that was so different from her black, and yet, the same, or the voices, or the eyes that stared straight ahead and not at her, never at her, like she was invisible, like it was her birthright to exist uninterrupted, like they did not care to dissect her body, or her hair, or her choice of clothes like everyone in Lagos did, and she loved America for the freedom in its air. She was America. *America-wonda*.

She continued to take in America as she popped acne on her chin in the ladies' restroom at the airport. As she waited for her hosts, arms outstretched, moony smile as warm as freshly baked chocolate chip cookies.

Her mother Adina had described her hosts as the kindest people she knew. *And don't forget their son*, her father Dumeje had chimed in from a corner of his lips. *A lawyer, no less. Handsome man*. There had been a vein in his temple. Adina had squeezed her palms. *First impressions are so important, Nne. These men know whether they want to sex you or marry you just from looking at you from head to toe.*

They will never look at my daughter and decide to sex her. Say amen.

'What are you doing, you devil!' Agbala coughed, gasping for air.

Ikemefuna blinked. She was back in the present, and hungry. She could sneak into the kitchen, cook something, or she could—

She stared at her outstretched arms. Thin and veiny and curled around the loose skin of Agbala's neck.

3

'The devil lives in you,' Agbala cried, tightening her rapa around her waist. 'Did you hear me? You are the devil herself.'

'I don't know what happened,' Ikemefuna whispered. She clutched her forehead as she sank to the marble.

'*Shhh*,' Eke hushed her. 'Enough.' He led a shaken Agbala up the stairs, his eyes on Ikemefuna till he and Agbala were out of sight.

Alone in the living room, Ikemefuna listened for the click of their door. She hobbled past the heavy-duty Mesa Brown upholstery and towards the sliding glass door in the kitchen that led to the backyard. She tugged the door's edges. It did not budge, had not moved an inch since she arrived at the house. She pressed her ear to the cool glass. She could hear snatches of muted conversation pouring out from the neighbor's backyard.

She missed Lagos. The predictable hum of bus conductors and hawkers. The mallams who left their wares to pray for her when she arrived at their kiosks with a busted lip. Houston was a fever dream, her head bowed, her hair parted, her body scrubbed clean for her husband.

The blackouts were just as bad in Houston.

She'd first experienced the blackouts as a child. They showed up when she was frustrated by her parents or her classmates, brief lapses in time during which she flung the nearest stationary objects at the people around her. In recent months, they had increased in frequency, overriding her senses at the slightest provocation. The last blackout happened towards the end of the dry season in Lagos, in her bedroom, swirls of dust-laden Harmattan wind pounding against the louvers as she watched her best friend Nneka and Nneka's boyfriend Obinna wrestle with their tongues by her bedroom door.

Ikemefuna eyed the digital clock on her phone. 3:15 p.m. Two hours till her parents returned to the flat. She contemplated asking Nneka and Obinna to leave. She couldn't bear the thought of her parents walking in on Nneka and Obinna's pelvic thrusts in the searing afternoon heat.

'Nneka. Obi,' Ikemefuna called out, her voice low, cautious.

She'd met Nneka at a neighborhood Afrobeats dance class a decade ago. At the time, they were rangy teenagers with seeds for breasts. Their friendship relied on Nneka's talkativeness and Ikemefuna assuming the de facto good listener role.

'Ike, what is it now?' Nneka groaned.

A bout of nausea washed over Ikemefuna. She tried to speak but only managed a low retching sound.

'*Nawa o!*' Nneka cried. 'Will you act like this if Bobo toasts you?'

She'd confided in Nneka that she had a crush on Bobo, their soft-spoken new dance instructor. Bobo – rumored to be in his early thirties, had arrived in Lagos from Oyo after losing his engineering job at a local plastic sheeting supplier.

Ikemefuna clutched her forehead. The bedroom shifted in and out of focus. She stumbled across the room and reached for Nneka's arm to steady her feet.

'What are you doing?' Nneka cried.

Ikemefuna pushed Nneka's voice out her head. She needed to concentrate on …

Squeezing Obinna's neck.

The realization of what she was doing hit her. She gasped, let go of Obinna's neck.

'What is wrong with you?' Nneka screeched.

'Psycho,' Obinna sputtered, his thick fingers massaging his neck.

At the time, she'd blamed the Harmattan, chucked it up to poor sleep.

She was wrong.

4

It was a quarter to midnight in Sugar Land.

Ikemefuna paced the Nwosus' living room and eyed the stairway leading to the house's upper level. All three Nwosus were upstairs. She hadn't seen or heard a peep from them since Agbala and Eke bounded up the stairs.

Her entire sex education comprised of steamy Harlequin novels and Nneka's sexcapades with Obinna.

Ike, you shoulda seen the way I jiggled my nyash for Obinna!

Nene, why would I want to see that?

So you can learn a thing or two! Heh!

Ikemefuna stilled her nerves as she climbed the stairs ascending from the foyer to the bedrooms on the second floor of the house. She hurried past the door to Agbala and Eke's bedroom and into a tiny bedroom next to it. Surrounded by the burnt clementine walls and damp stench of her bedroom, she peeled off her clothes and shut her eyes. Nna's face crowded her mind. His hooded eyes and gap teeth. His tubular bottom lip. Was he a twin? She was certain she'd seen him somewhere.

She racked her brain for where she'd previously seen Nna, listening to the sound of American wind rustling

American shrubs. She imagined the bluebonnets and carpet grass in the garden below her window, the feel of the twigs beneath her feet.

Her first night in America, she'd stood by the barbecue grill in the backyard and watched the dragonflies hop from stem to tarpaulin. Eke had whispered to her, matter-of-fact, that only white bodies and hardworking olive, brown, and black bodies could afford to live in the neighborhood. That his and Agbala's work ethic had earned them the right to live there and the neighbors respected them for it.

She'd imagined a real barbecue, pictured the neighbors filling the hot summer air with impressive tales of their kids' college admissions. They would whisper apple pie recipes, recommend lawnmowers, politely decline suya, take enough jabs at Mr Trump to distance themselves from his rhetoric, then bite the heads off their hot dogs.

Agbala and Eke had given her a tour of the house she would live in for the next two weeks. An open-concept living room and kitchen flanked by high stucco walls and shuttered casement windows. A windowless dining room with a glass-top dinner table and pastel walls. Wrought-iron banisters that curved up towards an upstairs hallway.

Upstairs – a bedroom-turned-study with engineered hardwood floors and book-dust air. An upper-level living room with arched windows and rolled-arm couches. A master bedroom that smelled of fish oil and soursop. Nna's room – sunlit and speckled with outdated posters. A tiny room with burnt orange walls. In it, a twin bed with wrinkled sheets. *Yours*, Agbala and Eke crooned in unison.

All of that was a long time ago.

Ikemefuna rose from her bed and gave herself a pep talk. Harlequin had taught her that sex was nothing but scouring a body for sensation, or a gold star, or acceptance, or apology, or love. Sex was a gift to be given, or it was taking. She channeled Nneka's carefree swagger as she sauntered out of the room.

She stood in front of Nna's room, heart in mouth, fist poised to knock. Then she was in the room, giggling loudly as she tiptoed to his bed. The sound coming out her mouth was hers, or it was not hers at all. She tiptoed faster, until she stood by the bed and next to a wall flecked with posters of Kobe and dead rappers from the nineties. Nna lay on his bedsheets, wrapped in chest hairs and Fruit of the Loom boxers. He was fiddling with a laptop. He raised his eyes to her face and arched a brow.

She sat at the edge of his bed, untied her rapa and let it pool at her feet. There was a dull weight on her flank. The laptop disappeared. Nna's palms pulled her closer till she was on top of him and lying on his chest. The purple bruises on her back were quiet. Not a murmur of protest. Not even laughter.

A pungent stench filled the air as Nna pulled down his boxers. The closest description – a whiff of rotten cheese. Ikemefuna swallowed the warm rush of bile that bubbled up her throat. She ran her palms against the sides of Nna's face, his eyelids. She scoured his body for sensation. He did the taking, emptying her of all she could give, once, twice, again and again, and then it was over, and she was clutching her rapa with shaky fingers, tying it against her skin, and tucking the excess cloth in the space between her breasts, and scurrying out of his bedroom.

She returned to her room with its damp air and darkness.

Her skin hummed softly, its buzz indistinct from the surrounding quiet. She ran her palms along her breasts, then against her belly to silence the hum. She fanned the damp heat between her legs. She'd had the sex Nneka always bragged about, but it was nothing like the sweet ecstasy Nneka had described to her. It was rushed and uncomfortable and required a great deal of holding one's breath.

She never wanted to relive the experience, but it was out of her control, wasn't it? Agbala and Eke had insisted that she must sleep with him every day until she was pregnant with his child – a baby boy with Nna's tarry skin and meaty cheeks.

Then what?

Then there would be the down time, losing the baby fat, falling in love with her body all over again, or for the first time. A wedding. A thing to plan, to incite a shedding of fat. She would adopt the paleo diet, or intermittent fasting, or Whole 30, or all the above. It would be a small ceremony at a courthouse, only open to close friends and family. She would pose for photographs on the courthouse steps. Adina and Dumeje would send their well wishes via WhatsApp. It was better than Dumeje spending fifteen hours on an airplane. Gritting his teeth through microwaveable airplane peas. Adina smiling nervously as Dumeje cursed at airport security for seizing his stockfish.

Then what?

Then she would taste America, extend her tongue to suck its skyscrapers, and its metro rail, and its cowboy hats, and its pepperoni pizza slapped on paper plates. Agbala's smile would reach her eyes, and Eke would stop watching her like she was an endangered thing. She would apply for a job as a cultural dancer at Disney, focus on her Atilogwu.

Ma, do you think he'll let me be a professional dancer?

Who?

My husband.

Of course he will. Being a wife comes with so many freedoms. Now, stop looking at me with those sad eyes. This arrangement is a good thing, you know?

Then Nna would take her to Philadelphia. He would show her his row house in Fairmount. She would make him show her a speakeasy, a comedy club, the Liberty Bell, frozen margaritas, chicken biryani, a fortune cookie, a thick pile of Philly cheesesteaks.

Then what?

Then she would settle into that new life, the new her – Ikemefuna, the wife, or Ikemefuna, the mother, or all the above. She would get a job and she would try her best to befriend the other dancers. It would be hard, what with her accent, and her natural penchant for the edges of rooms, and her distinct ability to drown in other people's worlds, in their awfully cliché crooked smiles.

But she would try.

She would learn to small talk, watch YouTube tutorials if she must. To pay a lot of compliments. To flash a non-threatening smile. To flaunt her accent. To stumble on her English then pick herself up. She would make the Americans love her. She would let them touch her hair.

Then what?

Then maybe she'd finally remember why Nna looked so familiar. Maybe he was the man of her dreams. Maybe she'd seen him in a dream—

Ikemefuna's rambling thoughts froze in place.

She knew where she'd seen Nna.

It had taken her hours to remember, because how could one make the connection?

His hooded eyes and gap teeth. The smatter of moles on his cheeks. That unusually thick bottom lip.

Nna was the spitting image of her mother, Adina.

5

January 1990

Adina Azubuike was not a very Christian woman.

It was true that when she was younger, she attended St Mary's Catholic Church in Amawbia every Sunday with her father, mother and seven sisters, and bible study on Wednesdays, and choir practice on Saturdays, a wilting daffodil in her hair as she sang 'Ave Maria' for the ninth time in a row. It was also true that she knew the King James' version of the book of Mark by heart and could dry fast for seven days without taking a day off from the fresh fruit stall she manned in Yaba. She was Christian, all right. A fact as clear as broad daylight. But she was not, you know, *Christian* Christian.

Somewhere between memorizing the gospel and singing out her lungs in choir practice, her faith missed a step and wobbled.

It was a quiet faltering, that. It kept to itself and swallowed its tremors as Adina continued to buy different colored bibles at her church retreats. She strategically placed the bibles in the nooks of the flat she shared with her husband, Dumeje.

A blood-red bible stashed beneath the threadbare divan in the living room.

A worn leather bible that carried the faint smell of herbal pomade simmering beneath her pillow.

A Hebrew bible, its words as foreign as her faith, greeting visitors from where it leaned against the ocher vase on her dining table.

Adina secretly hoped that her bibles would distract onlookers from the fact that the Sunday praise and worship that fell off her lips did not stick to her heart. She worried that if they burnished their horn-rimmed lenses and looked closely enough, they would see that she was exactly that brand of sinner in the bible parable. The one who heard the word and knew the word but did not let its roots sink into her heart.

Yet even with all her lack of God, she felt particularly Roman Catholic on that night, for how else could a woman who knew nothing but pulpits process the fact that she was sitting on the cold concrete of a backyard, her legs wide ajar? There was, after all, nothing more Christian than her righteous indignation at the moment's barbarity.

She took a deep breath and swatted a mosquito with the back of her hand. She shut her eyes so that her lashes gently caressed the thin bags beneath each eye. The moment was reminiscent of an old Nollywood set with all its provincial charm. She only needed to tilt her head to the right to see the ominous cowry shells in Tupperware, the red wax candles and their devilish gleam, the chicken feathers matted in dark brown blood, and the palm wine sprinkled against the wall.

To add fuel to fire, her neighbor, Agbala suddenly broke into tongues as Eke, her neighbor's husband, struggled to keep a tatty black yarmulke on his head.

A faithless woman does not land on the cold cement in the quiet of a Tuesday night without motivation.

On the night in question, she was a shapeless shadow. The skin of her belly and the back of her legs glittered with open wounds. She wiped the fresh blood on her stomach and said a silent prayer to her old friend, the Christian God.

6

August 2019

Nna woke up with Ikemefuna on his mind.

It was exactly two years since he last woke up with a woman on his mind (Bunmi, and before her, Zainab), and the realization caused a doughy lump (of excitement, fear) to rise up his chest.

He lay beneath his sheets, thinking of Ikemefuna. Fun-sized. The eyes of a hawk. Talkative, shy, then both at once. Beautiful from a distance, beautiful through eyes tired from a four-hour flight, eyes drawn to small, firm buttocks (his Achilles' heel). But something else too. Something not beautiful (that word suddenly tired), not striking (too cliché) when one came close enough to notice the intricate details. The face stitched together with care, each herringbone a near-perfect zigzag. The nothingness in her eyes. The odd slant of her grin.

He was haunted by his brief forays with love, like that one time it caused him to co-sign a two-year lease and co-parent a rescue pug before he learned of Zainab's chest hairs and her herpes problem (or HP, as she fondly nicknamed it) or the nonexistent hairline beneath Bunmi's signature Mongolian tresses from Alibaba.

But he would be careful this time. He was sure of it, what with all the growing up he had done since Bunmi yelled 'It's over,' vintage Nollywood-style, in the bustling parking lot of a Target. He would watch Ikemefuna closely. Inventory everything about her. He would make her rip herself open for him, then he would crawl inside. He would sample the texture of her navel and the viscosity of her ribs, till he knew the parts of her that were more bone than flesh. Then he would make a reservation or demand a full refund, because ultimately, he was the one who decided whether Ikemefuna was worthy of *Wife*.

That word.

Ikemefuna had spat it at his feet, like it was a threat, him a lowly prisoner, his rights revoked. *Wife*. It was a person one met, dated, and proposed to. *Wife* went through a rigorous vetting process and came out unscathed. *Wife* followed the walking down an aisle and the two-week vacation in Bali. *Wife* rode the elephants gracefully, knew the perfect poses to maximize Instagram likes, had a slight British accent.

Wife slipped into a man's vocabulary as it cozied up to him in bed. *Wife* was beautiful even upon close inspection, smelled of rosehip oil and honeysuckle, had an aliveness to her eyes, flashed a nonthreatening smile that revealed straight white rows. *Wife* was not thrown around in vain, and yet, Ikemefuna had declared it last night, in the kitchen of his parents' house, then again when she slithered into his room clad in nothing but a rapa and held him between her legs.

Nna heard the clatter of pots and pans as he reached for the work laptop he'd pushed beneath his bed in the moments before last night's lovemaking. He scrolled through Outlook for missed emails as he pictured Ikemefuna cavorting around the kitchen in her flimsy rapa. Notwithstanding his study abroads in Sydney and Madrid, he was Nigerian enough to know that arranged marriages remained the norm in Nigerian backwaters.

It was how his parents became husband and wife. Eke's father handpicked Agbala out of her nine sisters. He saw beyond her diaper rash to the childbearing hips that would grow out her flank, a fact that Agbala wore like a badge of honor. He was Nigerian enough to know that arranged marriages were a reality, and Nigerian enough to be righteously repulsed by them. To put his foot down.

But Nna's foot did not stay down for long. It hovered above the parquet as he stood by the sliding glass door in the kitchen and stared at Ikemefuna.

She looked younger than the previous day – face scrubbed clean of blush and lipstick, hair in donut buns. Younger than the version of her who kissed him fiercely in bed the previous night, dug her nails into his back.

'Eggs for you,' Ikemefuna announced, a sweet smile on her cherubic face.

Nna raised a brow. Ladies loved a raised brow.

'Ah. I see you're feeling better today,' he murmured. He still remembered the previous night, her back to the living room's wall, her eyes cold and vacant.

'Sorry?' she croaked.

She lowered her eyes to his lips, his jaw.

He let his eyes roam too. To the baby hairs sticking out the perimeters of her head, their tendrils clinging to the sides of her face. The smile that managed to be larger than her face without extending to the corners of her eyes. The chipped interstellar blue nail polish coating her nails.

'You seemed out of it in the living room last night,' he said.

Realization flooded her face. She turned away from him and stirred the scrambled eggs on the cooker.

'It was a long day. I must have been tired,' she mumbled.

Not too tired for sex, he wanted to add, but it would be ungentlemanly of him to bring up the previous night's lovemaking without cause. He took the flat-top ladle from her hand, started to scoop eggs from the skillet.

'Don't!' Ikemefuna yelled, her voice hollow. She smacked his hand. The ladle bounced off the parquet.

'Stop it!' she shrieked.

Her shallow breaths filled the kitchen. Nna massaged his knuckles. She held Nna's eyes then looked away.

'I – I'm sorry,' she whispered, her eyes averted. 'I didn't mean to hit you. It's just, I get jumpy when people are in *my* kitchen.'

He looked at her crestfallen face and sighed. It was impossible to be mad at her.

'Come here,' he murmured into her hair. He planted a kiss on her forehead. She pulled away from him and raised her eyes to his face.

'What?' she said.

'Huh?'

'You're grinning.'

'You turn me to mush, okay? I can't help it.'

It was true. She did. He liked how he felt around her. Like big spoon and farm hands, all grisly and manly, and – archaic cultural practice aside, he had to admit there was something inherently romantic about an Igbo woman flying thousands of miles to be with him. His real-life woman, to be loved and cherished till she was as wrinkled as a Meishan pig.

'You turn me to mush too,' she said, the corners of her lips lifting into a smile.

'Say it like you mean it,' he said, his voice low and gravely. Women liked it when men asked them to repeat their words midway through charged flirtation tennis. It amped the sexual tension.

Ikemefuna scraped the eggs from the skillet. She seemed flustered. Like something he said had offended her.

Nna swallowed his frustration. She was sensitive, which meant he must tread carefully.

'Eat,' she said, placing a plate of eggs on the kitchen table.

'My Nigerian friends are obsessed with Igbo girls. *Igbo girls are beautiful. Igbo girls are heartbreakers*,' Nna started. He gulped a forkful of eggs. Peppery, just like he liked it.

'Only us? *Nawa o!*' she laughed.

He didn't mention the other things he'd heard about Igbo girls, like how they made a man wait for sex, beg for it. Ikemefuna was the exception to the rule. The sex was a welcome surprise.

'*Nna'm*, are you liking the eggs?' she yelled as she bustled around the kitchen, throwing silverware into cupboards, and cleaning the granite countertops with a paper towel.

Nna'm.

His parents were the only ones who gave him that pet name. *My Nna* – an enduring reminder that he belonged to them. She must be taking pointers from them.

He swallowed a second forkful of eggs. Agbala must have given her cooking lessons too, he thought to himself as he savored the fluffiness of her eggs.

'They are delicious. Want some?' he said through a mouthful of eggs.

'Nnaemeka Nwosu,' she sighed. On her tongue, his name was a song. 'Has no one in this America cautioned you against talking with a full mouth? Finish chewing, *biko*. Then tell me more about yourself.'

'Let me get this straight,' he said. He paused for effect, a bewildered expression on his face. 'Is my *wife* admitting she knows nothing about her so-called husband?'

She shrugged.

He cleared his throat.

'Look, Ikemefuna. I'm not sure how things work in Lagos,' he started. 'But over here in America, we go on dates to be sure we like each other. We do the relationship thing for at least a year or two. We don't just rush into marriages.'

'*I'm not sure how things work in Lagos, but out here in America,*' she bellowed. She broke into giggles, the loud infectious kind that caused the skin to stretch.

'What's so funny?'

'For starters, your accent. You speak like an American. You rush your words like you are in a hurry to get to the end. Why are you rushing, Nnaemeka Nwosu?'

Nna felt a tightness in his groin. He stared at his thighs, at the knuckles pushing against his papery skin. He released his fists and threw an embarrassed look at Ikeme-funa, prepared to explain away his knee-jerk reaction to her teasing.

Hot tempered was how his fifth-grade geometry teacher described him to Agbala and Eke on open day.

Ikemefuna stood by the cooker, her back to him as she scraped the charred egg remnants off the skillet.

'If this thing, this *arrangement* …' The word was sour on his tongue, '… is to work, we must do it right. I insist on a date.'

Dates were all he knew, a ritual of sorts with the girls who stormed in and out of his life. Two-day cruises to the Bahamas. Disney-themed weekend getaways. Home-cooked dinners in makeshift restaurants (his backyard, his bed). The clinking of fluted champagne glasses as Oliver de Coque filled the air. He would watch the girl swoon over his attention to detail then stumble into her love for him beneath the soft glow of a rattan pendant. He would savor the imagery of her teeth sinking into a moist slice of lime-macerated tres leches as she sketched her custom-made Andrea Iyamah wedding gown in her head.

He would ease Ikemefuna into loving him, take her to Larry's ice-cream parlor in Westheimer, study her from a corner of his eye as she licks butter pecan off her fingers. He would roll his eyes at her when she sticks out her tongue like Genevieve Nnaji in that one movie with Ramsey Noah. He would take her to the comedy club downtown, learn the varied notes of her laughter. He would capture her raunchy photos in an empty parking lot in a seedy part of town for the 'gram. She would kiss him hungrily in the backseat of his car and he would remind her to breathe, to take things slow, to not be too in love with him, to enjoy this arrangement. She would listen. She would be slow. It would be different from last night, their foreheads and teeth bumping, the soles of her feet running for the door.

'No.'

'No?' Nna repeated.

He stared at Ikemefuna's back, stunned. None of the girls before her had ever turned him down when he proposed a date. He would say the magic words and they would instinctively search their closets for low-cut tops and taffeta skirts. They would beam with pride when he showed up to their buildings in his Porsche Cayenne.

He swallowed. An unsettling thought crossed his mind.

'Were you being honest when you said you didn't have a man?'

'I wasn't.'

He inhaled sharply. The moment came into focus – the industrial kitchen table littered with breakfast remnants. An open loaf of bread. Spilled Coffee-Mate. Black pepper flakes. A broken fingernail, likely Ikemefuna's.

There was another man.

Did he have a broader, hairier chest, a softer smile? Did she like that he had a broader, hairier chest, a softer smile? Did he live in Lagos, in the thick of her world, front row at the Fela musicals and Atilogwu flash mobs? Surely, he could not out-earn Nna. It was mathematically impossible. Not with that sorry naira-dollar exchange rate.

'I have a man. His name is Nnaemeka Nwosu,' Ikemefuna continued with a wink.

Nna exhaled.

'You got jokes,' he said, a playful grin yanking at his lips.

'I'm saving the best one for our first date,' she said, and when he caught her eyes, there was something in them. A wildness, fevered and pulsing – like she was waiting for him to sweep her off her feet and out the door.

7

David. Blond, stocky, perpetually tousled hair. Pressed his forehead to the windowpane in his bedroom and peered at the quiet street below. Any minute from now, his mother Mary would return from Pilates, upsetting the house's serenity as she pranced from room to room in her Chloé kitten heels, recounting the minutiae of her day to an entirely ambivalent David.

If you were any more lethargic, you'd be dead, David!

David winced at the sound of his mother's voice in his head. He looked up from the empty stretch of road outside his mother's house and eyed the upstairs bedroom in the neighbor's house. He felt his cheeks flush as he waited for movement from behind the fiberglass.

'Come on,' he hummed beneath his breath, his tongue wet from anticipation. 'Come on.'

He'd first seen her a month ago.

She'd raised her blinds just as he walked to his window to draw his curtains. He'd stopped in his tracks. It was the first time he'd seen anyone in that window since *forever*.

He'd not left the windowsill. He watched, just like back in seventh grade when Leila's pencil fell to the floor and he dove to get it, only to meet the crotch of her bright peach panties. He'd known, just like he'd known in seventh grade, that he was looking at something someone had forgotten to hide, and that he ought to look away.

But he couldn't stop looking. At the woman. At the contours of her body. And not for the obvious reasons. She was not his type. A little too curvy for his taste. And yet, watching her peel off her clothes as she bustled around the room was cinema. Looking away would be a disservice to art.

He watched her shoulders. She might have been dancing but he wasn't certain. Her movements were nothing like he'd ever seen before. Something about the way her shoulders hunched together – the hesitation in each forward motion – felt like a trainwreck on standby, the rush before a collision, and every carnage needed a witness.

He'd remembered to breathe only after she drew the blinds shut, completely oblivious to him. Since then, he'd been desperate for more. Just one more look.

'Come on,' he moaned into the sweet dust of his bedroom.

8

Early mornings were her favorite time of the day in America – the Nwosus tucked away in their bedrooms as the morning sun softened the asphalt in the driveway. Gusts of warm air puttering out the air vents in the house. The ritual of massaging her facial muscles. Of readying them for her rehearsed smiles.

She stood by her bedroom window with its iron sash locks. Her fingers wandered to the locks though she knew that trying to unlock them was futile.

A week had passed since her first night with Nna.

She'd since learned he liked to have sex in the dark, with his shirt and socks on. Sometimes, she tolerated the smell of his penis. Other times, the stench was so bad that she held her breath till she feared she would die. On some nights, she pretended he was Bobo, her beautiful instructor from dance practice.

On others, she would catch a glimpse of his eyes or his teeth and it would take everything in her to remember that he was not her mother.

She'd spent a week coming up with the reasons he resembled her mother. A cursed coincidence. A trick of the light. Except the resemblance was as uncanny in daylight as it was at night, the warm amber of the living room's rice lamps emphasizing the shape of his eyes and the indentation in his jaw.

The more she looked, the more she saw. The slight skip in his walk. The falter in his smile, its left side wavering mid-curl. A vine of moles climbing up his cheeks.

Was he her mother's cousin, twice removed? Her mother's brother? And if that was the case, who were the Nwosus?

The possibilities were endless. Just thinking about them made her skin crawl.

It was impossible to ignore his face. It stared back at her every day.

She racked her brain.

Nna had no recollection of his Lagos days, so he likely didn't know of the glaring resemblance.

She could confront Agbala and Eke with her observation, but she wouldn't. She did not trust them to tell her the truth.

What to do?

According to Nneka, men loved snooping around their woman's things. Granted, Obinna mostly snooped because he suspected Nneka was cheating on him, but men were more or less the same, weren't they?

She dug through the side pockets of her luggage for the browning photograph of Adina she'd brought with her from Lagos. It was an old photograph from her mother's younger years, but it was all she had. She scanned the room for a hiding spot – somewhere Nna could find the photograph if he decided to do some snooping of his own.

A door slammed open. She could hear the patter of feet tumbling down the stairs. The voice of a man belting out the lyrics to an Adekunle Gold jam. She should be out in the open, staring her husband in the eye. She should be bending her knees and bowing her head like the good wife.

Ikemefuna scuttled down the stairs in her shimi and a pair of drawstring shorts. She jogged past the foyer, through the living room and into the kitchen. Nna stood by the sink, drawing up the blinds. Sunlight spilled into the room. It illuminated the oak panels and granite countertops.

She could try her luck, ask him to take her on a walk. But what if her voice gave her away and he suspected something?

She must be careful. Just the other night, Agbala caught her tugging at the front door of the house.

Madam! I am watching you, o! Don't force me to kill you.

'You're awake,' Nna announced.

The kitchen came into focus. Nna walked towards her, his smile faltering at the sides. Just like her mother's.

9

A door swung open.

Two pairs of slippers descended the stairs.

'They are awake,' Ikemefuna whispered, her features frozen in place as she stared darkly at the stairs.

'Do my parents scare you?' Nna asked, a puzzled expression on his face.

'Nigerian parents are scary, Nna'm.'

Ahem!

A loud cough blasted through the kitchen.

Nna turned to the kitchen table where Agbala stood in her floral nightgown. Her eyes were red from too much or not enough sleep. Behind her, Eke – a pair of tight navy boxers gripping his manhood in all the wrong ways. Ikemefuna, seemingly devoid of her earlier fear stood between them, holding Agbala in her left arm and Eke in her right. Kissing the one's cheeks and curtsying to the other.

Nna slipped out of the kitchen with his coffee just as Eke launched into a colorful tale about his time in Nibo Boys, an all-boys secondary school in Anambra. Like many things about Eke, Nna found his father's childhood tales to be longwinded and dull. He clambered up the stairs and away from the trio.

He would use that time to get to know his alleged wife better. She'd given him the highlights reel – a thirty-second montage of her best bits. He'd appreciated the teaser for what it was, but he wanted more. The dirty laundry he could only unearth by poring through her cell-phone. Her filterless selfies. Her sordid confessions in the girls' group chat.

He walked into her room, a matchbox-sized space that smelled of mothballs. It was supposed to be a guest room but up until Ikemefuna, his parents never had overnight guests.

A pair of bathroom slippers lay at the foot of the narrow wood bed. Nna's eyes roamed the bare orange walls. He squinted at the metal bars enclosing the windows. When were those installed? He didn't remember the bars from his last visit. He would mention them to his mother. She loved when he feigned interest in her home improvement projects.

If she caught him, he would say he wanted to push the windows open, get rid of the room's damp smell.

He pulled open drawers and raised a pillow. There was a battered blood-red bible beneath the pillow. *Adina Azubuike.* A name scribbled in blue ink above the title page. The name felt familiar. Like he'd seen or heard of it.

He scanned the room for Ikemefuna's cellphone. He'd learnt from experience that a woman's cellphone held the answers to his most intimate questions. Bunmi's cell-phone, an iPhone 5 on its last breath, had revealed to him in 'lol'-heavy sentences and a string of eggplant emojis that he was not the only man who knew of the birthmark on her inner thigh. The abbreviated texts on Zainab's bubble-gum pink flip phone unceremoniously announced that Zainab had a thing for her weed woman.

But there was no cellphone in Ikemefuna's room. Not beneath the mattress or in the pockets of her boubous.

Ikemefuna's laughter, full-bodied and false, bounced off the railings and rang into the upstairs hallway. He pictured her throwing her head back to expose the red scars fracturing her neck. Her laughter drew closer as she bounded up the stairs. The bible that once belonged to Adina called out to him. He flipped through its pages. There was a photograph, a rectangle with a woman in it. A brown patina had formed along its edges, and it looked like it was encased in a cheap, weightless frame. He slid it into the left pocket of his khaki shorts and slipped out as silently as he had slipped in.

What was this light breeze fluttering in his chest? It had to be the onset of love. Nothing in his life was as exciting or as terrifying as the potential of new love.

He *loved* that Ikemefuna was not a silver-tongued girl who smelled of American freedom and late-night McDonald's fries in the backseat of other men's cars, or a prude who read him his Miranda rights when he tried to spice up the sex. That he felt bigger around her, his shoulders and heart expanding each time her fingers brushed against his arm.

That she was different, foreign, entirely un-American, from her accent to the okirika tee she wore with a fading *HOUSTN* splashed across its front in yolky yellow. He *loved* her for her newness and for her misdirected outbursts, and he was ashamed of himself for all that loving, but he was proud of his capacity to love a thing.

'Nna'm. Do you have a minute?'

Agbala stood in the doorway of his bedroom.

How long had she been standing there?

A dark grey turban leaned to the left of her head and there was a distant look in her eyes. He was familiar with the turban, with the look in his mother's eyes. She channeled that look each time she disappeared into the toolshed in the backyard to speak to Ala, her god.

Nna glanced at his wristwatch.

'We've got roughly fifteen minutes before my first work call of the day. We're negotiating a funky purchase and sale agreement for a Hilton hotel.'

Agbala walked slowly to his bed. 'Good. I don't have much time either. Eke is having stomach trouble again. He's been vomiting for an hour. I need to be by his side.'

'I've told him to watch his diet,' Nna muttered, a strain of irritation creeping into his voice.

Agbala sat at the edge of his bed.

'Nna'm, this is about our guest.'

'Ikemefuna?'

'Ikemefuna.'

'What about Ikemefuna?'

'As you know, she is your wife.'

His immediate inclination was to laugh at his mother's words. Dismiss it as maternal desperation for wedding festivities – a reception with trays of jollof rice and big-chested Abakiliki women in colorful lace or towering Sunday hats. A litter of grandkids. But Nna knew better than to take his mother's words for granted.

'What do you mean?' he asked, his right brow raised.

'We are close friends with her parents,' Agbala said, her tone measured. 'When she was born, they married her off to you.'

'What is this? 1963?'

'This is not the time for jokes, Nna'm.'

'I don't get a say in any of this?'

'You don't, Nna'm,' Agbala murmured. She stretched a bony hand to his cheek and stroked it. Her fingers felt like sandpaper. Hard and scratchy. 'Some things are decided by gods long before they are revealed to men. What matters is that Ala has your best interests at heart.'

Nna knew that his mother meant business. She was not the joking type. Her prodding was never a suggestion. It was an FYI.

He could think of a thousand examples too.

He'd contracted malaria on a cultural exchange trip to Ghana some five years back. On learning of his poor health, Agbala rushed into her toolshed. She emerged an hour later with her turban and the distant look in her eyes. She paced the house and whistled Bright Chimezie's 'Life Na Teacher' to herself. Then she said *Nna'm, do you have a minute?* He did. *It is well with you.* It was.

Then there was the time he sat for the LSAT following two weeks of bare bones studying. Agbala raised a palm just as he launched into a lengthy tirade about the exam. She ran to the toolshed, her flowing skirt ploughing through manure, one knocked knee banging against the other. She returned with her turban and the distant look in her eyes. *Nna'm, do you have a minute?* He did. *You will pass that exam.* He did.

There were the less flamboyant indicia of her prowess, like the leftover oha soup where minutes ago, there was none, and the spare change in Agbala's fanny pack at the sight of a gas station.

'Can I at least talk to, er, Ala? Can I hear Ala speak for once?'

He managed to keep the sarcasm from his voice. The only thing Agbala hated more than perceived insolence was insolence targeted at her beloved Ala.

Once, when he was a teenager, he'd snuck into the tool-shed. Agbala and Eke were at the annual Umu Igbo Unite convention in Maryland for the weekend. He'd braced himself for the worst. For floating skulls and rotting teeth. But inside the toolshed, he'd found a flashlight, spanners, screwdrivers, car batteries, deflated tires gathering dust, his beating heart, and an unremarkable figurine with a long torso.

He'd ogled the figurine's flaws, the bits of wood that hung awkwardly from its sides, the slash of its lips. He'd left the shed with a heavy ache in his arms, one he later identified as disappointment.

'Watch your words, Nna'm. You know Ala doesn't take kindly to disrespect.'

'I like Ikemefuna, Mom. I do. I'm taking her out on a date today. But I want more time with her before I commit to a marriage.'

'Time is not our friend, Nna'm. There is no time to get to know her better. Just trust that I have personally searched this earth and she's the girl for you.'

'Mom, this is insane. I haven't even met her parents. What if they hate me?'

'They won't hate you, Nna,' Agbala whispered, her eyes on her feet.

'You don't know that, though. They haven't even met me.'

'You know them,' Agbala insisted. 'They are close family friends. Or they were,' she added. 'We were neighbors in Lagos.'

'That's not nearly enough intel on my future in-laws.'

'The Azubuikes were one of the few families that kept in touch with us after we left Lagos for Houston. We would place monthly calls to Dumeje and Adina. They always asked to speak to you. They were fond of you, you know.'

Nna squinted at Agbala's turban. He recalled his earliest memories in America. A cramped two-bedroom apartment in Southwest Houston. Eke teaching him to ride a bike on the potholed roads of a rundown apartment complex. Agbala pressing kisses into his hair and holding him close to her chest before the school bus turned the corner. Long distance phone calls to faraway Nigeria. Nna on Agbala's lap as Eke pressed a black cordless phone to Nna's ear. The muffled squeals coming out of the receiver. A woman's voice. Or was it a man? Their unbridled joy. His curiosity and confusion at that odd ritual.

And then it had ended, and he had gone on to live his American life.

'This is insane,' he mumbled into his chest.

'Life is insane, Nna'm,' Agbala murmured, her palms cradling the back of her neck.

His row house in Philadelphia was too contained for an extra body. He would break the lease, move into a bigger space, a brownstone in Old City. He would give up his

Friday nights at Fat Tuesday's, part ways with his weed guy, set a reminder for Valentine's Day, make room in his shower for fruity scents. He would share a toothpaste with her, smell her on his bath towel. Or he would move back to Houston. Buy a condo in Midtown. Drop the kids off with his parents on the weekends. Agbala seemed to think she was his missing puzzle piece, and if she was not, he would chip away at her until she fit.

He nodded; his gaze averted.

'That's my boy,' Agbala said, flashing her teeth and stroking his cheeks. 'Now what is this thing you mentioned about a date?'

10

A checkered tablecloth flapped in the wind. Fat fruit flies zipped in and out of Ikemefuna's line of vision. The moment – warm Chablis fizzing in thick-stemmed glasses – was not the lavish first date Ikemefuna envisioned when Nna accosted her with the idea the day before. She reached for a fork and pushed coleslaw around in her plate. She raised her eyes to the house's asphalt shingles and the murder of crows flying above the roof. She dabbed the sweat rolling down her sternum and waited for the wind to carry the voices from the house next door.

A grasshopper crawled up her shoulder blade. She observed it, stunned by her encounter with new life outside of the Nwosus. Only remembering to scream when the skeletal insect hopped off her shoulder and onto the grass.

Across from her, Nna swiped the beads of sweat trickling down his hairline. His eyes darted around the backyard of the house like he was expecting something. But what? An extra bowl of burnt coconut fried rice. Agbala's watchful presence presiding over their date like a compromised referee?

Ikemefuna watched Nna from across the plastic table in the middle of the backyard. It was her first opportunity to observe Nna without the gloss of LED dimmers and rice-paper lamps.

Beneath the sun's glare, his hair looked arid and uncombed, its unflappable roots cemented into Basquiat-like lumps from a lack of trying. He ran his palms through his hair with too much force, the pressure from all that tugging exposing a hairline in its earliest days of recession. Its dips, not quite a rollercoaster but the blueprint for one.

'I'm sorry the wine is warm,' he said.

'Who needs cold wine anyway,' she replied, smiling brightly.

'Thanks for being a good sport.' He reached for the napkin next to his untouched plate of coconut rice.

Agbala had insisted that they make good use of the backyard. *Don't take her anywhere, Nna'm. I need her help around the house. I'm growing old, you know!*

'You deserve a proper date. Valet parking, fine dining, you name it. I'm sorry, Keme.'

Keme.

Ikemefuna frowned. She'd never been called Keme. The name felt wrong and foreign, like it belonged to a different girl. She stared at the oval patch of scalp peeking out the center of Nna's afro. She resisted the urge to lean in and press her thumb against the skin.

'Don't worry about it, Nna'm. The coconut rice is spectacular,' she said.

'I mean it. I'm sorry. My mom can be a real pain in the neck.'

She raised her eyes to his face, met his hooded eyes.

'Shhh,' she murmured. She placed a finger on his lips. 'Lighten up. Let's enjoy the quality time.'

'Cheers to that,' Nna said with a grin. He clinked his glass against hers.

She sipped on the Chablis. She scanned the backyard. The manicured carpet grass. The padlocked toolshed. The spiked metal fence that rose from the earth. She could hear faint traces of conversation in the air. Someone on a phone call. Peals of laughter ringing through the humid afternoon.

Nna raised a fork of rice to his mouth and swallowed. Grains of rice fell out of his mouth.

'Take it easy o,' she teased, giggling into her palms.

He rolled his eyes. She rolled her eyes back at him. He stuck his tongue out. Something in her chest softened. She uncrossed her legs and shifted her plastic chair closer to the table.

'So,' he continued, mischief in his eyes. 'Since I've already lost brownie points for the date – might as well ask some spicy questions.'

'Ha!'

'You down?'

'Try me.'

'What turns you on?' he asked.

She shut her eyes. Thinking of Bobo felt . . . wrong. And yet, he was all that came to mind. Those long dance sessions, his lean frame glittering with fresh sweat. His lips brushing against her earlobe as he advised her to whine her waist on beat. 'Slowly dear,' he would say, his palms guiding the movement of her hips.

'I'm a lady, Nna'm. We hold our cards close to our chests.'

'The rules don't apply anymore. You're my wife, remember?' he teased. 'We're past the coyness.'

'Fine. I'm a sapiosexual. I'm turned on by men with big brains.'

'Big *brains,* eh? Is that what Naija girls call it these days?'

'I don't know what you're talking about,' she giggled. 'My turn.'

'Go for it.'

'What's a dealbreaker for you?'

'Not getting along with my folks, for sure. I've dealt with that in the past and it's not a pretty sight.' He cracked a smile. 'Thankfully, my folks love you.'

Ikemefuna pretended to scratch an itch on her thigh.

'Think you can handle something heavier?' he asked.

'Try me.'

'What's your greatest fear?'

She met his eyes.

What would Nneka say?

Nneka would play it cool. She would blurt out something lighthearted and funny.

'Go on. Don't be shy,' he cajoled. He undid the first two buttons of the stiff polo shirt pressed to his chest and wiped the beads of sweat on his collarbone.

'I don't have any,' she shrugged.

'Liar.'

'That's not a very gentlemanly thing to say, Nna'm.'

'I apologize. Is truth-concealer, more apt?'

'Can we go with unbothered?'

'Nah.'

'Fearless? Fearless has a nice ring to it.'

'Come on. Give me something.'

'I'm scared of feeling trapped, Nna'm,' she admitted. 'Does that scare you too? Not having the freedom to live a full life?'

He shook his head and laughed.

'I've always been free as a bird, much to my parents' chagrin,' he said. 'Where do you think the fear comes from?'

She shrugged.

'My parents are very strict. Other than dance practice, they don't let me go out much. And when I do, I must be home before evening, or my father would be furious.'

'Does he get mad often?'

'He has a hot temper.'

Nna raised a brow.

She shook her head.

'Forget I said it.'

'It's fine, Keme. You can tell me anything.'

She stared into his eyes. She tried not to think of Adina's eyes, hollowed from years of Dumeje's violent outbursts.

'He gets angry sometimes, Nna'm. He hates it when I wear certain dresses, or stay out too late, or serve him leftovers from the previous day. He says his rules are for my own good, that they'll make me a good wife.'

Nna placed a palm on her arm and squeezed it.

'I'm sorry to hear that. My parents are anal too. I've lost count of the number of arguments I had with them when I told them I was moving to New York for college.'

Ikemefuna released a dry chuckle.

'At least yours wanted you to attend college. For the longest time, my father didn't want me to. My mother convinced him that Igbo men of nowadays prefer to have educated wives. Even with that, my father only allowed me to major in English so I could speak the Queen's English to my husband.'

The crows on the roof flew off the slats and across the backyard. Nna ran his fingers against Ikemefuna's knuckles, his eyes trained on her.

'Woah. That's heavy.'

'Anyway, all parents are flawed in their own way,' Ikemefuna murmured. She regarded him coolly. 'Even yours.'

'Tell me about it,' he muttered.

'I mean, they've been such gracious hosts,' she continued, her tone measured. 'But I bet you can think of times they have acted out of character?'

Ikemefuna watched Nna from across the table. She waited for him to tell on his parents. To confirm everything she already knew to be true about them.

'Mmmh,' he grunted as he shoved more rice into his mouth.

11

Ikemefuna squinted at the kitchen blinds as warm tap water filled the sink. Through the blinds, she could make out the tar that spanned the block. The flash of a bony arm. Streaks of platinum blonde hair like polythene strips in the air.

Away from the backyard's fecund heat, she reflected on her date with Nna. She'd hoped she would be out in public, surrounded by Americans with cellphones and big, bleeding hearts. Americans who would stop in their tracks and crane their necks if she raised an alarm. Still, she'd made the most of the backyard. She'd basked in the sun and smelled the earth.

He'd brought her back to earth with his questions. They were light at first. The kinds of questions she wished Bobo would ask her one day.

Then he'd switched gears, and before she had a chance to notice the shifting in the air, she was telling him about her parents and all the ways they were wrong.

He'd listened to her, nodded along to her words, squeezed her arm, all the while training those hooded eyes on her.

You look like my mother, she'd wanted to scream.

Why do you look like my mother?

She bit her tongue. The last thing she wanted was for Nna to think she was crazy. Worse – she didn't want him discussing her with his parents, telling them she was asking strange questions.

She'd settled for safe, chomping the dry rice and gulping the Chablis.

Nna lingered after the date. He stood beside her at the kitchen sink as she washed the dishes, running a hand towel against each saucer to soak up the moisture. He landed a kiss on her forehead each time she turned towards him. She nestled her head in his chest as he whispered sweet patronizing nothings in her ear – *You're beautiful. You know that, right?*

She cooed along to his words, like Nneka would.

Ike, do you know the secret to keeping a man?

No, Nene. I've never had a boyfriend, remember?

Oya, remember this for future purposes. Smile at him and look pretty. It's as simple as that.

Outside the Nwosus' kitchen window, Mary Schultz (bony arm, platinum blonde hair) watered the grassy knoll in front of her sprawling mansion. Well, not *sprawling*. Certainly not as *sprawling* as some of the other houses on her street. Modest. Respectable, even. Held its own. Which was good enough for the former veterinarian and Kyle, her freelance photographer lover.

There were more important things than sprawling mansions, like the fact that it was six in the evening and she was sick and/or tired of waiting for David (teenage son, blond hair, stringy) to do the watering. He never listened to her. Preferred to listen to John, and James, and Justin, and all the other Js the hue of condensed milk, from swim practice. Surely, teenage boys were more than scowls, slammed doors, and perfumed sweat?

She rolled up the hem of her jeans.

A car engine puttered.

She looked up, squinted, her tiny heart engorged and hopeful. Of course, her David was more than a scowl, a slammed door, and the sickly-sweet smell of sweat. He had returned home early to attend to his chores. Or to stare pointedly at the second-floor window in the neighbor's house, his latest obsession. And before that, the haka. And before that a classic pompadour.

No – it was not David at all. Her tiny heart sank to her feet. It was the Jamaican (or was it Nigerian?) woman from the house next door. The wrinkled one (could use a hot iron to her face) whose name sounded like an incantation. All jagged and heavy on the tongue.

Mary waved at the woman as she hobbled out of her tan Toyota. The woman managed to wave back despite the cardboard box crammed under her arm.

Mary studied the woman's face. Not even the moldy bones of a smile on that face. A cultural kink, maybe. No. She knew a half dozen other Nigerians – doctors, and cabbies, and poets. Each one of them capable of cracking a smile.

The neighbor never smiled at Mary, a fact that made Mary queasy, or grumpy, or both. A fact that needed fixing, like rumpled sheets or skin. And there was a quick fix. A knock on the neighbor's front door. A peace offering in the form of home-made snickerdoodles.

No, not good enough. Mary would extend a dinner invitation to the woman. *No men allowed*, she would whisper with a conspiratorial wink. The woman would bare her teeth and wink back at Mary. They would ditch the booth for the bar. They would spend the evening smiling warily at each other as they run their fingers along the perimeters of their cocktail menus. They would throw jabs at her photographer lover and the neighbor's couch-potato husband. Innocent little jabs at first, until the sauvignon blanc hit. Then, they would curse out their men in spurts of alcohol-induced giggles, palms to lips, each woman racing to out-crass the other in that nameless Olympics.

But first, Mary would have to remember the woman's name. Malaria. Child soldiers. KONY. No, that was Somalia. Or was it Eritrea?

If only she would crack an effing smile.

12

Nna walked into his parents' bedroom, his head in the clouds. He'd felt his heart flutter as Ikemefuna's teeth sank into the peppered chicken. He'd watched his hands tremble as he topped up her wine. His in-love friends often told him about the physicality of love – the poorly timed hard-ons and vacuous grins. But up until that afternoon, he'd never believed that a woman could cause his body to short circuit.

Ikemefuna had been generous with her smiles in the backyard. She'd thrown around pliant words like *please* and *thank you* for the smallest of requests. When she smiled, her eyes retreated into her face. He didn't know that one's eyes could do such a thing.

'Nna'm,' Agbala called from where she lay in bed, her head peeking out a tufted comforter. Next to her – Eke's eyes jumped from the Al Jazeera on the screen to Nna.

'I'll do it,' Nna announced, the words toppling out his mouth before he could take them back. 'I'll marry her.'

He'd spent the previous night wondering about being a husband and how it would change him. He would have to ditch the bar crawls with his single friends for poker nights with his married friends who wore their wedding bands on their fingers till the zirconium left permanent incisions on their skin.

'Eh? Say that again,' Agbala croaked.

Nna eyed the doorknob. He felt protective of his love for Ikemefuna. It was tender and neonatal and in no condition to be handled by outside hands.

'I'll marry Ikemefuna.'

Agbala sat up in her bed.

'Ah! I should have known when I saw you shining your teeth!' she rejoiced. 'This is very good news! I'm glad you see what we see in her.'

Eke stood from the bed and hobbled towards Nna.

'Very good, son! You will make a wonderful husband,' he huffed as he patted Nna on the back.

'I told you to trust me, didn't I?' Agbala cawed. 'I told you I would never lead you astray.'

'Mom, Dad, let's not get ahead of ourselves,' Nna cautioned. 'I still think this is batshit crazy, but for now, I'm certain she's the one.'

'*The one?*' Agbala repeated, a perplexed look on her face.

'You know – my soulmate.'

'Ah, you children of nowadays and your words,' Eke said with a fat grin.

'Ehen! Tell us everything that happened during the date,' Agbala begged, her eyes bright and burning. 'Did she share anything important? Did she mention us?'

Eke sat beside Agbala on the bed and raised his face to Nna, his gait expectant.

Nna squinted at his parents. Something seemed off about them. Agbala's lilting voice. Eke's pointed stare. Their paused breath as they waited for his words.

Was he imagining things?

He shook his head. Of course, he was. Save for his lunch with Ikemefuna, he'd been running on black coffee and Ritalin for two days straight thanks to a challenging new CRE deal working its way down the pipeline at his firm.

'Nothing that you need to know,' he said with a chuckle as he turned his back to leave.

His parents had good intentions, but they must learn to stay out of his business.

At night, Nna stood by his bathroom door and watched Ikemefuna layer her night-time skincare products in their adjoining bathroom. Cleanser. Toner. Serum. Cream.

Walking to his bed, he wondered about the brief unease that had enveloped him in his parents' bedroom as they waited on the details of his date with Ikemefuna. It was no secret that his parents were eccentric. Through the years, he'd seen them rationalize the abnormal – firing squads and burnt offerings and short-lived secessionist states. He'd long chalked up their quirks to the singularity of their cultural background. What did his friends' parents know about surviving the Biafran War or presenting burnt offerings to a god?

But there was no explaining the moments of unease that jumped out at him from dark corners. Moments of tucking discomfort between his teeth as the fear crept up his throat. Something fell to the bathroom floor. A hair-brush or a bowl. The sound of running water filled the air. He sniffed Ikemefuna's half of the bed for her scent. That sweet metal finish. He swept his palms against the bed-dings for her cellphone. He'd been searching the house for the thing for weeks.

Was she hiding it?

Why would she?

He dug his arm out of a pillowcase.

Clearly, she'd hidden the damn phone. He squeezed his eyes shut, a rogue groan escaping his mouth.

She would learn not to keep things from him.

He would make sure of it.

13

September 2019

By the first week of September, Ikemefuna began to dream of pregnancy.

She dreamt of a rawboned boy in her womb who ate himself to pacify his growing hunger. Tentatively at first. Nibbling his toes and the sore skin of his earlobes. Then with gusto, tearing the meat from his kneecaps and the soft of his buttocks till all that remained was a lump of chopped liver.

She hated to think of her body, stretching to make room for a growing thing. The darkening belly and fatigue. She did not care for maternity dresses. She wanted Nneka's bodycon. A house party with deafening Afrobeats. Bobo's big, strong palms guiding the sway of her hips.

On a quiet Sunday night, Agbala tore open a cardboard box in the downstairs living room and sent a confetti of pregnancy strips to the marbled floor. Ikemefuna shut her eyes. She imagined the living room with its kitsch brown throw pillows and blown-up brass frames of a younger Agbala, Eke, and Nna was a Hookah lounge that tasted of flavored Shisha and Shish Taouk. That the red plastic cup in her hands held vodka, and not urine.

She opened her eyes as Agbala dipped a strip in the cup. The reality was simpler, stranger. Two months into what should have been a two-week trip to Houston, she was still in the Nwosus' house. They would not let her leave the house until she gave their son a child.

She scoured the living room for Nna. She could use his kind smile, his firm hands on her shoulders.

When Agbala purchased the pregnancy strips from Walmart, she commandeered her lips into a smile to match that of the cashier with the bubble-gum pink hair who asked her if she was going to be a grandma. She caused her eyes to wink at the cashier like the cashier was an old friend, her tongue to hum a discordant *best believe* in what she hoped was an AAVE drawl, to perform casual American friendliness, that itchy scarf she often draped around her clavicle each time she left her house.

'Now, we wait.'

Ikemefuna imagined a boy with her long lashes and slender neck, his father's fleshy lips and berry black skin. Agbala and Eke would marvel at his bigness and his good health. Everyone would gaze in awe at Ikemefuna, a vessel solid enough, and virtuous enough, and wide enough for a god.

With time, she would no longer long for her old life. The chatter of kube kube. Nneka and her off-white shimi. The rumpled roll of Obinna's boxers peeking out the top of his sagged jeans. The brand new ogene at the back of her wardrobe. Bobo – his kind smile and big hands.

Or she would appeal to the Nwosus to let her go home. It would be their gift to her for her gift of a son. She would promise them she'd return to Houston with the same child-like awe from her first time around. That she would widen her eyes and gasp when Agbala points out the Chinese buffets and Old Navy. That she would erase all memory of the long and trying first night – Eke prying her passport from her palms then chewing it slowly, in small, bitesize pieces, till all that remained of it was his gaseous belch.

'Now,' Eke announced, his eyes on his pocket watch.

Agbala snatched the strip from the cup. One second piled on top of the next. Agbala squinted. She reached for her reading glasses and held the strip to a floor lamp. Eke clasped his palms and stared at his feet.

'Negative.'

Ikemefuna hid her face in her palms. Agbala's earlier warning rang in her ears.

Wives are like germs, child.

If you can't give him a son within a month, we'll find a woman who can.

She braced herself for what came next, a slap or a screaming match. Agbala was quite skilled at both.

'It can't possibly be,' she whispered weakly.

'Shut your devil mouth,' Agbala gnarled, her brows furrowed in anger. 'You are not trying hard enough.'

Eke's palms tightened against Agbala's shoulder.

'Let us give her an extra month,' Eke whispered to Agbala, his tone cautious. 'Maybe her body was just getting warmed up.'

Agbala eyed her husband. She hissed and stomped off. She would save the rest of her anger for their bedroom.

14

Agbala was not the kind of woman who avoided confrontation. Had never been. Not when she was a wisp of a girl and was forced to put up with the jostling of her older sisters. In those days, she had stood on top of her mother's ákpàtị̀ and glared at her useless sisters and their even more useless boyfriends. She had refused their requests that she polish their school shoes or run into town for fresh loaves of bread.

'Why don't you do it yourself?' she once hissed at Ebuka, her oldest sister's slimy lover when he demanded that she cook him a pot of Abacha with plenty palm oil. 'Don't you have hands?'

Her questions had earned her a swift slap, one she returned with equal gusto, her flattened palm repeatedly drumming the side of Ebuka's surprised face. She'd gotten away with it too. Everyone in her father's compound had been too stunned to see a small girl put a big boy in his place.

Then puberty struck.

Agbala joined the rare breed of young Nigerian women who commanded a certain respect from their peers and their elders – a strange deference that all who crossed her path clamored to uphold.

They said she spoke with authority. Something about her carriage, that she placed one foot in front of the other without swinging her hips. That she covered her breasts with just enough tarpaulin to throw men off her scent. Everyone, young and old, had their theories, but the consensus was that young Agbala had earned her keep.

So when Agbala's mother took ill with kidney failure and, surrounded by all of her daughters on her deathbed, announced that upon her passing, Agbala was to become Ala's chief priestess, Agbala's sisters merely nodded in agreement and proceeded to discuss the business of their mother's death.

American immigration was a humbling experience. It did not care about Agbala's storied past. It hacked at the sacrosanct till Agbala feared that all that would remain of her earlier mystic would be allusions to her once-upon-a-time at boring dinner parties with the Igbo wives in Sugar Land. Not that she was the type to attend such parties.

'Eke, don't try that again,' Agbala hissed, wagging a finger at her husband as he shut the door behind him. She was back in the comfort of her bedroom, afro-kinky wig off and surrounded by the familiar scents of bitter kola and wood. Soon, Eke would stick a dry chewing stick in his mouth, let it dangle from its side.

'What are you talking about?' he moaned, his voice laced with an innocence that made her want to slap him in the mouth.

Agbala sat at the tail end of their king size bed and eyed her husband, his frail build, the mounded skin of his belly.

'Don't challenge me again. Especially not in front of that girl.'

'I was not trying to challenge you. I just wanted us to be a little more reasonable in our approach. The girl is doing her best.'

'And how exactly do you know that?' she hammered.

Eke started to protest in his whiny voice so she stuck ear plugs in her ears. She'd had a long day. Weaving in and out of Houston traffic as she attended to the rote chores of American life. The dealership for an oil change. All three *Agbala's Braiding, Inc.* locations to monitor her workers. Walmart for pregnancy tests and soy milk. The dry cleaner to pick up Eke's sport coats. She did not want her argument with Eke to be the cherry on top.

'You're right. I don't,' Eke eventually said with a sigh.

When it came to Agbala, Eke knew he had to pick his battles. Decades of marriage had shown him that Agbala prided Nna above everything else. And he couldn't blame her. They had endured seven childless years before Ala blessed them with their son.

Eke watched Agbala stand from the bed. He eyed her as she made her way to him. His shoulders stiffened. Sweat dripped down his chin. He smiled tightly and pretended to look out of the window at the quiet street below.

She stood in front of him. She was maybe an inch taller, a disparity he struggled with when they were out in public, their arms entwined. She reached for his shoulders. He recoiled, but she was faster. She pinned him between her palms. Then she drew him into an embrace, her left palm running up and down his neck as he trembled in her arms.

15

March 2019

'Oya now. Do something!'

'Leave me, *jare*.'

'Come on! This is your chance!'

The medley of Afrobeats in the hall's charged air crackled to a stop. Ikemefuna and Nneka eyed the rest of the dancers as they stood to their feet and dusted the hall's soot from their buttocks.

Dance practice was particularly rigorous that afternoon, partly due to Bobo's high standards (there were rumors that his late mother was one of Fela's dancers in the seventies), and the small role the women would play in an upcoming musical at Terrakulture.

Bobo stood next to two dusty grey speakers in front of the dance hall. Ikemefuna and Nneka sat on the floor at the back of the hall and watched him fiddle with his Beats by Dre headphones.

'Even the way he holds his headphones is sexy,' Ikemefuna moaned.

'Don't dull yourself o,' Nneka said. 'If not that I'm trying to be loyal to Obinna, I would be all over him myself.'

'Good for you,' Ikemefuna grumbled as she zipped her duffel bag. She eyed the small clock on the wall to her left. 2:48 p.m. Adina and Dumeje were expecting her at home by 3 p.m. and she couldn't afford to be late. She massaged her earlobes. They still hurt from the previous week when she had returned home from dance practice a whole thirty minutes late.

'Ah ah, don't be like that now,' Nneka laughed. She tugged Ikemefuna's cheeks and giggled. 'You know I'm just playing with you. Don't be angry o. I don't want what happened the last time I was in your room to happen again.'

Ikemefuna shot Nneka a withering look. She'd made Nneka promise to never speak of the incident.

'Oya sorry now! You know I enjoy teasing you. I'm just trying to look out for you before these vultures swoop in on him and mark their territory,' Nneka said. She eyed the women filtering out the hall with suspicion.

'I don't even know him well enough to like him,' Ikemefuna protested.

'But you're always shining your teeth at him when he looks at you, coming early to dance practice when he's the instructor, and bragging about how he gives you the tightest hugs, and you even noticed that he hasn't given any other girl a hug, and—'

'Oya, it's enough!'

'I'm just making my point,' Nneka exclaimed, a fat smile on her lips.

'Okay, fine. I'll talk to him. I'll let him know today's class was good.'

'That's lame.'

'Ah ah. What should I say?'

'Sweetie, it's not what you say. It's what you do.'

'What do you mean?'

'Men can't resist women who ooze sex appeal. Just like me,' Nneka added with a wink.

'I knew you'd toot your horn,' Ikemefuna said. She shook her head at her best friend's antics. Nneka was something else.

'It's true *naw*. Anyway, I think you should adjust your blouse small. Pull it down so that your cleavage shows a little. Then soften your voice and maintain eye contact when you speak to him.'

'That's too much, Nneka! He'll think I'm an *ashawo!*'

'Men like ashawos. Trust me.'

'Fine, I'll try. Wish me good luck.'

'Wait first. Your lips look like they've not been moisturized in 100 years. Use my lip gloss.'

'Ah! Are they that bad?'

Ikemefuna patted Nneka's lime-flavored gloss on her lips and made her way towards the front of the hall. Most of her fellow dancers were gone and only a handful of stragglers remained. Two girls made a beeline for Bobo just as she opened her mouth to say his name. Her heart sank. She started to return to Nneka.

'Ikemefuna.'

Bobo's voice caught her by surprise. It was so deep and creamy. He sounded like Idris Elba. She wished she could wrap herself in his voice.

'Ah, Bobo,' she squealed like a mouse in lard. She cleared her throat. She would soften her voice like Nneka advised. 'Ah, Bobo,' she repeated, but softer.

'Were you looking for me?' he asked as he closed the gap between them, a bright smile on his face.

He should be a movie star, she thought to herself. She tugged the hem of her striped V-neck tee till her cleavage peeked out the top.

'Yes. I just . . .' She trailed off. Bobo was staring at her boobs. 'I just wanted to say today's class was great! Your etighi is so smooth.'

'Thanks dear! I thoroughly enjoyed teaching you ladies.'

Dear. There it was again. He was flirting with her, wasn't he?

'Anyway, I'm looking forward to our next class,' she added.

'Cool! See you next week,' he said as he made to leave.

Her joy slipped off her face. She'd been hoping for a longer conversation, a chance to show him she was fascinating and sexy, but the conversation had ended before it began. She caught sight of Nneka at the back of the hall. She was laughing (and/or flirting) with one of the other instructors, a wiry middle-aged father of triplets who once suggested to Nneka that she could be his mistress. She could hear Nneka in her ear, prodding her to return to Bobo.

Come on, Ike! Leave him wanting more.

She took a deep breath and turned to Bobo. He was fiddling with his phone as he made his way towards the exit.

She rushed forward, threw her arms around him, and planted a kiss on his cheek. He let out a gravelly moan and held on to her waist.

'Ikemefuna,' he whispered, his eyes wide with surprise as she tore her arms away from him.

'Just wanted to say goodbye properly,' she said before sashaying away from him.

She could feel his eyes on her bum as she walked away. It was equal parts embarrassing and gratifying.

Was this what Nneka enjoyed? This knowing that she could stop a man in his tracks if she so desired. It seemed like a practical skill to have when dealing with Nigerian men, she thought with a chuckle.

16

September 2019

Nna would barge into her room at any moment.

Ikemefuna had grown accustomed to listening to the night for his raspy laughter and the persistent cough that followed his feet. She waited, and washed her eyes with cold tap water, and held her eyelids open with her thumbs.

Then she heard it from somewhere outside her door. His raspy laughter. His persistent cough. His large feet stomping around his bedroom as he ran bath water.

The ringlets of skin around her throat whirred to life.

She clutched her throat. It was warm to the touch.

Run.

She froze. Run where? Run when? It was the middle of the night, and she was a tourist in America and its terror-filled night – drug lords, college kids in tank tops high on Percocet, trigger-happy cops, that one dead serial killer from the Crime & Investigation channel, resurrected. Her phone was gone, had been for a while now. It mysteriously disappeared in the blur of her first week in America.

She could run to a gas station. There was always a gas station.

But there was safety in the daily routine of the Sugar Land house. Breakfast in the morning. Dicing tomatoes and onions for lunch and dinner. Tidying floors. Burnishing countertops, then her skin, for Nna. Smiling on cue if he stuck his head between her door and its frame. Waving at him with her fingertips. Throwing her head back. 'Nna'm, what do you want tonight?' she would ask. 'Depends on what you're serving,' he would reply.

Run.

The voice was a headache, pounding against her cranium. It was true. She was running out of time to give him a son.

She would wear stockings tonight. She pulled two crumpled black stockings from beneath a stack of old newspaper clippings.

A distant knock.

More knocks.

Faint.

Insistent.

Nna's head between her door and its frame. His grin, slow and sure.

'You okay?' Soft. Everything about him was soft.

He inched closer. He was naked, his penis at attention. She worried about its smell. It was particularly foul at night.

She smiled. She waved at him with her fingertips. She threw her head back.

'Nna'm, what do you want tonight?'

'Depends on what you're serving.'

17

Nna was rarely sure of anything. In the years since moving out of the Sugar Land house and into his row house in Philadelphia, he had fine-tuned his knack for miscalculating his utility bills and the amount of water and time needed to boil two cups of rice.

Nna's poor judgment transcended domestic life. He guessed half the multiple-choice answers on the Pennsylvania bar exam and was known to French kiss lovers seconds before they broke up with him.

But tonight, Nna was right.

He basked in his rightness as he massaged a palm of lotion into his calves and sucked on the inside of his cheek. The browning photograph from Ikemefuna's bible lay on his sheets. There was no mistaking the thick monobrow above the woman's oily eyelids, or the smattering of moles that ran from one nostril to the farthermost corner of an eye, or the hooded eyes and full bottom lip, or the elf ears that stood at attention, vehemently refusing to lie flat.

The woman in the photograph was a spitting, revolting image of him. The him captured in the throes of an all-nighter, his bloodshot eyes gleaming in the dark. The him that drank himself to sleep. The him that wept on the front stairs of his ex-girlfriend Zainab's brownstone. The him he hid from prying eyes, buried beneath expensive cologne, teeth whiteners, impressive degrees. She was the him beneath his rabbinical beards – a jawline angular in all the wrong parts.

Nna eyed the woman's dandruffed hair, the careless middle part, the singe of the hot comb tugged through sections of that hair, the hooded eyes, the peeling rouge cheeks, the gap in her front teeth, the crucifix that dangled from a thin silver chain. He hid the woman's eye bags with his thumbs like they were dirty laundry on a dinner table and the guests were arriving. Then he hid her practical grey blouse with his index fingers, closed his eyes, imagined her in something prettier, a bouncy off-shoulder chiffon that complimented her clavicle.

Her crucifix glinted through the baryta paper. He imagined she was a Christian. A prayer warrior-type. Entirely un-American. And yet, as American as Chick-fil-A's spicy chicken sandwich.

Ikemefuna knew the woman in the photograph enough to carry her across continents. To hide her between scritta paper. To press her to her chest at night. To bow her head and pray to her like she was a shrine.

He closed his eyes and swept through his memory till he arrived at a fuzzy memory of Agbala and Eke huddling together. Whispers of *Adina* in the living room of the Southwest Houston apartment. Eke throwing furtive glances at him as Agbala wrapped a telephone cord around her wrists. *Adina*, Agbala would mouth, frantic and feverish. Sometimes, Agbala would appeal to the woman for patience. Other times, she would pass the phone to Nna and he would stutter his greetings in bad Igbo. Then the phone call would end, and he would return to the *Flintstones*.

Looking at the picture, he tried to unsee his face on her face, his moles crawling up her cheeks.

He ran a comb through his beard.

He released dry laughter, stopped abruptly.

He was being ridiculous. Of course, Adina was not wearing his face. His face was not for sale. She could not take out a mortgage for the hollow in his cheeks.

Still, he couldn't shake off the feeling that he was missing crucial information. He would ask his parents about their relationship to the Azubuikes. Perhaps, he would also keep a closer eye on Ikemefuna, find her phone for a start. The latter was better than driving himself mad with the strangest of theories.

For now, he would distract himself with thoughts of Ikemefuna. He could ask her to move her things to his bedroom. Lay some ground rules as she makes room for her dresses on his rack: (a) his bedtime, (b) his breakfast favorites, (c) how not to press the toothpaste tube.

He could broach the sex too. There was nothing inherently wrong with the sex, and maybe that was the problem. The sex was functional. It did its job, worked its forty hours, paid its bills on time. But Nna did not want to make a good tenant out of sex. He wanted a homeless, drugged-out low life with bad credit and vodka breath. He wanted dirt and scraped skin in its finger beds. He wanted it to melt in his mouth like butter or a glug in a skillet. The sex could be no-name vegetable oil. Greasy in the best way.

He hurried over to Ikemefuna's room. She wore a plain black tee shirt with a browning stain. Braless – her breasts, the shape of papaya, straining against pilled cotton. Thick black stockings riding up her thighs. She leaned back in her bed, legs crossed and waiting, like she knew he would come. He was her so-called husband. Predictable. A scratchy blanket that smelled of mothballs and Tide. Home.

Nna did not want to be home, that balding thing that crawled into bed with a cheap briefcase beneath its sweat-stained armpits. That run-down employee recounting his day in granular detail – the cursing driver of the Camry, the mad boss, the food poisoning from cafeteria guacamole, the typo in the email from the mouthy first year who wore wrinkled violet bowties and a lip ring.

Ikemefuna kissed his cheeks.

'Long day, Nna'm?'

'Just long enough.'

He kissed her softly.

She bit his lips.

There was so much potty-training to do.

If he was to marry her, he must teach her to play fetch, throw a Frisbée at her, applaud her as she leaps in the air and seizes it with her teeth. She would learn not to kiss, or bite, or tug with too much teeth, because she was not just any girl in a bad wig at a street corner in Third Ward. She was not the opposite of a tender thing, the wrong amount of woman, her flaws manifesting as a small crack at first, then a chasm wide enough to fit a golf ball, or to swallow him whole.

He planted kisses between her breasts.

He would pry her out of the house, polish her bad bits with brown sugar, refine her taste. He would make reservations at an Eater-approved restaurant in Westheimer. Put in an order of Bouillabaisse for himself. Help her navigate the menu, steer her clear of anything too common, like Spaghetti Bolognese or Truffle Fries. Introduce her to Escargots à la Bourguignonne. She would reward him in the backseat of Agbala and Eke's RAV4, with tongue, lips, a little teeth.

Ikemefuna held Nna's tongue between her teeth. She tugged at his jeans hard. Always too hard. Too unbecoming for a wife. He grabbed her wrists and put them away. *Enough.* He could not bear another second of her hunger. His wife was not supposed to be a mouth. She was supposed to be the meal.

'I have a question for you, Keme,' he started.

She pressed her sweaty glass ribs to his torso, made a mewling sound.

'Keme, listen.'

She was so close to him, her blue-tinged lids and button nostrils squished like sardines on the round canvas of her face. Her lashes stirred. The veins on her eyelids pushed against its papery skin as she shut her eyes tighter. A stab of pain shot through Nna's forehead. He clenched his fists. More urgent this time, his patience worn thin, 'Stop, Keme. I need to ask you something.'

That someone so small could disobey him, could be so unmoved by the fact that he could hold her between his palms and squeeze her tight, till all that was left of her were dark red clumps of blood and a slick patch of manuka honey quickly drying into a crinkly glaze.

His anger ran wild beneath his skin. But only for a few seconds. He was not the kind of man to let his emotions get the best of him. He folded his anger like it was the rented tuxedo he wore at his last networking event (perpetual trays of pinot grigio, white bodies in Armani). He shelved it because it belonged to a lesser man who knew nothing of Goethe or *Architectural Digest* or spontaneous Labor Day weekend trips to the Poconos.

'What about?'

'This.'

He whipped the photograph of Adina from behind his ear.

'Where did you find that?'

Her voice was just above a whisper.

'Who is she?'

He watched a lump slide down Ikemefuna's throat.

'Who do you think she is?' she said. There was an intensity in her eyes that made him uneasy.

'I – I don't know. I found her in your bible.'

She continued to stare at him like she was waiting for something to give. He planted his elbows on the pale blue sheets.

She broke into a grin.

'That's my mother, Nna'm. You're so obsessed with me that you're looking through my things, eh?' she said. 'Find anything of interest, Mr Officer?'

Mr Officer.

He hated the way she mouthed the words, mockingly. Hated her wink, that sudden shift in skin, the crassness of the aesthetic. It aged her, made her ordinary, the opposite of a wife. He looked away from her face for her sake.

'Okay this is going to sound batshit crazy—'

'Trust me.'

'Keme, why does your mother look like me?'

She stiffened next to him. She started to open her mouth, then reconsidered her words, her lips slightly parted.

'It's one thing to love me. It's another thing to be so in love with me that you want to be my brother. *Na wa for you, o!*' she finally said, grinning up at him.

He sat up in bed, a scowl on his face.

'Come on, Keme! Don't bullshit me. I know you see it too.'

She gestured for him to come closer to her. He drew closer to her and held her in his arms. He could feel the thin confluence of bones beneath her expanse. She pressed her lips to his earlobe.

'Kiss me already, *my broda,*' she giggled in his ear.

My brother.

He shuddered.

'You got jokes, huh?' he growled. He rolled out of the bed, barged out the room and clambered down the stairs. She rushed after him, cornered him at the foot of the stairs.

'*Nna'm,* I was just messing with you. Don't be angry, please,' she pleaded, tugging at the band of his boxers.

He met her eyes. His irritation dissolved into the air as she kissed him squarely on his lips. He sighed. It was impossible to stay mad at her.

She'd told him she was a low-maintenance girl. *It's the simple things for me, Nna'm.* There was a Diptyque candle in the cupboard beneath the stairs. He'd ordered it online earlier in the week, placed it in the cupboard when it arrived. Just like he'd placed a lighter beneath the settee in the downstairs living room and leftover calzones in the refrigerator.

'Come with me.'

She did, arms folded across her breasts, lips drawn into a pout, a moving image of the quintessential brat. She would learn humility. He would see to it.

Nna lit the candle and unwrapped the calzones, placed them in the microwave, planted a kiss on Ikemefuna's cheeks.

'Nnaemeka Nwosu, is this a date?' she murmured.

'Ikemefuna—'

'Nwosu.'

'This is anything you want it to be.'

Eke once told Nna that a good union began with a colorful backstory. He'd first met Agbala at the market square in Nibo. Unbeknownst to them, their chance meeting occurred a week before Eke's clan arrived at Agbala's father's compound to ask for her hand in marriage.

Neither Eke nor Agbala knew that their families had arranged their marriage, but Eke was turned off by Agbala's talkativeness and had wondered out loud about how a woman like Agbala could be so unruly. In turn, Agbala raised a widened palm and yelled an expletive – waka! – at Eke before sashaying off with her girlfriends. So when Eke's clan demanded Agbala's hand in marriage, Eke returned the earlier favor by raising his palm and yelling a resounding waka at his horrified bride.

Earlier in the day, Eke called Nna into his bedroom under the pretext of showing him cufflinks he'd purchased for a discount at Harwin. There, Eke slipped him a plain wood ring.

'I carved it from the bark of a cashew tree in my parent's compound in Nibo thirty years ago,' Eke professed, his voice cracked open with emotion.

He'd asked a stupefied Nna to *do the needful*, and *be a man*, and *be the man I raised*. And what was more manly than Nna, bare-chested and hopeful, his one knee grazing the ketchup-stained parquet of the family kitchen, his right hand whipping out the wood ring from the front pocket of his jalabiya, his stuttering tongue asking Ikemefuna that age-old question.

'Keme, I know that this is nuts, but I promised I'd do things the right way, so …' A shaky pause. 'Will you marry me?'

18

Ikemefuna stared at the man kneeling at her feet. She bit into a calzone, savored the mozzarella. She swayed to the rustling leaves of the cedar elms scratching the kitchen's windowsill. She tried to pretend that she wasn't reeling from the earlier moment when he'd thrust her mother's photograph in her face.

Nna repeated the question. Louder this time, with all the right ingredients. More passion. More pain. Ikemefuna stared at a spot on her thigh. She stifled a yawn. Something dark passed through her face. When Nna raised his eyes to her face, she was smiling.

'Yes, Nna'm. Yes, I will.'

Her voice was apathetic and lifeless. A whistle fizzing out the floorboard cracks. The shrill sigh of water rushing out a rusty faucet. Entirely indistinguishable from the creaks behind the kitchen walls.

Still kneeling, Nna was struck by the wrongness of the moment. The flickering LED dimmers. The pungent calzones. The ring crumbling to dust motes in his fists. Ikemefuna, stranger than fiction. A stranger in his father's house, walking its hallways, sleeping in its rooms, painfully indifferent to his proposal.

Wasn't this what she wanted?

He observed Ikemefuna's small round face, the eyes that darted around the kitchen every so often. He wondered if he was making a mistake. If she was just another fling he was rushing heart-first into, another heartbreak in waiting.

He'd fallen fast, even by his standards. She'd carried the trappings of love right from their shared moment in that kitchen. The fullness of her laughter, the bite in her voice, the bits of saliva that sputtered out her mouth like fireworks. His name, sweet as toffee on her tongue. The earthy smell of her skin. Her body, ragdoll-limp in his arms.

Ikemefuna released a second yawn.

Nna raised his eyes to Ikemefuna, then to the kitchen parquet, the smile on his lips straining against his earlobes. He wondered if the faint crack in the parquet that ran between him and Ikemefuna was the thin line between love and hate.

19

Ikemefuna woke up to the wet flap of Agbala's lips humming a Bright Chimezie tune. To Agbala disappearing into thin air in the hours between lunch and dinner. To the medicated smell of the tiger balm Eke massaged into his spine. She counted the seconds it took Agbala and Eke to place one foot in front of the other. She tied a rapa to her belly to shield it from Eke's curious eyes.

'Nna'm. Can we talk?'

He stood in front of the flat screen TV dressed in outside clothes – a starchy white office shirt and black dress pants. He smelled of whiskey and Frangipani. She eyed the bulge in his front pocket. She could make out a key.

Was it the key to the front door?

She swallowed.

'I have a meeting with one of the firm's Houston-based clients, so let's keep it short,' Nna replied, cautious, distrusting. He ran his palms through his greased afro. 'What's the matter?'

Earlier in the morning, she had cut yams into thin pieces, fried the slices to a crisp brown and mashed pepper sauce.

She had plated the yams and pepper sauce and brought the ensemble to his door. A peace offering.

'Leave it at the door,' he growled from his bed, his back turned to her.

'What's wrong?' she whispered. She held his face in her hands. She'd watched Adina hold Dumeje's head a thousand times. Sometimes, it was enough to calm her father's erupting temper.

'What do you mean?'

'I don't know. You seem different today.'

Nna stared hard at her. A slight chill ran though her chest. The heat of his gaze took her back to Lagos, where she would stand before her father, her head bowed in penitence as she waited for him to decide to hug her to his chest or slap her in the face.

'This is about last night, isn't it? I'm sorry about my reaction to your proposal. Of course, I want to be your wife,' she continued. She glanced up at the ceiling, a somber expression on her face. 'It's just – I was still trying to process our earlier conversation. The one where you claimed to resemble my mother.'

She'd been worried about the appropriate response to his question. Worried that if she agreed with him too quickly or stoked the flames of his suspicions prematurely, he might read her earnestness as manipulative and question her motives. So she'd resorted to light humor.

He smiled. Her chest cracked open.

'It's all good, Keme. Do you have any other photos of your mother? I've been doing some thinking, and it's possible our features only seem similar in the one photograph.'

'I'd have to dig through my luggage.'

'If she wasn't my future mother-in-law, I'd think we were related.'

'There you go again, weasling yourself into my family tree,' she teased.

'You got jokes, huh?'

'*You got jokes, huh?*' she repeated.

They stood in the middle of the living room, her torso pressed to his chest, his raspy breaths falling against her hair. She struggled to shake off the moment's wrongness, her flank curving inwards to make room for his arms, her fingers curled against his neck.

Her time in America was plagued with mistakes.

Walking down that winding tarmac was a mistake. Boarding the Boeing 747 headed for Houston, her naïve hope bubbling beneath the scratchy sweater she'd worn to protect herself from frigid American air. A mistake.

'Never leave me in the dark again,' Nna murmured.

Sunshine spilled through the Venetian blinds, highlighting the high points of his cheeks.

She could tell him everything.

Right there and then.

She would tell him everything, but she must be smart about it, wait for the right time and place. She only had one shot to play her cards right and when she did, it must be powerful enough to set her free.

20

It was a weekend evening, and the Nwosus gathered around the flat screen TV in the downstairs living room. Agbala filled a russet plastic bowl with buttery popcorn and handed Vita Malt to the audience of three. They were watching Trevor Noah's Netflix special.

Free-flowing laughter.

Nna announced he'd be speaking to HR at his firm about permanently switching to the firm's satellite office in Houston. 'The timing feels right since I'm about to start a family.'

Agbala nodded approvingly. She said she knew he would come around.

Eke kissed Agbala's forehead.

Nna kissed Ikemefuna's forehead.

Ikemefuna excused herself.

'Let me change into something more comfortable,' she whispered into Nna's ears.

He nodded, a coy smile on his lips.

Ikemefuna released herself from his arms and bounded up the stairs. Three pairs of eyes followed her feet before returning to the flat screen on the wall. She ran into her bedroom, shut the door, and pressed her back to the frame. Then she hurried to the window and pushed against the fiberglass, tugging at the sash locks. Outside her door, someone laughed. She inched away from the window and rummaged through the dressers, like she told Nna she would.

The sky flashed neon white. The first drizzle of rainfall bounced off the cedar elms. Ikemefuna returned to the window and pressed her forehead against it, staring at the neighbor's backyard. She missed rainy days in Lagos, the city's red soil thick with earthworms and centipedes. She missed Adina's jangled laughter and how it transformed her mother into a younger woman – the kind who still believed the world was her canvas. She even missed Adina patting a blob of iodine into first, her sores, then Ikemefuna's, feeling along the edges for open wounds.

She listened for Nna's laughter, shrill and clattering, like nails on chalkboard.

She could learn to love him in the unrehearsed way some women loved their husbands. Some of those women were products of an arranged marriage. Take Nneka's mother, Nwanneka, for instance. Nwanneka first met her husband on the eve of their wedding. Thirty years later and she still sang his praises to all and sundry. Was she not proof that a woman could love a script?

So Ikemefuna could trace the swirls of Nna's chest curls and love each strand of hair. She could beat her chest till it pattered to the sound of his voice. She could continue to cook, and clean, and smile. Spread her legs and herself thin for Nna, then Eke, then Agbala, till her belly swelled with child, a boy, her son, black and ruddy.

A light blue sleeveless dress.

She pressed the fabric to her nose. She twirled in the mirror. She rubbed lavender on her wrists, then behind her ears, then her navel. She tied her hair with a nut-brown scarf, untied it, laughed at her reflection in the window, the earnestness in her eyes. She walked towards the window. She could bring herself to wear some lipstick – rouge, or a dusty brown, the color of a cherry mango.

Her breath caught in her throat.

There were eyes in the upstairs window of the neighbor's house.

Human eyes.

Tousled blond hair and piercing blue irises.

Do something!

A ticking pulse beneath her right armpit.

Scream! Wave your hands!

Pooled sweat in the hollow of her spine.

The eyes were gone. In their place – drawn blinds.

Had she imagined them?

No. She was positive that they were real. That they had stared back at her, seen her. The reds of her eyes and the limp in her walk as she hastened to the window.

'I knew you were hiding in here.'

Nna, her husband-to-be, stood at the door. A half-smile, the shape of a tusk, spread across his lips. He was handsome. Something about the goatee left unattended, the afro sticking out in all directions, the tiny welt on his aquiline nose. She could turn her fear into gratitude, be kinder to him, to herself.

'Don't be silly, Nna'm.'

She tucked a loose curl behind her right ear and steadied her trembling hands, still shaken by what she thought she'd seen in the neighbor's window. She hoped she was radiant enough to pull off the talkative, twinkle-eyed girl from her first night with Nna. The one who gave him a reason to stumble over his tenses. To thirst for new skin.

'Turn around.'

She spun around to face him.

'Do you have a little black dress? Those are sexy. Plus it's a turn-on when you show off your thighs, babe.'

He looked at her with big, hopeful eyes. She stared at her feet. Did he not notice the rouge on her lips, the lavender in her armpits, that she had fluffed out her afro so that she looked young and free in that baby blue?

'Nna'm, I like this one.'

'Pretty please?'

She sighed. She crouched, fumbled through the dresser for *black* and *short* till her fingers found a simple black dress. It had once belonged to Adina, who folded it into a ball and stuffed it into Ikemefuna's luggage on the morning of her trip to Houston. Who had been so confident that it would come in handy.

'This one, nko?'

She held up the dress for inspection. Pieces of lint dotted its rumpled length. But it was *short, black* and Nna eyed the dress, its lint and its creases. He nodded. She waited for him to leave but he did not. They stood in place, him rocking back and forth on the balls of his feet, her running her palms against her neck.

'I'd like to watch you undress.' Then a blushing afterthought. 'If you're fine with that, of course.'

She sighed. Yes, they had been intimate on multiple occasions. Peeled off their clothes till they were down to the bones. But that was different, their bodies entwined and awash with the soft glow of the moon as they concentrated on fleeting pleasure. Their eyes tightly shut, unconcerned with registering the ridges, or out-of-place ribs, or the fat swinging from the wrong angles.

She shielded her breasts with her forearms as she slid off the sleeves of the sky-blue dress. She rushed to throw on the black dress, but it caught on her big toe and for a few horrible seconds, she was a half-naked form struggling to free a hem from a toe.

'Not so fast,' Nna murmured. He inched further into the room. 'I want to see your belly.'

She held up the dress inches above her belly and focused on the black concave dent next to the light bulb on the ceiling. Nna ran his palms along her belly, tapped its skin, lightly at first, then with increasing pressure. He rolled a fold between his thumb and index finger, once, twice, again, until she smacked his palm and tugged down the dress.

He laughed and it jangled, like bobby pins in a tin.

'Aren't Igbo girls supposed to be confident?' he asked. 'Why is my woman the exception to the rule? We've got to work on your confidence, Keme.'

Keme.

That name was growing more aggravating by the minute.

She rolled her eyes and turned her back to him.

'See you downstairs.'

She could hear his retreating feet and laughter. The air returned to her lungs, the color to her cheeks. She swept her palms along the hardwood for the pieces of her splayed across it – droplets of sweat, rouge stains from her lips, remnants of dignity, and the rusty hook of a dreamcatcher earring.

'A word?'

A stout figure with a headscarf on its head.

Agbala.

How long had she stood in that spot, shifting her weight from thigh to thigh? How much had she seen? Was the entire Nwosu family trying to interview her in the middle of Trevor Noah's set?

Agbala marched into the room with wide, graceless steps. She inventoried the room's contents – the bedside lamp, the fingerprints on the window, the girl, the heap of clothes at the foot of a bed, the balled bedsheets. She pressed her palms to her back. The backaches were getting worse. They had stopped responding to the tablets she chewed at dusk.

'I have been doing some thinking,' Agbala started, her throat trembling. 'It's been over a month since you met Nna, yes?'

'Yes.'

'And you've been sleeping with him every day, yes?' Agbala continued, tightening the grip of the head scarf swinging loosely from her hair.

'Yes.'

Agbala inched closer to Ikemefuna, so that the front of her headscarf rubbed against Ikemefuna's temple.

'Yet, your womb is the same as it was on your very first night in this house, yes?'

'Yes.'

Agbala did not mention that she'd locked herself in the toolshed in the backyard with its mounds of unstretched braiding hair and cardboard boxes gathering dust. That she'd asked Ala why her grandson was dragging his feet on his way to Ikemefuna's womb. That in return, cockroaches had scurried over her feet, and cobwebs had stuck to the whites of her hair. Nor did she recount how she had held on to her faith with her fists and it had paid off because Ala herself had come to Agbala in her sleep and shown Agbala the problem. A low-hanging fruit. A body. Ikemefuna.

'At first, I was convinced there was something in you,' Agbala continued, a rivulet of anger gushing into her voice so that each word shook as it left her mouth. 'An evil spirit was eating up your sons just as they formed in your thankless womb. I mean, you tried to strangle me for godsake!'

'But then I looked at you,' Agbala continued, lowering her voice and pressing her lips against Ikemefuna's ear. 'And I saw the truth, clear as day. You are too tiny, too weak. Spirits prefer bigger bodies, you see. Stronger bodies.'

'I just need more time,' Ikemefuna whispered. She tried to steady her voice, swallowed. 'Tonight ma. I'll try again tonight.'

Ikemefuna wished she was in the living room with its LED dimmers and buttery popcorn. She wished for the shock of blond hair from earlier, sirens, a 911 call from a kind stranger, a tip, a visit, feet knocking down doors, a bevy of police dogs, yellow tape, a frazzled survivor (*her*) led away in a bath towel or a robe, disheveled but alive, a blaring ambulance like in the movies. Ginger tea with a drizzle of honey. A concerned nurse (*it's all gonna be okay, sweetie*), her southern drawl, a job prerequisite.

'I know of women like you and all of your tricks,' Agbala whispered. Her spicy breath fell on Ikemefuna's upper lip. 'Yes, child. This morning, I took it upon myself to search your possessions while you prepared breakfast. I did not stop until I found every last one of your pills.'

Agbala bared her teeth, threw back her head, and laughed.

Ikemefuna shut her eyes.

The pills: flesh-pink and tiny.

Omoye had wrapped them in a small, black nylon and stuffed them in Ikemefuna's purse just before she left her nail salon. *These Naija men in America have large appetites,* Omoye said. *Before you know it, you fit carry belle you no want.*

They had giggled conspiratorially, but deep down, Ikemefuna had been grateful. She had shielded the nylon from Adina's prying eyes and Agbala's careful inspection on that first night, wrapped it in a balled hairnet, opened it at the break of dawn every morning, dipped her finger into the nylon till it connected with a pill, pressed the pill to her tongue and swallowed. It was a ritual she performed without thought. But Agbala had searched her things, and found the pills, buried beneath hairnets, and socks, and hope.

A bout of nausea hit Ikemefuna like a gut punch. She wrestled for control of her body as she swayed sideways and staggered forward. She widened her eyes. She caught snatches of her fingers tugging at the thicket of hair beneath Agbala's head scarf. Of her arms tightening around Agbala's legs.

Agbala slipped through Ikemefuna's arms and rammed her elbow into Ikemefuna's chest till Ikemefuna fell against the bed frame, glaring at Ikemefuna as she moaned softly on the bedroom floor.

Ikemefuna opened her eyes. The room came into focus. There was a heaviness in her chest. From the corner of her eyes, she could see Agbala advancing on her. She leapt into the air and ran for the door. She felt a dull thud at the back of her shoulder. Something bounced off her shoulder and clattered to the floor.

A thick grey heel, the shape of a gun.

Blood, sticky and red, trickled down her arm. A rogue drop landed on the hardwood as she pressed a palm to the gash.

Behind her, Agbala reached for the bloodied shoe and aimed it at the wound.

21

Agbala paced her bedroom. She'd been in timeout since she pulled Eke into the kitchen on the pretext of fixing the clogged sink and told him what she'd done – that she had questioned Ikemefuna. Taken matters into her hands.

'Go on,' he'd huffed in the gruff voice he used to signal his disapproval.

She'd gone on. She'd told him everything. The way Ikemefuna rushed at her, her pupils black and pulsing, like a raccoon feeling for meat. How she'd acted on impulse, her old fight or flight response kicking into gear as she grabbed a stray heel off the shoe rack. 'You should have seen her,' she'd said to Eke's widened eyes. 'You would have done the same thing if you'd seen her.'

She was not proud of her actions, but what was the alternative? That she stood at attention while a gum of a girl punched and bit at her? Never. Over her dead body. She did not spend years of her life carefully building the resume of the woman she was today – a revered medium for Ala, the leader of the Houston chapter of Umu Ada society – to let herself down like that. Besides, someone needed to take charge and she knew Eke well enough to know that he would not. She was the one Ala trusted with her demands. The one who felt the cold draught of Ala's breath on her spine.

She had orchestrated the move from Lagos to Houston because Eke would not. Been a big girl about it too. Frantic months of clinging to the handlebars of danfos headed to the American Embassy in Lagos Island. Of gathering naira notes in rubber bands, first for visa fees, then for fat bribes that would expedite the visa processing. She had spent her last night in Lagos throwing scarves and rumpled rapas in Ghana Must Go bags as Eke snored into his pillow and Nna tossed around in his cot. Because she knew, more than Eke would ever know, that it was what Ala wanted for her son.

They had arrived in Houston on a warm afternoon in June. The air was sticky with the tang of smoked brisket. The people were a forceful kind of friendly, clobbering her with their *sweeties* and *sugars*. Reducing her to three-fifths of a woman. On her third night in Houston, she searched the yellow pages for a Nigerian immigration lawyer who would assist with their asylum petition. One willing to cut corners for the right price. She knew – through hearsay – of Nigerians who filed for asylum under all manners of guises, and wasn't her nuclear family a textbook case? Marginalized Ala worshippers in an increasingly orthodox West African metropolis.

She'd silently shepherded her family through each asylum hearing, shedding slow tears beneath the immigration judge's scrutiny. She had known, long before the postmarked green cards arrived in the mailbox, that the judge would grant their petition. It was what Ala wanted him to do. But there was no explaining to Eke that hurling that shoe at Ikemefuna was also what Ala wanted her to do. She would not put herself through his interrogation. Not anymore.

Only the day before, he'd suggested they let Ikemefuna out on daily walks – *thirty minutes or so. A little fresh air* – and she had reminded him of all the nights they'd walked in on the girl ramming her body into the kitchen windows. The mornings they'd found her standing by the front door, a wildness in her eyes.

He'd dismissed her words with a shrug.

'The girl just needs some air. Why can't we give her that?' he'd said. 'You are too hard on her, you know? Sometimes, I look at you and I wonder if you are Ala herself.'

The bruise was a dark mauve. It curled down the back of Ikemefuna's arm, nicking away bits of her skin.

'Just ignore it,' she muttered as she sat next to Nna on the stiff Mesa Brown couch in the living room. 'I slipped at the top of the stairs and bumped into the railing.'

He eyed the darkening sphere of skin, the knowledge of her new imperfection calcifying in his brain.

'Why did you let that happen? You should be more careful,' he said, his tone reproachful, frustration slipping through the cracks in his voice. He tried to ease back into himself, to mask his annoyance with a kiss to the wound. But trying only made him tenser. More annoyed at her carelessness and at himself for being so affected.

'Nna'm, cheer up,' she whispered beneath her breath, her eyes on Agbala and Eke who were making their way down the stairs from their bedroom. 'Imagine how I feel.'

He placed his left palm on her thigh, squeezed it. He intended the gesture to be endearing but she winced.

He lowered his eyes to stare at his palm, tugging at her skin.

22

The next morning, Ikemefuna told Nna that she didn't have any other photographs of her mother with her.

'I've been thinking about it, Nna'm,' she added as she stood by his bathroom door, toothbrush in hand. 'You look like my mom, *sha*. The more I look at you, the more I see it. You have the same eyes and teeth.'

Nna rubbed the sleep from his face and frowned.

'So let me get this straight. You didn't see the resemblance when I pointed it out a few days ago, but you see it now?'

'Nna, it's common for Igbo people to have similar features. People tell me that I look like the nerdy version of my best friend Nneka all the time. Besides, it's weird for me to see the resemblance to my mother so I dismissed it at first.'

He nodded slowly. He could show his parents the photograph. Adina had been their neighbor when they lived in Lagos, so it was possible that they knew something he didn't. Or he was reading meaning into the resemblance. After all, there were people whose entire personalities revolved around being celebrity doppelgangers.

His phone beeped to remind him of an upcoming networking event at his firm that would attract the firm's biggest clients. Dick, his partner mentor, had suggested that he show up to the event. Dick said Nna's presence would raise his profile at the firm.

He rolled around in his bed, the lean expanse of his bronzed skin tumbling against his sheets. He would make a quick trip to Philadelphia, attend the networking event, crack a few LIBOR jokes over deviled eggs and caviar. Then he would meet with HR to discuss permanently moving to the firm's satellite office in Houston.

He hated to admit it, but Houston was growing on him – the proximity to his family, to warm ogi and fresh laundry. He sniffed the air. Something was cooking. Akara sizzling in hot canola oil. His stomach rumbled from the thought of it.

Should he take Ikemefuna with him to Philadelphia? He could use her cooking in Philadelphia. She would marvel at the nuances between his pots (small, functional) and Agbala's pots. She would turn up her nose, and fold her arms, and refuse to cook until he bought her bigger pots, and thicker mittens, and an apron. He would get to know her beyond the stucco walls of his parents' house. He would quiz her on her mother.

He frowned. No, it was too late to get her on his flight. Besides, she barely cared to leave the Sugar Land house.

'Nna, America excites me. But it's also terrifying!' she'd said to him as they picked at dinner the other night.

'How so?'

'Too many skyscrapers and packed highways.'

'That's part of its allure, no? Anyone can be anything here,' he'd murmured, leaning across the glass-top dinner table to plant a kiss on her cheek.

'Yes. And anyone can disappear here,' she'd replied darkly.

He smiled to himself. She was terrified of America and its capitalist morass of trigger-happy cops, and school shooters, and neo-Nazis, and used-car salesmen, and sparkling water, and bubble-gum pink hair, and televised chants of *lock-her-up*.

Agbala was a part of the problem. She encouraged Ikemefuna's fear. The night before, Agbala pulled him to the side and reminded him to protect Ikemefuna from America's excesses. 'Remember it's her first time in America so don't take her anywhere just yet,' she'd said. 'You need to ease her into it.' Agbala said that America changed a body when there was no supervision. It fattened it, flaunted it, gutted it, and left it for dead. He hated to admit that his mother was right.

The previous night, he'd left her side for no more than a few minutes and Ikemefuna had reemerged from the darkness of her bedroom with a gash on her shoulder, a flap of crimpled pink flesh spanning the fresh wound's edges. He had spent the rest of the night hating himself for it.

He should have stood at the entrance to her bedroom, watched her every move, rushed to her side just as she lost her balance. And if she could bleed in his parents' house with all of its soft landings, how much more would she bleed if he threw her to the rabid dog that was America?

It was decided then.

He would leave Ikemefuna with his parents for now. He would return to Houston in a week or two. When he returned, he would dress her in a low-cut floral jumpsuit, like that one Zimmerman jumpsuit his ex, Bunmi, wore on special occasions. They would go to an expensive restaurant in River Oaks. He would try not to stare at the wound or lecture her on how she must do a better job of taking care of herself.

Women did not like the truth. They wanted to be coddled like eggs. He would know. He'd been vocal with Bunmi. Expressive with his words. With his gesticulating hands. Some would call it passion. She had called the cops on him.

Nna flashed a lazy smile as he walked into the kitchen. Something was different about Ikemefuna. Her hair. The way it stood at attention in two space puffs. He swallowed, his eyes lingering on the lime-green rapa fastened beneath her armpits. She was every bit his wife in that moment, a thing to be loved, and held, and sucked on, and picked apart bit by bit, till flesh slid off the bone.

'How long are you gone for?' she asked as she stuffed akara balls into a foil wrap for him.

He could see her worry, the way it rounded out her shoulders and caused her to slump forward. She looked undone, her falsies peeling at their edges. He squinted at her lips. He would remind her to use a chapstick.

'A week or two. I'll be back in no time.'

He pressed his length against her back, kissed an earlobe.

'You miss me already, don't you?'

'Maybe.'

Her eyes rose to the ceiling then fell to her fingernails.

'Can we not do this?' he sighed.

'Do what?'

'The thing where you don't tell me what's bothering you.'

It was meant to be sweet, reassuring, but his jaw throbbed as he spoke, his frustration thickening, pushing up his throat.

She folded her arms.

He folded his arms.

'Am I being childish?' she asked, looking up at him through guileless eyes.

A small bead of heat pushed its way up his gullet and spread across his tongue.

'Just a little.'

She lay her head on his chest.

'I'm sorry,' she said.

'Mmmh.'

'Don't leave me,' she sighed.

Her words gurgled out of her mouth before becoming a trickle of saliva on his chest. He tried to pull her off him, to search her face for answers. But she held on to him with her nails and her hot breath, her fists pounding against his back.

'Stay.'

'Please.'

'Nna, Please stay.'

'Please don't leave me here.'

Her words ran into each other, shattering in the air and clattering to the floor around his feet. Her fingers tugged at his collar, then against his mouth.

He tried to make sense of what was happening. His emotions rose and fell. Fear. Confusion. Attraction too – a strong gust that drew him to her in a way that terrified him. For the first time, he could see her clearly, in all her raging madness, and it was intoxicating. He tingled with curiosity, his palms tightening against her arms. What would she do if he fought back? Matched her punch for punch? Would she hit him harder? Would he like it a little?

Agbala and Eke walked into the kitchen.

Ikemefuna released Nna's shirt collar. She reached for his neck, straightened the microscopic wrinkles on his collar. Her lips unfurled a smile.

Agbala eyed Nna's overgrown afro and the bandage jutting out from Ikemefuna's shoulder. She grinned, revealing a chipped incisor.

'You will get a haircut before returning to Philadelphia, yes?' she said to Nna.

'Yes Mom. Whatever makes you happy,' Nna sighed.

She turned to Ikemefuna.

'How is your shoulder today?'

'Better. Much better,' Ikemefuna said, her eyes averted.

'Very good.'

Agbala traced the outline of her pots with her right thumb and shook a plastic bottle for thyme.

'You are drinking my potion, then?' Agbala asked.

'Yes. It's helped a lot with the swelling. See,' Ikemefuna motioned. She pulled back the dressing. Nna grimaced.

Eke shuffled around the kitchen. He sniffed overripe bananas for rot. He rearranged loaves of bread. He inventoried pantry items due for a replacement (onions, table salt, tatashe). He struggled to lift a yam tuber.

Nna held back a groan.

Eke was so mild-mannered and wispy, so different from Nna in his physicality and temperament. He often joked that he was lucky to have Nna as a son because how else would he protect himself from America's miscreants?

Eke was right, Nna thought to himself bitterly. The man could barely rub his medicated balm on his back without pleading for assistance.

'Remind me to dress your wound tonight,' Agbala said to Ikemefuna.

Nna raised his head just in time to catch Agbala winking.

23

Two hours and a fresh haircut later, Nna stood in front of Ikemefuna's bedroom door, a moleskin briefcase in his right hand and a boarding pass in his left. He looked at the briefcase as a tightness formed in his forehead. He clenched his fist, prepared to knock.

His flight to Philadelphia would depart in exactly four hours and he was minutes away from leaving Sugar Land for the airport. But he couldn't leave without seeing Ikemefuna, not after what happened in the kitchen, her fingers tearing straight lines into his skin with manic precision.

She had some answering to do, and if she gave the right answers, he thought with a chuckle, he would reward her with a quick romp between, beneath, and without the sheets. He would kill two birds with one stone. Her unfounded worries and the teenage boy lust in him that often caused him to turn to less flattering outlets – like the recently divorced Liberian woman who lived next door to him in Philadelphia.

He knocked on her door.

'Come in.'

He smelled her in the air and on his skin. Last night's panties swung from a nail on her door. A lacy bra poked out the back of a headboard. The coconut and sea breeze of her shower gel mixed with the metal in the air. She stood in the middle of the room, a shower cap on her damp hair.

She raised her eyes to him. Her shoulders jutted forward. She stamped her feet, began to march, left, right, left. She jumped. It took him a second to realize she was dancing. But to what? There was no music playing. Just the gentle hum of the air vents.

'Don't just stand there, join me!' she called out to him as she shimmied towards him, her arms flapping in the air.

'You must give me a heads-up next time,' he said with a chuckle.

He undid the top buttons of his dress shirt.

She was in front of him now, her eyes bright with excitement, her feet stamping the floor with more fervor, her shoulders ramming into his chest. He tried to shield himself, but she was faster, hitting his chest seconds before he could block her blows with his arms.

He shook her.

He didn't mean to.

He just wanted her to stop.

One second she was in his face, her elbow ramming into his ribcage. The next he was sweeping her off her feet.

'God, Ikemefuna,' he yelled at her limp frame on the floor. His body felt electric, like he was more alive than he'd ever been, the blood in his veins redder. 'I'm so sorry.'

She looked up at him, a wave of nausea washing over her body.

What just happened?

The preceding moments came to her in blurs of imagery, her body moving to its own rhythm then falling into his as her world spun on its head. Damp blasts of air from the vents puffed against her face. Her eyes tore past him as she scanned the stuffy room before settling on its shuttered windows.

'Nna'm, your flight leaves in four hours. You should get going. It's a long journey to the airport,' she said, nudging him off her and standing to her feet.

He gathered her in his arms.

'Not when we're like this.'

'Like what?'

'You seem off. Talk to me, Keme. What is the matter?'

Silence.

Her silence rang in his ears. He hated to see her in that state – the welts on her skin exposed, the back of her shoulder mummified in swaddling bandage.

'What's the matter?' she repeated slowly. 'I hear those words a lot, you know?'

There was something in her voice, its edges jagged.

'My father says it to me whenever he thinks I have an attitude. He stands so close, and he leans into my ear. He says it and it sounds like a threat.'

'Just him? Or are there others I should know about?' Nna asked, staring sharply at Ikemefuna.

He pictured the other men in her life. Young, black Lagosians with dada in their hair, broken English in their throats, and the smell of diesel fumes on their blue-black skin. Men itching to lay their large, grubby hands on her. To sink their teeth in her breasts.

A bellicose vein pushed against his temple.

Nna stared at Ikemefuna, a strange shock of repulsion beating in his chest.

She let the men get away with it. He was sure of it.

She let them read her like poetry, memorize her like scripture, moan her name beneath the streaks of a half moon. If they asked her to be their *forever*, she would say yes, and she would mean it.

He glared at her shower cap and felt the urge to pull it off her head.

'Sometimes, my father says – *open your mouth and speak. He says it when I am in a foul mood,*' she whispered.

'Good man.'

'He is not a good man, Nna'm. His words are usually followed by a backhand slap,' she said drily.

He groaned. Daddy issues, then. He should have known from the jump. The tell-tale signs were there – her stage-four clinginess, that air of despair.

'Nna'm, my father is the worst man I know,' she said.

He regarded her closely. He was overprotective of his parents and could not imagine discussing them with such vitriol. Once when he was fifteen, his childhood best friend Brian spent the afternoon in the Sugar Land house. They tapped away at Play Station consoles and yelled expletives at the TV screen until his mother marched into the living room and banned them from playing more games for the rest of the day.

Brian, whose parents spared the rod and spoiled the child, mumbled *bitch* as Agbala walked away. Even years later, Nna remembered latching on to Brian's smooth cylinder neck and pressing its slimy length with all his strength until Agbala tore his palms off the boy, one finger at a time.

'You don't believe me?' Ikemefuna asked. She loosened the knots of her rapa till it bunched at her waist. She pointed at an ugly yellow dent in her flank. 'See.' Rows of purpling zigzags above her navel. 'See.' A deep tan scarification that ran the length of her stomach. 'See.' A charred patch of skin three centimeters away from her spine. 'See.' A light peach wetness beneath her left breast. 'See,' her agitated body twisting and turning to reveal the parts of her where debris, or dried flesh stubs, or air had replaced skin.

'My God, Keme.'

'Abeg, my name is Ikemefuna.'

He was surprised to hear the irritation in her voice, the broken English in her mouth.

What else was she hiding from him?

'Hey, look at me.' He cupped her face in his palms. 'You know I'm not your father, right?'

He tried to be gentle with her skin, to avoid its bruises. But he found himself pausing, wishing for a pair of gloves or a paper bag to wrap around his palms. For the honk of an Uber. The cool cabin of a plane in midair. A door marked *Exit*.

He tried to peel her skin from his chest, but it was a clumsy dance of limbs and teeth. Him patting the top of her head with the tip of his fingers. Him kissing the air above her cheeks. His lips hovering over her lips. Their overbites bumping as he stood to his feet. Another whispered assurance – *I'm nothing like your father*. He imagined Ikemefuna's father – a tall man with a horse whip. He took a step back from her body, smelling her wounds on his tongue.

'Nna'm, I'm scared,' she moaned, reaching for his neck. He took another step back, tried to swallow the panic.

'Please. Not now. I have a flight to catch.'

Ikemefuna bit her tongue. She considered shutting up. He was right. Her timing was off, and she should wait for him to return from Philadelphia. But she couldn't. Not anymore. September was nearing its halfway point and when she shut her eyes at night, she could still see Agbala's glare as the older woman commanded her to fall pregnant by the end of the month. She feared what would become of her if she failed to meet those expectations.

She opened her mouth. She would begin at the very beginning. Adina picking her wriggling body from the banks of the Lagos lagoon. Adina and Dumeje raising her as their child. Dumeje showing her how he liked his Peugeot washed. Nkemdili teaching her to sweep the cobwebs from the ceilings of the Lagos flat. Adina stuffing recipes in her luggage and shaving her privates. *My daughter will never carry a jungle to her husband's house!* Dumeje warning her not to disgrace the family. *I didn't spend thousands of naira on that yeye degree for you to rubbish my name, o!* The George Bush airport with its whirring conveyor belts, and buffalo chicken wings, and University of Houston sweatshirts, and Houston Press bookstand. Travelers barnacling in and out of stores with wild abandon. The hope of American freedom – a mustard seed in her heart.

Agbala and Eke ushering her into the RAV4. Agbala's fingers pointing out the Beyoncé billboards, the Minute Maid stadium and a boarded-up Forever 21 as the Toyota sped away from the city's speckled lights. Eke, silent and watchful, leading her into the house. Her quiet awe at

American ostentation. Framed diplomas and a year's supply of Ritz crackers.

Ikemefuna, watching with confusion, then horror, as Agbala's smile hardened into a grimace. Eke yanking her passport from her grasp as the house's yolk walls and barred windows caved in on her. Eke's yellowed teeth clamping down on her passport's pages.

'Nna, I need to go home,' she blurted out.

'Home?'

'I need to go home,' she repeated. It bounced off the room's clementine walls. The shuttered windows.

'What do you mean you need to go home? To whom? The father who treats you so badly?'

'Nna, I need to go home—'

Nna clenched his fists. She was not making sense. How could she romanticize her old life in an abusive home over the bottomless reservoir of his love? Could she not see that he could be a leather-skinned black man in that Lagos, fraternizing with those Lagosians, *his people*, in thick, beer-battered English?

'You don't understand,' Ikemefuna spat, her voice raw with emotion, that new-school Nigerian accent. 'They – they took my passport, swallowed it.' She grabbed her throat, her words slurred and breathless. 'They smashed my cellphone. They threatened to kill me if I leave this house. Before you got here, they – they punished me each time I tried to leave. Hit me. Starved me. Nna, they said I must – I must have your baby. Your son. They won't let me leave this place until I do, Nna'm. I'm not ready for a child. I don't want …' Heaves. Dry gasps. 'Not now. Maybe sometime later. I just want to dance …' A queasy smile, there, then gone. 'I just want – I want to dance. Anywhere. I just want to dance, Nna'm.'

'They?'

He felt a coldness in his chest as he held her by her neck, tightening his palms against the cold flesh to keep her head in place.

'Your parents, Nna,' she croaked.

Pooled saliva dribbled down the corner of her lips.

'What are you saying, Keme?' he asked, and it was not a whisper. It was something lower, laryngitic, a rustle in the air.

'Listen to me, there's something wrong with the two of them,' she said, her eyes flitting between the door and his face. 'If you pay attention, you will see the way they watch me. Nna'm, I've been here for months and I've never left the house. They won't let me.'

'My parents are overprotective.'

'I lied to you. The wound on my shoulder isn't from a fall. Your mother hit me with a shoe because she found out I was on birth control. Please Nna'm, you have to believe me. They make me take pregnancy tests. They are forcing me to have your child!'

Nna swallowed.

'Your parents are not who you think they are, Nna'm.'

The honk of a Nissan blasted through the window.

'There's something wrong with them. You have to believe me,' Ikemefuna pressed. 'You saw the photo of my mother, didn't you? Isn't it odd that you look exactly like her?'

Nna clenched his fists.

'Didn't you say Igbo people share similar features? Besides, it's an old photograph.'

'It's still her face *naw*.' Ikemefuna shut her eyes, a pained expression on her face. 'Look, I'm scared and I'm sure you are too. I just want you to know that there is something going on in this house that you don't know about.'

Agbala called for Nna from down the stairs.

Nna'm, hurry!

Nna shot a fearful look at the door.

'I don't know what you're talking about.'

'Please. Just think about it.'

Freshly cooked akara filled his nose, his throat.

Bright Chimezie tinkled in his ear.

Nna released himself from Ikemefuna's grip, slowly, carefully. He pictured Agbala rushing towards him, her left knee knocking against her right. Eke at her tail, his sallow face and aching gut. He thought of Ikemefuna's missing cellphone. Of the other night in their bedroom and the disquiet that had enveloped him. Of all the other moments carved into the recesses of his mind. Slight shifts in temperature. A smolder in Agbala and Eke's eyes. There, then gone.

He exhaled.

'Look around you, Keme.'

She looked: at the clementine walls; the bedside dressers and their overflow of knickknacks; the lopsided lampshade; a tub of Dark and Lovely.

'Look carefully,' he whispered.

She looked at him, her eyes bright, a flame.

'This is home. Get used to it.'

24

Adina sat on the floor of her balcony. She watched the neighborhood children kick a deflated soccer ball. She envied them for their lack of care, how they could just stand there, kicking up sand as the sky darkened around them.

Adina did not have the luxury of carefree evenings, not since she was thirteen and scuttling up ebelebo trees in her father's obi. But those days did not last. She'd become her mother's backbone after her father married a second wife and began to insult her mother at every turn. She'd watched her bright, mouthy mother retreat into her carapace till all that remained of her was a painful devotion to family life.

Adina had sworn she would not be her silent, cowering mother. That she would make the right choices and avoid potholes. Then she met Dumeje at an end-of-year party in her final year at the University of Nsukka. She was blinded by his potential. A second-class upper in geophysics from UNIBEN. A Chevron job in Lagos. Great dentition. An intimate knowledge of English, not the Ngiligbo that came out the mouths of the boys in her South-Eastern town – their English, marred by fissures they filled with Igbo.

Someone cackled from the streets below. A small girl with a swollen face, her pinafore muddied with sand. Adina stared at the girl. The girl stared back at her. Her amusement stretched out her cheeks as she pointed at Adina and laughed.

Adina's breath caught in her throat.

Was the girl laughing at her?

Adina tried to feign indifference. She stared straight ahead at the flat opposite Number 25 Uyime road and tried to block the girl's horrid little laugh from her mind.

Why was she laughing at her?

Had she heard something about Adina from her parents?

Adina folded her arms against her breasts and eyed the girl. Something about her looked familiar. The up-turned nose. The crowded teeth.

She sighed. It was clear now. The girl reminded her of Ikemefuna. She had not always been Ikemefuna's mother, but she had become her mother early enough. Ikemefuna was only a few weeks old when Adina watched from behind an Iroko tree as the birth mother, a teenage girl with thinning red hair who worked for Adina, stepped out of a molue in Makoko with a large paper bag.

Adina had observed Ikemefuna's mother in the days leading up to that afternoon in Makoko and had known that the poor woman was struggling. That it was only a matter of time until she gave her child up.

Adina wiped the gathering moisture from the corners of her eyes. Thinking of Ikemefuna made her emotional. She had hoped it would be easier to let go. That she would be logical about it. Eventually, all girls left their mothers.

Adina had left her mother, and so had her mother and the women before her.

And yet.

She could have stopped it.

She could have tried harder instead of letting Dumeje call the shots as usual. Instead of punctuating his sentences with her nods.

She had contemplated reaching out to the Nwosus on Ikemefuna's behalf. She would send a care package to Ikemefuna through them. Iodine for her sores. Kayanmata to sweeten the sex. But history had taught her that the Nwosus could not be trusted to deliver her packages.

Adina tightened her rapa against her chest and clenched her lips. She wasn't entirely to blame. She had tried her best with Ikemefuna.

She remembered her *trying*.

When Ikemefuna was ten years old, Adina was delirious with buyer's remorse. She needed to let the girl go. So she grabbed Ikemefuna by the lapel of her gingham dress and dragged her to Akande market, palms clammy with sweat as she imagined Dumeje following her. She pushed the thought away. Dumeje was working as a fuel attendant at a Total fuel station, not the white-collar Chevron job he'd told her about. She would have another four hours before he returned to the flat. She marched through the untarred streets of Akande market with Ikemefuna in tow, Adina strumming clay-glazed stockfish and avoiding the greasy arms of the traders.

'Before you know it, you will grow breasts and buttocks, and a man with a big stomach will live in your house, and he will call himself your husband, and he will be very hungry all the time,' she'd said to Ikemefuna. The words had come from nowhere, but they'd felt urgent. 'It will be constant, that hunger. An everyday hunger. Every minute of every day hunger. And it will be for the rest of your life. Is that what you want? Ikemefuna, look at me when I'm talking to you. I said is that what you want?'

Ikemefuna looked her dead in the eyes and Adina looked away, unable to bear the heat of her daughter's gaze. Around them, the market was a breathing sphere of sweaty black bodies towing machetes, and wheelbarrows, and empty coca cola crates, and yam tubers, and glass boxes filled with puff puff or meat pies, and rifles, and babies. The bodies twisted and unraveled in and out of shapes to fit into the nooks of the market's narrow streets, breasts pressed to bare backs like sardines.

Ikemefuna tightened her grip around Adina's wrist.

The air bristled with heat. Half a dozen teenage boys kicked around a punctured car tire in a clearing and ignored the sweat dripping from their jaws. To their left, a woman in a wife-beater and a rapa the color of a black eye, fanned four corn cobs on a grill. To their right, a band of drummers beat their dundun to the market's rhythm, their vocal cords ululating as the melody crescendoed.

Adina shook her wrist free from Ikemefuna's grasp as her daughter, distracted, watched the bodies around her. They were laughing, and exchanging naira, and gulping from Maltina bottles.

Adina ran.

She dashed into the crowd with its sweat, and its Maltina, and its dundun.

She ran past stalls, and fallen moi moi leaves and torn tires, her slippers slapping dry earth. She ran fast, faster, picking herself up when she collapsed to the earth, ducking, and diving, and whipping beneath the armpits of traders and behind toolsheds. Blending into raffia baskets of tomatoes and dry fish. Dashing past the harsh glare of Volvo headlights. Sailing past bus conductors leaning out the sides of emptying molues, blindly, then with purpose, till she arrived at the fenced compound on Number 25 Uyime road.

She was home.

She had successfully returned Ikemefuna to the street.

She began to concoct a story for Dumeje. She would tell him that she woke up and Ikemefuna was gone. She would say that she called all the neighbors, the police stations, the army barracks.

She sat at the dinner table. She ignored Nkemdili's timid queries about Ikemefuna (*Where is she, ma? Won't you tell me?*) and stared at the framed photograph of Dumeje from his early years in Abagana, a catfish dangling from his fist.

Then the brass front door of the flat burst open and Adina's shoulders stiffened. She opened her mouth to greet him. Except it was not Dumeje. It was Ikemefuna. The little girl hobbled into the flat with its cement walls and its empty soda crates.

'Mother,' Ikemefuna whispered, the flinty browns of her eyes digging into Adina.

The louvers lining the living room rattled in their hinges.

Adina shuddered.

She pushed the memory of that day out of her mind. She must stop thinking about Ikemefuna. Nothing good came from dwelling on the past.

25

The ceiling fan hummed steadily above Ikemefuna's head at night. She ran her palms along her arms and shut her eyes. Earlier in the day, Nna had gone to Philadelphia for a networking event so she had all the time in the world to sit with her thoughts. She pictured Nna's chiseled jaw. The crepe laugh lines shooting out the sides of his eyes. The vertical cracks running up his bottom lip. So similar to Adina's jaw, the sides of Adina's eyes, Adina's bottom lip. She shuddered at his resemblance to her mother.

She would never get used to seeing Adina's face each time he climbed on her, his naked weight pressing her into his sheets. His rapid breathing, the sound of phlegm shifting up his throat. The stench from his penis filling her mouth. She rubbed the spot he'd bitten on her belly the previous night.

'This is home,' he'd said in the afternoon, and there was something about the way he said those words that caused her eyes to glance nervously at the door. She'd wanted to fly across the room and run down the stairs.

'I know you think I'm crazy, Nna'm,' she'd whispered pleadingly, her eyes on his. 'But please believe me. I'm not making any of this up.'

She waited for understanding. He was supposed to be fond of her. She was supposed to be able to wield his desire like a wand. *Release me,* she would chant, and he would turn the key in its lock.

'Think about it, Nna'm,' she continued. She softened her voice, tried to make it pliant. 'Why did your parents keep this arranged marriage from you? What else are they hiding from you?'

His eyes fell to her shoulder.

'You're crazy,' he whispered, but his words lacked conviction.

'Nna'm, I know I sound crazy—'

'You do.'

'Then explain your resemblance to my mother. Your eyes. Your mouth. The shape of your ears. You must see it too.'

'It's just one photograph.'

'It's not just one photograph. You look exactly like her, Nna'm.'

He did not respond. He just stood there, staring down at her. Her eyes darted to his fists, the way they clenched and unclenched.

'You're accusing my parents of a crime,' he stated slowly.

She swallowed.

Was that a statement or a question – him confirming the scope of her accusation before he dialed 911?

'Nna'm, I'm telling you what happened to me.'

He nodded. She sighed, relieved.

He extended his arms. She started to fold her body into his chest, to brace her chest for his tight embrace. He pushed her. A little push, but still – he pushed her. With enough force that she stumbled on her feet and grabbed the headboard for balance.

She watched, stupefied, as he walked out the door and slammed the door shut.

It was like she was back in Number 25 Uyime road where she would lean forward for Dumeje's embrace and meet his cold indifference, his palm stopping her in her tracks and directing her towards Adina or Nkemdili.

She sat on her bed and stared at the ceiling.

She was tired of blending into the worlds of men who did not love her. Of picking the chaff from their beans, dusting their furniture, making their eggs all fluffy, just the way they liked it, contorting her body to fit the crooks of their arms till she was a sponge, or a dish rag, or a pair of briefs, sheets, threadbare, colors faded.

'Where is that girl?' Agbala called from the kitchen.

She froze.

What if Nna had relayed everything to his parents?

She needed to focus. Think fast. Nneka once told her that Obinna prided himself on making unilateral decisions for the both of them. *Ike, it's all about planting a seed in their ogologo heads and sitting back to watch it grow*, Nneka had added with a flourish.

When Nna returned to Philadelphia, she would take Nneka's approach and resist the urge to revisit their last conversation. She would trust that she'd sown enough seeds in his mind to cause him to doubt everything about his parents, down to their very identity. She would watch him realize that his parents were hiding important details about his life from him, like he had walked into that conclusion by himself.

If Nneka's approach failed her, she would play the long game. They would sign a lease in Houston, or he would take her back to Philadelphia, to his bachelor pad, and he would let her make it her own.

Then one day, they would return to their townhouse from the grocery store or the movies, and she would stand on the front steps, and just before he turns the key in its lock, she would yell at the top of her lungs, and all the good Americans would peer through their blinds, and they would see her distress, and they would fasten their capes, and dash out their front doors, and save her from him, or herself. Or they would see her Black, and mistake her for a crime in progress, and call 911, report a disturbance and hope for the best.

But I still have to kiss that man for now.

She groaned.

He was so good at turning her off. Right from the start – her narrowed eyes watching his tongue glide across his teeth as he locked eyes with her from across the kitchen table. The rancid fat that clung to his penis as he forced himself into her mouth, the bass in his voice and the way that he pressed her to his chest like she was a loaf of bread, like she needed less oxygen and more him. Everything about him gave her the ick, down to him abbreviating her name to a simple, nonsensical, *Keme.*

'Is that girl still hiding in her room?' Agbala screamed from the foot of the stairs.

Use your feet.

Ikemefuna stilled her feet.

Use your feet, Ikemefuna.

She would. It was just a matter of time.

A matter of time, as in that evening. Exactly four hours since Nna stormed out of her room and out the front door of the Sugar Land house. Without her.

Ikemefuna stood by the kitchen's casement windows. The good news was that Nna hadn't revealed their conversation to his parents. Or if he did, Agbala and Eke were doing a great job of pretending he didn't.

She caught her reflection in the kitchen window. The 4C hair in thick, tangled clumps. The boogers in the corners of her eyes. The tomato paste smattered across her left cheek. She giggled despite herself, a hearty round ricochet that fleshed out the sides of her face. The moment passed. The giggle settled into a garish smile that caused the tip of her nose and the veiny crisscrosses on her eyelids to scrunch into a ball.

Agbala and Eke were in the upstairs living room, their voices ricocheting through the open kitchen space below. Without thought, Ikemefuna climbed up the kitchen counter. She felt along the window's perimeters till her fingers settled on the lock. She grabbed a knife from the kitchen sink and rammed its tip into the lock, twisted left, then right, then left – nothing. She pressed her palms against the plexiglass. Pushed. Pushed with all her strength. Then with her head. Once. Twice. A steady knock reverberating through the kitchen walls.

'What are you doing?'

Eke's voice flooded her senses. She didn't hear him come down the stairs.

She climbed off the granite.

'I said what are you doing?' he said, his voice steadier, more commanding. He took a few steps towards her.

She glanced at her hand, at the knife in it. She raised it till it was level with her face.

From the upstairs living room, Agbala yelled for dinner. Now. Right now. *Make yourself useful for once, Ikemefuna.*

'I – I was drawing the blinds.'

Eke stared at the knife, his lips a tight slash.

'But the blinds are still open?' he said, his left eyebrow arched.

She eyed the knife. She could charge at him with it. Push it through his belly. Twist and turn it. Then head upstairs. Charge at Agbala. Rinse. Repeat.

But there were so many unknowns.

Like how much blood would she have to clean up? A shallow stream of red, pooling around her feet? A shapeless sphere spreading to the yam tubers leaning against the kitchen table?

The knife could get stuck in Eke's sinewy muscles. Maybe he was stronger, he could overpower her, snatch the knife out of her hand, deliver a fatal thrust. It would be in self-defense. He could get away with her murder.

She threw the knife in the sink.

She rinsed soup bowls.

She dished a tray of pounded yam and ofe nsala beneath Eke's watchful gaze.

She served Agbala and Eke the meal in the upstairs living room and waited for Eke to say something. For Agbala's suspicions to rise into the air.

Nothing.

Just the sound of Agbala and Eke's throats, widening to make room for balls of yam glazed with soup.

The night was still young.

She could still make a move.

She could hear the neighbors from across the street. They were having one of their garden parties. The ones Agbala and Eke never attended. The nausea was back. It was stronger than it had ever been. She clutched her head and slid against the yolk walls.

Hello.

A familiar voice broke through the air. Ikemefuna stared hard at Agbala and Eke. They continued to eat, oblivious to the voice.

Hello.

Clearer. Stronger. It was real. It was her mother, Adina's voice.

Ikemefuna sucked on the roof of her mouth and concentrated on the voice. Were her parents colluding with the Nwosus in whatever yama-yama business was going on? Didn't they know the Nwosus were holding her hostage?

Wait a minute.

A second voice. Her father, Dumeje. She could see it now, the cellphone planted between Agbala and Eke, the voices coming out the speaker.

Laughter.

Her parents were laughing.

They were not grieving, or yelling at the Nwosus, or threatening to alert the American police. *What have you done to our daughter? Let her go. Let her go, or else.* They were laughing, like her suffering was their entertainment. Like she was invisible, her absence inevitable.

Another wave of nausea, a heavy draft sweeping her off her feet and hurling her towards Agbala and Eke. She snatched the Falu red vase on the coffee table in the living room and hurled it in their direction, striking the side of Agbala's neck. The vase clattered to the floor in three shards.

Agbala pressed a palm to her neck. It was bleeding, drizzles of rust blood leaking out the gash.

'Give me the phone. Now!' Ikemefuna shrieked. 'Let me speak to them.'

Agbala and Eke stared back at her in silence.

She reached between them, swept her palms against the patterned couch. Nothing. There was no phone in sight. It was gone. Along with Adina and Dumeje's voices. She broke into a cold sweat as she tried to find her bearings. She leaned against a ledge, steadied her harsh breathing.

'I . . . I think I blacked out,' she cried weakly.

'You little devil,' Eke cursed at her. He tore off his singlet and pressed it to Agbala's neck. Agbala held her bleeding neck in her palms and sniggered, rolls of her neck skin sliding in and out of place.

26

'Kimchi pork sliders, sir?'

Nna opened his eye to a skeletal waiter with a buzzcut lowering a dozen pork sliders on a tray till it was level with his nose. Beside him, his work buddy Bode cozied up to a VP at Banco Santander.

The evening sky was a cloudless peach. The networking event at the Barnes Foundation was in full heat. Men in tailored Armani and women in Ann Taylor-esque silhouettes reached for prosecco and tartlets, pausing to throw noncommittal laughter at the finance-appropriate jokes floating through the air.

'No, but thank you,' Nna said to the waiter, an apologetic smile on his lips.

He turned to Bode and the VP and attempted to join their conversation, emitting forced chuckles and dazed *Oh*s during awkward pauses. In the end, he gathered the remnants of his dignity, leaned away from the duo, and slid his palms in his pant pockets.

'I'll be right back,' he announced to no one.

He walked around the Barnes' sweeping grounds, drifting from circle to circle, catching winds of conversation, bland grievances, and exultations about the upcoming CREFC conference in Miami, a whispered recount of the last networking event at the Barnes and who remembers whatshisname getting so drunk he kissed that one paralegal on her forehead?

Nna inched away from the crowd, slid between the tables of veiny blue cheese and brie and through the glass doors. Then he was in the gallery, the cool blast of conditioned air tingling the hairs on his arms. He found a bench, fell against it with a thud. He held his face in his palms, massaged the waves of exhaustion running through its muscles. He'd tried to keep his parents off his mind but the more he tried, the more they crept in – Agbala first, then Eke – the lines running down the sides of their mouths furrowed in concentration as they inched closer to him in his head.

Ikemefuna's voice rose through the faint traces of conversation filtering through the gallery's windows, her accusations ricocheting in his cranium.

Kidnap. To intentionally or knowingly restrain another's liberty by using or threatening deadly force.

It was Criminal Law 101. Fodder for law school arguments in study rooms with padded walls. In fact, in his first year at NYU, he had dissected the elements of a kidnap, explored defenses to its prosecution. But his library outlines were theory.

Ikemefuna had insisted that his parents kidnapped her. Watching her performance had been an out-of-body experience, him observing her from a safe distance as her eyes filled with tears. The cool pressure of her fingers on his neck. The loud squelch of a hose sucking him down to earth as he struggled to free himself from her grasp.

Muscle memory was a funny thing. Isolated events melded into one. He'd watched Ikemefuna and thought of his old best friend Brian lying on the settee in the upstairs living room. His ragged breathing and clammy palms.

He stood from the bench, wiped his palms on his pants, clenched his jaw. He was not the flawed protagonist of a box office thriller, and his parents were not wanted criminals. They were hardworking Nigerians who picked themselves up by their bootstraps and earned their keep on foreign soil.

He shut his eyes and exhaled.

Ikemefuna was just another fresh-off-the-boat Nigerian trying to capitalize off her trauma. She was addicted to victimhood. With each little white lie, her deceit seemed to become more vicious. He would do something about her lies. He would put an end to them before they tore his family apart.

Then explain your resemblance to my mother.

Your eyes.

Your mouth.

The shape of your ears.

Ikemefuna's voice thumped in his head. He punched his arm to get rid of her voice. Nna raised his head from his thighs. He locked eyes with a mid-level associate at an investment firm just as she released a soft gasp. He sighed. He'd assumed he was the only one in the gallery.

'A fly,' he said, flashing her an apologetic smile.

27

Wake up.

It was the crack of dawn. Tangerine streaks in the air. Blackbirds pausing on windowsills in search of early breakfast.

Wake Up.

The ceiling fan had stopped whirring, its background noise replaced by a jangle of bangles and the peppery scent of tiger balm.

WAKE UP!

Ikemefuna blinked. She was in her room in the Sugar Land house, the air filled with the stench of spoiled milk and old books. She raised a hand to her eyes to shield it from the sunlight filtering through the blinds. She stifled a yawn and started to shut her eyes again.

Then she saw them.

A pair of balding heads hovering above the bedpost. Agbala's smaller and rounder than Eke's. She'd tied an indigo scarf around her temple and pressed rouge blush into her cheeks. A ball of dressing jutted out of her neck. Eke's head – oblong and gaunt, bobbed beside Agbala's, each clad in matching blue-white pajamas that smelled of fried eggs.

Ikemefuna sat up in her bed. Her eyes darted between them.

What did they want to discuss now? Her womb? No. She still had two weeks till October. Two weeks to be pregnant with their grandson. Then bits of the previous night came rushing back to her. Her body. Running into the front door of that house and lurching forward. A hipbone rammed against a metal knob. Then a shoulder. Then a forehead. Then her teeth. Against windows. A windowpane. Plaster.

'We're going to lunch today, all three of us,' Agbala announced, her palms clasped, her gaze steady, her bangles glinting in dappled sunlight. 'Don't look at me like that. Save those eyes for Eke. It was his idea.'

Ikemefuna struggled to keep her face blank.

'The new Nigerian restaurant in Southwest Houston,' Eke announced. 'Clearly, you need some fresh air. A refresher on how to behave like a human being and not a goat, yes?'

Ikemefuna nodded. They would be out in the open. She would feel real sun, not the nothingness of the rays that pierced through her windows. She would be in the middle of the city. Nna had warned her about the humid Houston air, but she did not mind humidity.

Ikemefuna smiled at Agbala and Eke. Agbala glared at the ceiling. Eke looked at the sunspots on his arm, uncomfortable with the visuals of her joy.

'Stand up from that bed then,' Agbala growled, baring teeth. 'Get ready. We don't have all day.'

Fatima. Senegalese. The owner of the Nigerian restaurant at the end of a strip mall speckled with empty shopping carts, spilled coke, plastic bags stuck to granite, and homeless men with capes of tartan bedsheets.

Fatima. Who did not particularly like Nigerian food (too spicy, too many bell peppers and periwinkles), or Nigerians (too spicy, too many bells and whistles), but was business-savvy enough to know a good business in Southwest Houston was a green-white flag glued to a store front, the overpowering scent of jollof and suya, and the chaos of Nigerian accents laughing or cursing, the former indistinguishable from the latter. Thieboudienne and yassa could wait. Jollof took priority.

Fatima's Nigerian restaurant had quickly gathered a cult following in Southwest Houston. The room, a small square of dull orange walls pockmarked with expired RCCG calendars and an oval clock whose long hand had long stopped moving, was packed with black bodies of different shapes and accents. Pidgin flowed in and out of patois as they demanded more jollof, more meat, more shitto, less oil, softer plantains – no, harder – faster service, cooler A.C., and *where is Ngozi*, and *where is Laide*, and *why has quantity gone down, and prices already gone up*, and *two boxes to go, ejo*.

Agbala, Eke, and Ikemefuna sat at a table pushed to a wall. They eyed the menu. They would occasionally glance up, take turns to size each other up, slice their lips with their teeth so that it retreated into their skin, and shake their heads to the Davido pouring out of the twin speakers beside the door marked *employees only*. They took giant swigs from the bottled water on the table, each washing down the previous backwash then leaving fresh backwash in its wake.

Ikemefuna's ears bristled each time the restaurant's door swung open. Her eyes took in customer after customer, assessing each new body for strength (of bones, of lungs, of arms). Two chatty girlfriends ran past her on their way to the restroom. An elbow brushed against her arm – *his father asked me if I can cook ayamase, can you imagine!* Two waiters burst through swinging doors, one sporting twin tribal marks on each cheek – *maybe I would attend HCC in the fall, get some credits* – teeth disappearing into warm meat pie.

A chubby woman, skin the color of sandpaper, marched to the table. She smelled of cayenne peppers and onion juice. Her smile revealed a chipped tooth. Ikemefuna stared at the woman's gaping mouth. Was she small enough to fit through that opening, squeezing past teeth and sliding down throat, till she was far from Agbala and Eke?

'What can I get for you?' the woman asked the table, her voice a jingling note.

'Swallow for me,' Eke announced. 'And edikaikong.'

The woman scribbled something on her notepad then turned to the left to address a cluster of middle-aged women in rapid-fire Yoruba. Then she regarded the table, an apologetic smile on her face.

'No edikaikong today, sir. But there is egusi, and okro, and ogbono I think. Maybe even efo riro.'

Agbala started to complain, but Eke nudged her and she snapped her mouth shut. It was one of the little pleasures she afforded Eke – the illusion that he had the final say in anything.

'I want the egusi.'

'The ogbono soup for me,' Eke added.

The server nodded.

'And you?'

Ikemefuna met the server's eyes, held her gaze to the point of discomfort, until she looked down, eyes glued back onto the notepad in her hands.

'She will have ogbono,' Agbala interjected, her voice cutting through the silence.

'Anything to drink, then?'

'Water for me. Water for all of us,' Agbala barked, eager to get the server out of her hair.

'Okay ma. Fifteen minutes.'

The server (she'd introduced herself as Funmi) retreated into the door marked *employees only*. Ikemefuna followed her with her eyes, her breath easing as the server increased the distance between them.

'What was that about, *eh?*' Agbala barked at Ikemefuna.

'Nothing. I wasn't sure. That's all.'

A man seated at a table next to them – broad-shouldered, with kind eyes, skin the color of bamboo – chewed the lips of his dinner companion. The companion laughed too carelessly, her eyes wide open, her nostrils flared, her body rocking back and forth from the heaviness of her joy. The duo made plans to see a movie that night, or the next night, or for the rest of their lives.

Ikemefuna watched with a quiet longing. She wanted to be careless. To stretch a little, stand on her feet, place one leg in front of the other, attempt a pirouette, feel the crackling air sneak up on her cheeks. Her movements would be rusty. She would topple over once, then again. She would catch herself in time to place one foot in front of the other till she was in front of the exit.

'What do you think you are doing?' Agbala asked.

Ikemefuna looked at Agbala and Eke, then at the life buzzing around her. She was standing up, the legs of her chair scraping concrete. She was placing one foot in front of the other. The whole thing was a little too easy.

'I'm leaving,' she murmured, more to herself, than to Agbala and Eke. 'Can't you see?'

She'd begun to quicken her pace. Fast. Faster. Past the necking couple, and the waiters, and the men in their polos and chinos, and the girls deconstructing last night's date, towards the door, her feet quickening. Quicker. A jog. A slow sprint.

'Going where exactly?'

She could smell Agbala and Eke behind her (onions, bile, bangles, runny eggs, sweat). On her.

'Away.'

She pushed the weightless door, *EXIT* bonded to its glass in cheap Vinyl. She tasted the humid air. She was free.

28

Funmi walked out the door marked *employees only* with a large plastic tray in her hands, three saucers of pounded yam, three bowls of soup and her million-watt smile. She grimaced as she hobbled to her customers. Her leg was acting up. She would book an appointment with her doctor again, insist on a full examination. If he refused, she would get mouthy. Let go of her immigrant graces, her *pleases* and *thank yous*. She would embrace the sassy in her black. *DO YOU TREAT YOUR WHITE PATIENTS LIKE THIS OR IS IT BECAUSE I'M BLACK, DOCTOR SMITH?*

An article she once read said doctors were less likely to give black women pain meds. That they assumed black women could bear pain better, like their bodies were more than tissue. Articles like that were the real-life consequences of *black girl magic* tautology. White folks were starting to think she was magic and here she was, limping about the place with a stupid smile on her face. She would not care what the doctor thought of her, or that she could be accused of playing the race card. Sometimes, the race card was her only shot at a checkmate.

She heard a commotion in front of her. She looked up at the scene unfolding in the restaurant. The group of three she'd been heading to were headed for the door. The girl – their daughter, Funmi imagined – was ahead of her parents. If Funmi didn't know better, she would think the girl was trying to get away from them.

'Ah, don't leave *naw*,' Funmi cried. All that time spent ladling egusi and cow leg into deep-dish bowls. It seemed like they were leaving. All three of them, now huddled around the exit door. 'The food is here, oh.'

'No, we are not leaving,' the man assured her, a tight smile on his face as he grabbed his daughter by her shoulder.

'Yes, we are returning to our table. Are we not?' the woman echoed. Her voice was dry. It reminded Funmi of constipation, a montage of clenched butt cheeks.

Funmi stared at the girl.

Then at the girl's feet, one leg suspended above the ground.

She raised her eyes to the girl's face. Her facial expression unsettled Funmi. There was something swimming in her eyes.

'No,' the girl yelled.

Funmi frowned at the girl.

'You heard me,' the girl seemed to strengthen her resolve. 'I said no.'

29

April 2019

The night Dumeje revealed Nna to Ikemefuna like he was her ticket to greener pastures, he asked her to sit beside him on the forest-green leather divan in the flat's living room with its clutter of Milo tins, old newspaper sheets and Coca-Cola crates.

Ikemefuna stared with suspicion at her father. He never addressed her directly or by name, preferring to speak to her through Adina. *Tell the girl to boil me potatoes*, he would say to Adina as she stood beside her mother. *Tell the girl to stop wearing dresses that don't reach her knees*. And yet, there he was, patting the spot beside him on the divan and wagging his sparse brows at her.

She swallowed.

'Come on,' Dumeje mewled, an ornery grin contorting his features. 'I don't bite.'

She took quick steps to the divan, afraid that anything less than quick steps would earn her a sermon or a slap. She half expected that he would renege on his invitation before she made it to the seat, her legs rushing towards the divan, determined to outrun anticipated disappointment.

He was still sitting on the divan when she got to it, his legs crossed, his fingers strumming his kneecaps as she adjusted her buttocks to its scratchy width. She was just starting to relax when she spotted Nkemdili, a bumbling figure nervously pacing the living room's fringes.

'Daddy, any problem?' she whispered, her stomach tightening into a ball.

She scanned Dumeje's steely gaze, surveilled her mind for wrongdoing.

She could swear she'd done all Adina and Dumeje expected of her. She had ditched the neighborhood boys who clung to the pavement outside Number 25 Uyime road with their insta-poetry pickup lines and melted chocolate. She had bought the longest loosest dresses, trimmed her hair into a vintage Bieber bob, and emptied her make-up tin to throw gluttonous men off her scent.

'Calm your nerves,' Dumeje said. He released another one of his chuckles. 'As a woman, you must learn to be patient. Or hasn't your mother taught you anything?'

She bowed her head in penitence.

Dumeje grunted. He reached for the remote control and turned down the volume on the TV screen so that the only sound in the air was of Ikemefuna's engorged heart pushing against her chest.

'Your mother and I have been talking to our, er ...' Dumeje threw a sharp look at Adina. 'Our family friends. One Mr and Mrs Nwosu. You don't know them. They used to be our neighbors, but they moved to the United

States a long time ago. Long before you were born. Anyway, the Nwosus want to host you in Houston.'

'They are doing well for themselves. I hear they run the biggest hair braiding salons in Houston,' Adina added from where she stood behind the quilted jade recliner in the living room.

'Well, the Nwosus, they have a son,' Dumeje forged on. 'I think I mentioned him before. Yes, I'm sure I mentioned him. Nnaemeka. A corporate lawyer.'

Ikemefuna held her breath.

'I spoke to them last night, and we agreed that Nna will marry you. Oh yes. In fact, Eke Nwosu's brother who lives in Aba but runs an import and export business in Lagos will bring your bride price to our house before you leave for Houston. Eke Nwosu is a stand-up man, you know. He doesn't want to have any outstanding debts before you join the family in Houston.' Dumeje released a raspy chuckle. 'And if the rumors are true, the apple doesn't fall far from the tree.'

Ikemefuna stared at her father's lips. She heard the words, the way the bass slipped in and out of his voice. But she could not make sense of what he was saying. His words were as obscure as Sanskrit.

Dumeje coughed.

'Daddy, I'm n—' she started to say.

Dumeje raised a palm. The press conference was over, and he would not be taking questions. He cupped her face in his palms, his lips pulled back to reveal the thick strands of goat meat wedged between his teeth. Adina stood behind him, stiff as a corpse, her papery hands stroking her rosary like it was a living thing.

Outside the living room, the dark sky broke into heavy rain that pounded against the red earth of Uyime road. The rain formed shallow brown ponds and deep grey puddles in front of the wood kiosks and overflowing gutters littering the road. The neighbors rushed out of their flats to snatch the bedsheets they had hung to dry on swaying cloth lines. The little girls playing suwe by the gutter packed up their pebbles, washed their feet in the rain, and disappeared behind the metal barricades of their flats.

Ikemefuna imagined that Bobo was somewhere out there, listening to the thunderstorms and thinking of her. Earlier that day, Nneka had convinced her to ask Bobo for his number at the next dance practice. For a brief moment, she considered leaving the flat in the dead of the night and hiding in Nneka's house. But Nneka's parents' bungalow was tight on space and Nneka's father was friendly enough with Dumeje to snitch on her.

Out of easy options, she hoped that Nna was a kind man. An educated man. Nothing like the local papas who frequented the neighborhood bars and groped any living thing with a hole between its legs. That he was a patient man. The kind to take his time to unravel her skin till he got to the bone. That he would not saw through her flesh for blood.

Dumeje shuffled to the kitchen for his Flomax. Ikemefuna stood to leave the living room and Adina cornered her to a wall.

'Don't be afraid,' Adina said, stretching her mouth into a wide smile so that her gap teeth peeked out her lips.

Ikemefuna pressed her back into the wall as Adina poked her rib.

'Be happy!' she shrieked, her voice fluty and breathless. 'You'll soon be an *Americana* with your very own *wanna gonna* accent.'

Ikemefuna faked a smile to pacify her mother, but in bed that night, she resolved to hide patches of her skin in the secret compartments of her suitcase so that her marriage would not swallow her whole. As Ikemefuna drifted into sleep, Adina slipped into the room and sat by her lolling head.

'Ike, are you still worried?'

She shook her head. It was a lie, but she did not want to bother her mother. There was nothing Adina could do about her worries.

'I spoke with your father, and we agreed you'll only visit Houston for two weeks. We want you to meet Nna and his parents for now. The wedding and everything else will come later.'

Ikemefuna nodded, relieved.

'Besides, I talked to a few of my friends who have been to America,' Adina said. Her tone was different, less fluff, more brass. 'It is nothing like Nigeria, Ike. Certain things we tolerate here, the women over there don't tolerate at all.' Adina's words tumbled out her mouth in a dizzying rush. 'In fact, all you have to do is dial 911 and the police will find you and save you if need be. Do you hear me? 911. Say it.'

'Yes ma.'

'I said say 911.'

'9—'

'Slowly. *Nain. Wan. Wan.*'

'*Nain. Wan. Wan.*'

'Good girl.'

Adina patted the bags beneath her hooded eyes with the hem of her rapa. She looked smaller and sadder than usual. Ikemefuna wished she could pull her mother to her chest and hold her in her arms. But their mother-daughter relationship was not the kind to withstand the weight of sudden hugs. So she pulled her blanket to her chin and watched Adina shuffle out the room.

30

This is What a Feminist Looks Like.

Nna eyed the inscription on the milky indigo tee he'd worn to class on many law school mornings, barreling down Furman's hallways on his way to Reproductive Rights. He'd chosen to sign up for the class, despite all his guy friends warning him against taking the class, because *that class is torture, bro!*

They were not entirely wrong. He'd been the sole guy in Reproductive Rights, which meant he had to work twice as hard to earn his keep. That was where the tee came in, his $35 attempt at virtue signaling. Then he'd bought a second tee. Blood red with black ink. *We Should All Be Feminists.*

'The woman who coined the phrase is Nigerian,' he'd bragged in Melissa Nguyen's ear a week before finals. They'd been sitting in Reproductive Rights class, waiting for Professor Margolis to make her grand entrance. 'Oh yeah?' Melissa queried, her eyes bright and curious. 'An acclaimed author,' he'd added with a flourish.

Nna was smooth like that. He knew it too. It was that dangerous upper-middle class Igbo son upbringing. He was not born with a silver spoon in his mouth – it was a gold spoon with his name inscribed in tight cursive. At five, Agbala and Eke began whispering to him about how special he was. They showed him off to their friends, made him sit between them during home visits.

At nineteen he was completing a gap year in Durban. He spent his weekends flirting in bad isiZulu at neighborhood braais, drove a Lexus and had a trail of broken-hearted girls to show for it. At twenty-seven, a law degree. A six-figure Big Law job. Women auditioning for wifey.

Bunmi. Tall, thin, and leggy. He liked her because she made him put in work. All those long-stemmed yellow roses and day trips to NYC for dinner at Kochi. Tickets to *Hamilton*. Two-night specials at Gramercy. And yet, she had her reservations. 'I just need time, Nna.'

He was relentless. Never mind guys who say they like it when girls do the chasing. Their egos like it. The men? They want the girl who makes them sweat from all the trying.

Bunmi made him sweat.

Long days spent holding open doors for her and belting Whitney Houston on the phone at her command. '*And I will always love you*. You know that, right?' he would say, the bass in his voice breaking in all the right parts. 'You don't have a choice,' she would reply with a coy giggle.

Then out of nowhere, she'd fallen *yakata*, without warning, and Nna had been forced to pick her from the floor. 'I love you too, Nna,' she'd said in bed. It was the first night he'd seen her without the Lancôme foundation and the twenty-two-inches Mongolian situation. He was supposed to say those words again? Dating was a scam.

It was mad of her to continue to expect everything, from the long-stemmed roses to New York, Lin-Manuel, flayed, well-done, brought to her on a stick. Mad that she blamed him for the edge in his voice instead of commending him for keeping it together. Mad that she blocked him on Instagram and Twitter when he shoved her off him on his birthday. He'd been frustrated by the disintegration of her illusion. He was only human.

Women wanted the fairytale. They wanted men that saw them in all of their ugly and loved them for it. It was unrealistic. Inhumane, truly, the way they balked at a man's humanity.

Suddenly, 'I love you,' turned to 'I never knew this side of you.' As if humans didn't exist on a spectrum of emotions. As if a smile stayed frozen to one's face, despite a change in circumference.

And what about Zainab? Bad girl Z. He was going to marry her. Swear down. Something about a woman who talked dirty and didn't give a shit about anybody, but wanted a man who would put her in her place. It was sexy. He liked it. He didn't think he would, but he did. He was even willing to overlook the STD. There were ways to navigate such things. He could play along. 'Expand your mind, baby,' she would drawl into his ears. He could.

Then Zainab met his parents and things went down the drain, a train lurching forward at full speed, forking left, without warning, falling off a cliff. *Bad vibes* was how she'd described his parents, her discomfort palpable from where she sat in the passenger seat. He'd refused to engage, turned up the radio's volume, drowned her foolishness in

Mariah Carey. Women of nowadays. Was it something in the water?

It was funny, really, how Ikemefuna existed in the intersection of the two. She had Bunmi's fear, the questions, the 'I didn't know this part of you' written all over her face. And yet, she wielded Zainab's thirst to offend, to question the people he held dearest to him. To place a target on their back.

He refused to think of all the accusations. The horrible things Ikemefuna said to him, and convincingly too, her tears big and easy. He was a black man in America for the love of God. The child of immigrants. He navigated the world with a target on his back every day he left his house. Every single day. Shoulders hunched, eyes to floor, body ready to defend his parents' honor.

Black immigrant parents deserved better, man.

Black immigrant parents who crossed continents for their children deserved better.

Agbala and Eke had crossed continents for him.

They were his heroes.

The ones he would die for.

He'd seen the news. The nationalists were becoming more brazen. A Karen at a Walmart spitting orange seeds in the face of a Mexican granny. A beefy redneck with a MAGA face cap heckling an Asian man, small stature like Eke, frail like him too. 'Speak English, Jackie Chan! This is America!'

Whenever he watched those videos, he was shocked by the breadth of his anger. The victims could have been Agbala or Eke. The mere thought of it, of people putting their hands on his folks, threatening their safety, the simple lives they had carved for themselves in America, set his Igbo boy pride on fire.

Nna tossed off his bedsheets. His restless left leg dangled from the foot of his bed. He'd wanted to get to know Ikemefuna inside out, till she was his worn-out favorite shirt, chewed out like the foreskin of udala. Till she spotted blood, a dime-sized hole, sweat spots, her loose threads unraveling at their seams. Till she was less fruit and more gum. Till all of her flavor was gone and his mouth hurt from all the chewing. Till all that was left to do was spit her out.

Getting to know a woman took its toll on a man.

She was supposed to be the shiny outlier – that small head, the big eyes, the pursed lips, the slender neck, those ankle beads, man. The way she'd caused his heart to bounce against his rib cage. He should have known she was a trick of the light.

The truth – Ikemefuna was dangerous. More than Bunmi with her irrational fear of his humanity, or Zainab with her imposing questions. She was dangerous in the way a woman who played victim was dangerous, with her tears, the presumption of her innocence.

The optics were terrible. Young Nigerian girl, tourist, abducted by her benefactors. Held against her will for months. Everything happening in what should have been the safest suburb on the outskirts of Houston. Fox News commentators at the ready. *This is what happens when we let these people infiltrate our country, our neighborhoods. This is what we let happen!*

He barely knew Ikemefuna, not in a way that mattered. All he knew was: she was laughter that began in the throat and stopped at the tip of the tongue. Laughter that did not ricochet from belly, to jaw, to the tips of her toes. A cool touch in the throes of passion. A compulsive liar. A vindictive little bitch.

So why couldn't he stop thinking of her words?

Listen to me, there's something wrong with the two of them.

No – she was wrong. His parents were good people. They had given him a good life. An education. The career of his dreams. He was grateful for all they had done.

But maybe he needed more.

An extended trip to Lagos, the city of his birth. A deep dive into his roots beyond Afrobeats and Naija Independence Day parades beneath the Brooklyn bridge.

He shook his head.

He must not let Ikemefuna get to him.

31

The dive bar on 17th and Sansom with muted neon lights was the perfect distraction for Nna. He'd texted his closest coworkers – Matt from Antitrust, Kevin from IP, and Bode – and they had answered his call. The night was young. They were second years now so work could wait. Two shots of tequila to the brain and he'd started to forget about his anxiety. Around him Bode, Matt and Kevin knocked back their shots and pressed lime wedges in the cracked skin of their mouths.

Nna reached for his third shot.

'Big Law has ruined us, bro,' Matt guffawed, his tobacco-stained teeth glinting in the dark. 'I'll be lucky if I feel a buzz after three shots.'

'Tell me about it,' Nna yelled above the clamor of David Guetta. He surveilled the bar, his eyes narrowing on a pair of rounded behinds belonging to two black women who were leaning over a counter to ask a weary bartender for something sweet and strong.

'Bro, focus!' Kevin yelled at him, his eyes flitting between Nna's face and the asses. Kevin's admonishment earned him cheap laughter from the group. The women whipped their heads back to glare at Nna. Nna winked at the prettier one. Narrow face. Thick lips. Just like Ikemefuna.

'Nna's always on the lookout,' Matt joked. He pronounced Nna as *Nah*. Nna grimaced. When he'd first joined the firm, he'd made a point of correcting every person who butchered his name, but he'd given up by the third month after he realized that his efforts were in vain. 'Can't take him anywhere.'

'Remember when Ted made partner and he hosted us at his cabin in the Poconos for the weekend?' Bode started, leaning closer to the other guys so they could hear him.

Faint memories of an alcohol-fueled blur flitted through Nna's mind. A hell of a weekend. Ted's sister was on the come up in New York, had walked the runway for Michael Kors or something. Ted put in a last-minute request and with her help, there'd been an excess of young, pretty women to impress. Every hotblooded Big Law recruit with a salvageable hairline made a note of pointing out to the women that although they were not quite New York sharks, the attorneys at the firm's Philadelphia location worked on the same multibillion dollar financings as their New York counterparts.

'Can we not talk about the Poconos?' Kevin groaned.

'What happens in the mountains stays in the mountains,' Bode added.

'Man, all I remember was Bode and Nna telling whatshername, Kavia, remember her? Redhead with big tits …' Matt started.

'Kaviaaaaa,' Bode groaned, his face in his palms.

'I still have her number,' Nna added, a sly grin forking across his lips. 'Saved as *Kavia with the Big Tits*.'

'Big teeth, you mean,' Bode groaned, clutching his crotch.

'… telling Kavia they made monthly donations to the Women's Refugee Commission,' Matt finished.

'I swear I donated $30 the very next day,' Nna yelled. 'I can dig through my emails for proof.'

'I mean, she made it clear she was a feminist. We couldn't get a word in without her mentioning Cosby,' Bode added.

'My thing is …' Nna started, his words punctuated with hiccups, his heart a warm puddle of gratitude for the heat of the tequila in his throat. 'Why are black men always the scapegoats? In a world of Harvey Weinsteins and Jeffrey Epsteins, why aim her spear at Cosby? That was my problem with Ka—'

'Kaviaaaaa,' Bode sang.

'Here we go,' Matt sighed, scanning the litter of shot glasses on the table for leftover tequila. 'Let's make it about race.'

'Everything's about race, bro,' Nna doubled down, daring Matt to challenge him. 'You wouldn't know, would you? You think Philly starts and ends in Rittenhouse Square.'

'Fine. But admit you only pretended to donate to the Women's Refugee Commission because you knew it was the fastest way to get Kavia to bust it open,' Matt insisted.

'Don't hate the player,' Bode slurred. 'Who says I can't be a perfect gentleman who donates to feminist groups but also appreciates good head?'

The men took turns hi-fiving Bode and laughing heartily at their archival history.

'Nna's the worst offender, really. You know what they say about the quiet ones,' Matt said, regarding Nna from across the table.

'Free my man,' Bode yelled.

'What's the latest on your love life, Nna?' Kevin added with a chuckle. 'Still trying to make things right with Bunmi? I hear she works for JPM now.'

'Pshh,' Nna hissed. 'Bunmi's old news. Your boy has a whole wife now,' he announced with a grin.

'Shut up. You're kidding, right?' Bode asked, doing his best to sober up.

'Bro. You know how Nigerian parents get. I go home to see my folks and there's a wife waiting for me.'

'Brooo.'

'Brah.'

'That's wild.'

'So what? An arranged marriage? I didn't think that was still a thing,' Kevin asked.

'Me neither,' Nna replied darkly, his murky feelings towards Ikemefuna cutting through the smokescreen of manufactured joy.

'How's that going? You're really following through with it?' Kevin pressed.

'Man, I don't know. I was down with it at first, but the whole thing is starting to sketch me out.'

'How so? She just lies there in bed? You gotta pry her open with alcohol, or else she'll have sex like her Nigerian parents are watching, bro,' Bode advised.

'I just have one question,' Matt started, raising a finger above his head.

'Make it good, Matt.'

'Does she have big teeth?'

The men burst into laughter and for a moment, Nna forgot about his life in Sugar Land, Ikemefuna, and everything she'd said about his parents.

32

Ikemefuna opened her eyes to an airless room with muted orange walls. She was no longer in the Nigerian restaurant in Southwest Houston. This room was smaller. Its air flowed less freely, standing at attention like a child bride on her wedding night. There were no yellowed RCCG calendars on the wall, or water marks from burst pipes, the pong of cabbage mingling with party jollof. The new room did not have that new room smell (sealants, sheetrock, wood). It smelled of armpits and damp clothes. It hit her all at once. She was back in her bedroom in the Sugar Land house.

She zoomed in on a stainless-steel bowl at the foot of the thin mattress. Soaked garri, a flotsam of granulated sugar and peanuts. Her first memory was of her body, hunched over the stainless steel, thin drops of saliva stretching from her lips to the bowl, and the door to the room swinging open. Agbala, dressed to the gods in a blunt-cut wig and a severe pencil skirt. So tight she could barely walk. Just enough to teeter to the edge of the bed. She'd squinted at Ikemefuna for what felt like a second but could have been much longer. Then she'd walked out the room, her heels clicking against the hardwood.

Ikemefuna sat up in her bed. She held her throat in her hands. It was scratchy and warm to the touch. She tried to scream but all she managed was a gust of stale air and a growl. She crouched on all fours, her eyes narrow, her nostrils flared, her teeth bared, her forehead speckled with glow-in-the-dark acne. How long had she been on that wafer-thin mattress, bits of skin hanging from her lips, head shaved clean of every strand of hair so that her skull jutted out her neck like a thumb?

There was no telling. She had lost all sense of time. She slapped an itchy spot on her back. She scratched her elbows, gently at first, ramping up speed and pressure as the itch intensified, tearing through her skin till she could see the peach sap underneath.

She shut her eyes.

Come on. A whisper. *Think!*

Trickles of recollection drizzled into her mind. She was back in the restaurant, standing at attention in front of the door marked *Exit*. Her impatient tongue tasting the air for freedom, that ice-cold thing, the consistency of gelato. Her smile, wide and discordant, even as the crew of diners shifted uneasily at the visuals – all those tawny teeth – and demanded their checks.

The waitress lost her grip of her tray, releasing a soft whimper as bowls of egusi and pounded yam slid off and bounced against the concrete, making a sudden carpet of glittering china poxed with diced vegetables. Agbala and Eke were shell-shocked, frozen in place, and she could have run, couldn't she? Flattening her skin beneath a Honda Accord or behind the bramble. Hopping into anything with wheels and making it move as quickly as she willed, till she was far from the Nwosus. She pictured it too, because seeing is believing. Ikemefuna, carving out a life in Houston. Owning a small dance studio in the city where she would teach her students to infuse Atilogwu in their Bachata.

The memory rushed back at once. She did not get a chance to walk out that exit door. One second she was staring at the diners and their apathy. At the waitresses mopping spilled egusi. At Agbala and Eke's calculating eyes, their mouths hanging open. At Agbala suddenly screaming like a banshee, a witch, a circus performer. The next, a multitude of grips. It felt like a pelting, each new palm searching for unclaimed land on her body, legs first, then belly, then breasts, clamping, squeezing, tugging, pounding. She was the earth, and it was a stampede.

The palms came in twos, threes, black, and hairy, and wiry, and built like Lego bricks; arms belonging to expatriates, and international students, and MDs, and PostDocs, and bloggers, and grandmothers, each determined to be their brother's keeper. Except Agbala and Eke were their brother and she was their brat.

The disbelief. She felt its presence in her spine, rigid with shock. Wasn't she in America? *The* America. Land of paved streets, and prom dates, and CNN, and watered lawns, and lemon ricotta pancakes. She could still hear Agbala's voice, pleading, persistent, cloying, impossible to ignore. *Please. Please, I beg you. Hold her. Yes. Hold her legs. Don't let her go. She's our daughter. Oh, the things she has put us through. Grief like you can't imagine. Please. Please, I beg of you. Don't let her go* – each syllable, fractured from stress.

Plastic forks glazed with egusi fell to plates as the diners' eyes raced from Agbala's broken face to the sheen of Eke's balding head, to the grin that was slipping from Ikemefuna's lips. They stood to their feet, confused, determined to be good.

Ikemefuna stared hard at the bedroom door. She needed to remember.

The weight on her arms and legs as the multitude of limbs held her down, each tightening palm a copy of the one before it. She could not tell Agbala from Funmi or the rest of the waitresses. From the men with flabs that doubled as bellies and the women who dreamed of semesters in the city's community colleges. She tried to raise her head above the tremble of knuckles and palms.

Please.

She was a hoarse croak.

Please. You have to listen to me. No. No! Listen to me. Just listen. Hear me out. She's lying to you. Please, I beg you. You have to believe me.

The arms of good black folk, folks with faces like her mother, pulled her farther back into the restaurant. Fatima, tall, black, a flowing brown kaftan, gave the orders – *To the back room. Bring her to the back room, quick quick! All this commotion can't be in my restaurant!*

Clear instructions were easy to follow. The diners did as they were told, grabbing, and tugging, and heaving, and reducing Ikemefuna's vision to a blur of elbows, loose arm skin, and plantains that rolled off kitchen sills and into the eye of the storm.

She tried to remind the diners that she too was one of them, a sister, a daughter, a friend. That they were in

America-wonda, with its sirens, and its streetlights, and its CCTV, and its forensics, and its law and order. That one 911 call and there would be helicopters, and choppers, and a swarm of bodies in oversized FBI jackets. That if her screams carried far enough, it would raise an eyebrow, a placard, and the microphones of the cable news reporters.

But public speech was not her strong suit, so the words did not work for her. They slipped out of reach, hiding behind the boughs and vines of her mind as she clung to the off-white plastic tables with palm oil stains the shape of bowl bottoms. Somewhere, a dusty, grey speaker blasted Lagbaja, as her eyes followed the outline of the parking lot with its empty Budweiser cans and piled trash bags.

She remembered more. Agbala made a bullet out of her tears, her breasts shuddering as she spoke to those who'd made it to the back room, her supplications generous, a mouthful: 'This girl has put us through hell and back. She's carried us from one police station to the next. She's caused us to file multiple missing person reports. God save us.'

A breathy gasp dashed through the crowd, shaking like foliage in a sandstorm. A sigh. A hiss. The synchronization of flexed muscles. Dozens of eyes shooting daggers at the tiny frame pinned down with arms and buttocks. Hands rising to heads. *Arueme!*

Ikemefuna could still see the sugar daddy with thick lips who ran his scaly tongue over his bottom lip and eyed her. She could still feel the cold palm of the keen waiter with twin tribal marks who leaned closer as if to get a better look, then pressed her forehead into the concrete with his elbow.

'Trying to abscond with her older lover. An oyibo man for that matter. Imagine our horror,' Eke chimed in, his voice trembling with false fury.

It was like bad Nollywood had overtaken the restaurant with a cast of first-timers reciting their stilted lines. Except the pain pulsing through Ikemefuna's head was real. The earful of prayers was real. One or two, humming hymnals, casting and binding demons out of her body.

These children of nowadays are very ungrateful – a stooped, balding man in a bright blue suit. *We do all we can to bring them to this country* – a thinning grandmother with a smattering of moles on her chin – *and they repay us like this. Same thing my Ifezuli did, dropped out of school, that one. Started following bad boys up and down. Next thing I knew, she don carry belle!* A collective gasp. *Ashakalakamakadaka Yashagadalagwaladakaka* – Bare feet Aladura churchgoers.

'My people, we can't thank you enough,' Agbala continued. She stood in front of the mindless crowd, supplicant and provider. 'Abeg, help us carry our problem child into our car. We can't carry her by ourselves. She will overpower and drag us to the police again.'

The crowd nodded their assent. They swung into action, pushing tables out of their way and hoisting bits of Ikemefuna's flesh against their shoulders and their backs as they marched out of the restaurant in single file.

33

The molue lurched forward with a sudden thump that caused the skinny bus conductor hanging onto its roof bars to almost fall off. Adina inhaled sharply. It was too early in the morning to witness a death. The ukwa she'd had for breakfast gurgled up at the bottom of her throat, two seconds away from shooting out of her mouth.

As the molue weaved through Lagos's potholed streets, she tightened her grip on the nylon of ahuji leaves she'd bought from the market. She would be adding it to the night's dinner of porridge plantains. Dumeje requested it the evening before, his torso straining against her back as he nuzzled her neck. He was like that sometimes, a gift basket of warm breath and pillowy arms. She'd acquiesced immediately, afraid to break the trance. Afraid that if she took too long to respond, hesitated for a fraction of a second, he would pull away, his large swaddling body taking all of the covers with him.

A passenger on the bus was selling boiled groundnuts. She was a teenage girl with tightly plaited cornrows, throwing derica cups of groundnut in translucent polyethenes and snatching nairas from customers. Adina contemplated buying some, had started to count her change when something caught her eye – a charm dangling from the girl's left wrist. Black with ivory corals, a red stone in the center. The homemade wristlet was easily mistakeable for a fashion accessory. Except it was more than that.

She recognized the charm from her years of watching Agbala prance around Uyime road with a similar charm on both her wrists. She'd asked Agbala about it once, because she was curious, had been curious for so long. 'Oh, this?' Agbala said with a chuckle, her left fingers strumming the beads. 'It's *arusi*. My protection. It shields me from harm.'

Adina still remembered that warm Sunday afternoon all those years ago when she'd looked into Agbala's hawkish eyes and decided that for once, she was going to trust someone with her pain. They had been making small talk by the clothesline in the backyard, when Agbala asked: 'That *yeye* husband of yours is still beating you, isn't he?'

Adina tightened her rapa and looked to the left and right to make sure Dumeje was not lurking behind the bushes hedging the mottled fence of the compound. Then she looked at Agbala askance, before falling into the woman's arms, weeping.

'Why didn't you say something about your pregnancy wahala? I could have helped you a long time ago. Haven't you heard that my mother was a medium for Ala, and she passed her gift to me before she died?' Agbala finally said as Adina's tears gave way to shallow whimpers.

She allowed herself to believe in Agbala's god because she was desperate for a solution. What did it matter that her only knowledge of Ala came from old wives in Aba with balding heads and sagging breasts who sat outside their clay homes as they waited for death to whisk them away.

The ahuji leaves were fragrant.

Adina pressed a bough to her nose and inhaled. She'd always loved the smell of ahuji, the complexities of its taste. That it could be used for multiple purposes. Medicinal by some accounts. Deadly by others. Some said the right recipe – crushed cloves, a little rat poison, a sprinkle of ahuji – could kill a man.

The Nwosus had not been transparent with Adina. Had withheld information. Had acted of their own will when they suddenly disappeared to America in the dead of night, reducing their relationship to years of infrequent phone calls and stacks of unacknowledged mail.

The molue driver hit the brake pedal with too much force. Adina's body flew from her seat, then fell back against it with a plop. She nudged the girl with the groundnuts, held out her five hundred naira.

She had spent the last twenty-nine years playing by Agbala's rules. She had followed the rules because Dumeje wanted her to. Because they were supposedly Ala's rules.

She needed to know the proper protocol for questioning a god. The science of jabbing her finger in Ala's omnipresent chest. She needed to grab Ala by her lapels and refuse to let go. She needed Ala to skip the middleman and whisper in her ears. She would tell Ala that she was running out of patience.

'How much, madam?' the groundnut seller asked, gesturing at her tray of groundnuts.

Adina shook her head, swallowed. She could feel the sun on the rind of her scalp. It was making her nauseous. She pointed at the woman's charm.

'Tell me,' she whispered.

The woman eyed her.

'Please. I need to know. Tell me about your god,' she cried.

She was louder than she intended to be. Heads turned. She couldn't bear their eyes on her. Their judgment. Their pity. She wedged her ahuji leaves against her armpit, her eyes on the molue's peeling floor. Then she stood up, squeezed past thighs, climbed out of the bus and into the street.

34

Ikemefuna's second introduction to the Sugar Land house was Eke's rising manhood responding to Agbala's chants of *Be a man! O nwoke k'ibu!* as he pushed Ikemefuna into her bedroom with all of his upper-body strength. The sunlight hitting the ugliest parts of the house – a burn, the shape of an iron's bottom on the sheepskin rug in the foyer; cobwebs swinging from the living room's ceiling; the scratch marks on her wasting skin.

A day later and Ikemefuna was still on that rail-thin mattress, her forehead pressed to its scratchy pillow. She tried unsuccessfully to fend off her exhaustion, to move her head and arms.

She thought of Nneka and Omoye. Would they believe her if she described the America she found at the end of that fifteen-hour flight from Lagos?

Then her thoughts trailed to the birth control pills she'd guarded jealously.

It was possible that the Christian God was punishing her for daring to be her own woman – one with a strong enough voice to say no to an unwanted pregnancy.

She burrowed into the mattress.

Strong voices were for girls with easy lives. Flamboyant girls in colorful hairpieces and gypsy skirts. Girls who lived on red carpets and in box office hits. *Seen* girls. Girls who did not lie on thin mattresses with stomach worms in their bellies. Girls who gesticulated with their hands and stroked their chiseled chins and expressed themselves through art. The limited-edition prints above their bedposts. The fingertips conveniently soiled with watercolor. The perfectly tousled curls. Girls who could afford to say no. Who expected others to take notes, impressed.

She was not that kind of girl.

Lagos did a number on her voice long before Houston and her twin cornrows and dopey grin. It silenced it before her eyes connected with the crimson of Agbala's kaftan as Agbala drew her into a long oud-scented embrace outside of the George Bush International Airport.

35

Agbala peeked through her bedroom blinds at her neighbor Mary's backyard. She could make out the small crowd lounging around a barbecue grill, the fingers stroking paper plates, the distended necks and belly skin swinging sideways as they laughed at God knows what.

Twenty-five years of America, of boneless chicken in cellophane, of rehearsed morning pleasantries, of battered Trader Joe's cards stuck in Ross wallets, and America was still foreign soil. She still felt a lump in her throat each time she stepped up to a counter and locked eyes with the customer service rep behind it. Twenty-five years and a flourishing hair braiding business and the CBP officers at the airport still treated her like a visitor.

America's foreignness did not bother her. After all, America was not home. It was her refuge, her relationship to it practical. America was a necessity, a boundary, her peace.

When she first arrived in America, she would go on long walks around their clustered apartment complex in Southwest Houston, pausing to watch young black kids congregate by the basketball court to talk smack and dribble. She liked the way they spoke to each other, how quickly they moved through words so that she rushed to grasp each one long enough to make sense of the whole. She'd wanted to drown in their words, in that new world.

She'd left Lagos because it had been too much to bear. It had begun to suffocate her, its heat and its people pressing down on her windpipe till she feared she would die.

In Lagos, women came to her from near and far, Lekki to Lokoja. They banged on the compound's gate, begging to speak to her. 'We heard of you,' they would say, gazing at her with awe or suspicion. 'We know the things you do.'

Word of mouth traveled fast. She'd always known this. She'd watched her mother blossom from a wallflower to Ala's hand, complete with a compound to her name. She should have been prepared for the crowds, all those desperate women selling the clothes off their back for a child.

In her last days in Lagos, she'd held each woman in her arms, spoken to Ala on the woman's behalf, relayed Ala's message to her, word for word.

It was always easy to spot the cowards, the way their shoulders dropped. The immediacy to their shifting gaze. She could not be bothered with such women.

Then there were the women who followed Ala's instructions to completion. Whose wombs still refused to hold a child. Those ones were personal, an affront to her power.

Adina was different.

At least that was Agbala's first impression. Unlike the other women, Adina's hunger for a child was not about her. It was about her husband. She'd co-opted her husband's hunger, pressed it into her belly till it became her own. She had followed Ala's instructions like her life depended on it, and maybe it did, considering that husband of hers. But in the end, Adina's acquiescence had turned to indignant questions and unsolicited suggestions.

'You didn't say it was going to be like this,' Adina once whispered on a warm Sunday evening in the weeks before Agbala left Lagos for Houston. Adina had been sitting on Agbala's front porch, her crestfallen face in her hands. 'It's so unbearable for Dumeje and I, you know. To be so close to all we ever wanted, and yet, so far away.'

'Just trust me,' Agbala had growled, her palm cradling the back of Adina's neck.

'Is it you I should trust, or should I trust Ala?' Adina pushed, a vexed gleam in her eyes.

Agbala smiled coldly at the woman. She did not mention that earlier that day, she had collected her family's American visas from the drop box on the Lagos Island. Or that Eke had sold his land in Ajah to fund the costs of their tickets and they would be leaving Nigeria in a month.

Agbala folded her arms and hissed into the tepid evening air as Adina gathered her wares and scurried into her flat.

She needed a fresh start. A new street with neighbors who did not flock to her house in droves. The quiet joy of uninterrupted motherhood.

Women like Adina would not understand her needs. They were too consumed with their own private longings to sympathize with another woman's hunger.

36

October 2019

When Nna returned to Sugar Land, October was spreading its cast across the city with its rainfall and pumpkin spice lattes, and the odd sighting of a jack-o-lantern in the front window of some Sugar Land houses.

He came back just as Mary, David, Kyle, and the Greens from two blocks up tied matching turmeric-colored scarves and drove to an apple orchard in Medina to immerse themselves in the spirit of the season. Eke stood by the living-room's vinyl windows, a wistful look in his eyes as he watched the picture-perfect Schultzs and Greens zoom off into the hazy distance. He floated the idea of the Nwosus taking a trip to the orchard and Agbala shot it down with her withering scowl.

Nna watched the interaction between his parents from the foot of the stairs. He shook his head. Some things never changed.

Other things, like sex with Ikemefuna, were different upon his return.

Their silhouettes moved with imprecision, toppling into each other as he pressed his palms to the back of her head. Their limbs bumped, one set of arms sturdy as rail banisters, smashing into the other.

There was a utilitarian quality to the sex, like it was paramount that they give only what they could afford to lose. No need for sweet talk, the empty words he'd whisper in Ikemefuna's ear before seizing her skin between his teeth. He let his body do the talking as he tightened his grip on her waist and pressed his frame into her.

'Nna'm. Nna'm please,' she moaned from beneath him.

She spread out her palms on the mattress, her fingers digging holes into the foam.

She groaned something. He wasn't sure what, or if it was a groan at all. He'd learned to be content with the grey areas of female pleasure, that shapeless thing that twisted and turned to the tune of feminine wiles so that one minute it was a sequence of lustful moans in quick succession as knotted bodies tumbled towards the vortex of an orgasm, and the next it was the flame of a tiki torch in the air with cries of #MeToo.

'Nna!'

Her elbow rammed into his groin. Once. Twice. He pushed it off him, wrapped his palms against her slender neck, slick with sweat. He laughed at the way she wriggled between his palms, beads of sweat falling from his brow bone to the small of her back. He kissed her shoulder blade, pressed his chest to her back, squeezed his eyes shut, imagined she was anything but the limp body beneath him.

'You tried to leave,' he said.

The quiet minutes after the sex, their naked bodies lying side by side, their eyes on the cracks in the ceiling.

'Nna, I—'

'It's not a question. I just can't believe you tried to leave me.'

Eke was the one who told Nna about Ikemefuna's strange behavior when Eke and Agbala took her out to lunch. He'd pulled Nna to the side once he returned; his forehead lined with the residual stress of having to keep Ikemefuna in line. *It was very strange, eh! She tried to leave the restaurant without us. But to where? We are the only people she knows in this country, yes?*

Nna had tried to respond but all he could think of was Ikemefuna's smell, how it never quite left the air. It left behind a thin sheen on the upholstery. A stickiness on the mouth of vases.

'I was scared, Nna,' Ikemefuna whispered into the heat.

She looked different with the gorimapa, her forehead wider, protrusive.

'Scared of what?'

'I've told you I'm scared of your parents.'

'Is that so?' he murmured against her nose.

She turned her head away from him. She'd hoped the seeds she previously planted in his head would lead him to distrust his parents, but it was quickly becoming clear that she couldn't count on him to draw the right conclusion.

'They should scare you too.'

'Here we go again.'

'They are hiding things from you, Nna'm. First it was our arranged marriage. Then it was your resemblance to my mother. What else are they holding to their chest, eh?'

'Why don't you tell me since you know it all?' A vein ticked in his temple. 'Look, I trust my parents. They may be a bit unusual in their methods . . .' He trailed off, his eyes on her shaved head. '. . . but they have the purest intentions.'

'If you trust them so much, why don't you ask them to explain why you look like my mother?' she spat.

He could smell the baby powder on her skin. With his one eye open, she almost looked like the beautiful woman from their first night.

'You won't because you don't believe they'll tell you the truth,' she pressed.

He grabbed her by the sides of her face.

'You're out of your mind,' he growled. She was testing his limited patience.

'Faces don't lie, Nna'm. You saw my mother's photograph. You know I'm not making this up,' she whispered.

'It's an old photograph.'

'Then let's go to Lagos. You can meet my mother for yourself.'

'Enough!' he yelled. 'I don't want to hear it.'

Nna massaged his temple. A headache was starting to form behind his eyes. His pride wouldn't allow him to come clean to Ikemefuna, but she'd made a valid point. In short – there was a woman in Lagos with his face and he would be an idiot to overlook that brazen truth. His likeness to her mother could be the coincidence of the century, but what if it was not a coincidence?

He swallowed. He would have a conversation with his parents about Adina and if he was unsatisfied with their answers, he would go to Lagos for answers.

37

Nna woke up early the following Saturday with Adina on his mind. Ikemefuna's constant mention of the woman's photograph burned in his mind. He had studied the image many times since he first looked at it. The more he looked the more he saw. Adina's pointed ears. The ovate shape of her face. He'd caught himself tracing the outline of his face in his bathroom mirror.

The woman in the photo could be his birth mother. He sat with the reality all morning, till it formed a soft lump in the center of his throat. Once or twice, he caught himself staring into the distance, his fists clenched too tightly. If Adina was his mother, who exactly were the Nwosus and what was he doing in their house? He walked up the stairs of the house just as Ikemefuna disappeared behind the door to her bedroom. The soft lump in his throat slid up an inch. And if Adina was his mother, what was his relationship to Ikemefuna and why would his parents or the Azubuikes encourage their union?

Since his return, he'd begun to watch his parents closely. The tenor of their voices when they spoke to Ikemefuna. The contractions in their facial muscles when they smiled at her.

He'd long overlooked his parents' eccentricities, and now, he worried that he might have turned a blind eye to their excesses.

He needed to confront them with Ikemefuna's accusations. That they chewed up her passport and threatened to kill her if she left the house. That he was a spitting image of Adina and, surely, they too noticed the resemblance? It must have struck them as odd, no?

But his parents were stubborn folk. If they were harboring a secret, confronting them would only make them guard it more jealously.

He would have to do some digging of his own, uncover his own truths, catch them in a boldfaced lie. In the last two days, he'd wandered every inch of the house, searching its crevices for old photo albums and unwashed film from his Lagos days.

Nothing.

Not surprising. His parents were dismissive of their Lagos days. Lagos was the grass before their grace, the interlude to their reality.

Just last night, he'd asked his mother for the key ring that held the keys to the doors in the house.

'C'mon mom! I know you like to keep the keys safe but it's hard to move around when everything's locked up.'

'Fine. I'll give you the keys, but you must keep them from Ikemefuna for now,' she huffed. 'She isn't part of the family yet, and I am protective of our valuables.'

While the rest of the house slept, he'd searched the downstairs study, sweeping his palms through his old law school casebooks and diving into the jumble of cords and adapters beneath its oak desk. Then he'd moved to the cupboard beneath the stairs, the living rooms, Ikemefuna's empty bedroom.

That Saturday morning, he snuck out through the sliding glass door in the kitchen. He pushed open the toolshed's creaking door and sucked in the musky dust as he felt along its wood panels for a switch. Warm orange light flooded mulch and bramble, makeshift cardboards of toys from the nineties, video cassettes in manila envelopes.

He walked around the shed, pausing to pick up odd knickknacks – a miniature American flag, the head of a hammer. He blew air into the trash bag he'd grabbed from Agbala's kitchen stash.

Something caught his eye from behind a cardboard box. A spider web dangling from the ceiling. He grabbed his broom and strode towards the web. For what it was, it was impressive. It stretched across the low hanging ceiling like translucent moss.

A flash of movement tore past his feet and scurried behind an empty Coca-Cola crate. Nna flung the broom at the web. It hit the cardboard box, causing it to topple over.

Nna stooped to pick up the contents. A Barney with a chewed tail. A Lego car missing its back tires. He vaguely remembered the car from childhood – a blur zipping beneath the TV stand in the living room of a small Houston apartment.

He stuffed the Barney in the box. He breathed in the shed's dust. He would need some fresh air before he got a chest infection. He reached for the car. There was something beneath it. An envelope. He raised the envelope to his face and squinted at the block letters scribbled on its smooth back.

A wave of nausea rushed up his neck.

Why was the envelope in the toolshed? He got the sense that someone had intended to hide it, but they'd forgotten to follow through with the task at the last hour. He had no recollection of any school projects from grade school that required his parents to pen a letter to him. Had Agbala fallen sick with a chronic illness? Did she hope that he would find the envelope upon her death? He'd seen similar scripts in movies, deceased parents bequeathing life lessons and fortunes to their children in riddle-heavy prose.

He tore the envelope, each finger a helix of nerves. He reminded himself to go slow. He traced the envelope's borders, slid a finger beneath its thin flap.

Two photographs slid out the envelope and landed on the mulch.

Nna picked the photographs and held them to his face.

The first – Adina. A younger version. And yet, she was easy to spot with her split ends and bulging eyes. She stood by a water pump with a toddler in her arms.

The second – Adina on a couch in a living room. Beside her, a tall man with umber skin. A crawling baby with an ovate face at their feet.

A headache formed behind Nna's eyes. He opened his mouth, sucked on his tongue for moisture. The block letters on the envelope stared at him, dared him to look away.

FOR NNA.

FROM MUMMY AND DADDY.

38

The disquiet crept up Nna's chest during his morning jog. It latched on to his ribcage as he threw forkfuls of scrambled eggs in his mouth. It crawled up his skull as Ikemefuna ambled past him in the kitchen, a tiny rapa fastened to her breasts. He considered reaching for her, engaging her in mindless conversation about Atilogwu and her favorite brand of nail polish. He would listen to her colorful description of the cowries that rolled along her waist as she swayed to the rhythm of an ogene and danced from compound to compound in Lagos. He would ask her about her parents. Make her start from the very beginning.

Sometime after sunset, he watched her pick at her porridge beans and plantains with a morose expression on her face.

What was she hiding?

She had given him crumbs; her curated information reminiscent of a social media influencer's online footprint. Her waist-to-hip proportions. A running list of her interests. That she chewed her nails till she turned eighteen and liked to suck her udala clean. But all of that was surface chatter.

He needed to know everything.

He watched her water the pothos by the kitchen window.

Maybe she planted those photographs in the toolshed. No, she couldn't have, he thought. She didn't have the keys to the shed.

'Tell me about your mother,' he announced abruptly.

Ikemefuna looked up from the pothos. Her eyes slid to his empty dish.

'You heard me. What's she like?'

Ikemefuna placed the watering can down.

'What do you want to know?'

'Everything, Keme. What's her personality? What does she do for a living?'

'She runs a fruit stall on the Lagos mainland, Nna'm. She's far from perfect, but she's a kind woman.'

'Tell me more.'

'You can ask her everything you need to know if you take me with you to Lagos,' she whispered.

She held his eyes for what seemed like an eternity.

The doorbell rang.

Nna frowned, rose to his feet. Agbala and Eke had few American friends, so who could it be? He hated to ward off August visitors. Their inquisitive eyes and their cheery smiles.

'Stay right here. Don't move,' Nna whispered.

He peered through the keyhole.

There was a shock of blonde hair. Bright green eyes. Healthy pink cheeks. A fine dust of freckles. The warm beige of curved lips. A set of teeth spreading apart to make room for tinkling laughter.

Nna opened the front door an inch.

'Oh, howdy,' the petite woman standing on the front porch exclaimed. She took a step forward, then a step back, a tin foil rattling in her hands. 'I'm Mary. Your neighbor.'

'Oh.'

The neighbor.

Nna did not know the neighbors beyond his perfunctory waves at vaguely familiar faces each time he entered or exited the Sugar Land house. His parents didn't see the need for conversations and invitations. Not before Mary and her freshly baked bait arrived at the front door of the house.

Mary made him nervous.

'Hello Mary,' Nna started, pausing to clear his throat. 'I'm Nna.'

'Nna. What a lovely name.'

Mary rolled his name around her tongue like candy, feeling along its sides till it fit the dips of her mouth.

'I've been trying to properly introduce myself to you and your folks for years now!' She laughed, pausing to lick the dry rind of skin hanging off her bottom lip. 'My busy schedule as a vet made it difficult, but I'm retired now. More free time. Cheers to that!' She shook the tin foil tray, the loose skin of her neck swinging with wild abandon as she grinned at Nna.

'I baked some brownies for y'all. Mind if I come in for a little bit?'

Nna eyed the petite blonde woman and her pale pink sundress. She stared up at him with all the goodwill in the world.

'Yes, of course. Please come in.'

Mary took long purposeful steps into the house. Her eyes wandered to the endless rows of yellowed Nwosu photographs (The Nwosus at a now-defunct Six Flags in Atlanta. At the Santa Monica pier. At a skating rink) plastered on the walls. She stared expectantly at Nna, willing him to hand her a cold beer. She would offer him his pick of IPAs if the reverse was the case.

'I'd love for y'all to stop by for dinner next Thursday. I have a mean chili recipe I want to try out. Now it's got some heat but I was raised on chili con carnes and fajitas so I'll be just fine. You know, us Texans can handle our spice!' she announced cheerily. 'Anyway, your folks home?'

Nna thought of Agbala and Eke huddled beneath the thick fleece in the master bedroom, Agbala's muscled body burrowing into Eke's chest. He should alert them to Mary's presence. He imagined their bodies swinging into action – Agbala adjusting the band of her hairnet and tightening her rapa. Eke pacing the length of the bedroom, a forlorn look in his aging eyes.

'They are here. Excuse me for a moment and I'll let them know.'

'Thank you, Nna. Very kind of y–oh, hi there!'

Nna followed Mary's eyes to a spot behind his back.

Ikemefuna stood behind him, her eyes wide with shock as Mary reached forward with outstretched arms.

'Hi! I'm Mary! It's nice to meet you!'

39

Mary Schultz was always curious.

When David grew out of all of his tee shirts in the span of three months, she hid between the pruned hedges at his school, her salmon J Crew bunched above her lolling knees. She watched with narrowed eyes as David devoured, first his lunch, then the lunch of the three scrawny boys huddled to a side of the playground. And when Kyle began to keep late nights at his co-working space in Montrose, she purchased a fiery red wig from a Sally's Beauty and found a quiet corner three desks behind him, from where she studied the growing tightness of the hugs he gave his lifestyle-blogger neighbor.

Which is to say, nothing got past Mary. Except the Nwosus.

The Nwosus arrived on the front steps of the brick-red house next to Mary's on a frigid November morning fourteen years ago. Man and woman donned cargo pants and loose cotton shirts. Surly teenage son, a crew neck and jeans.

Mary had taken one hard look at the trio through her kitchen blinds and her Southern sensibilities had moved her to act. She'd filled an old cardboard with gently worn fleece jackets and left the box on the Nwosus' doorstep moments after they retreated into the house. She'd been proud of herself for that gesture, for what it said about her – that she was a decent human who rendered aid to her black neighbors. Who harbored quiet longings for poker nights, and wine tastings, and the odd inter-family weekend getaway to Galveston.

The Nwosus did not say thank you.

Not that day.

Not the day after, when she'd flashed a toothy grin and a palm at the Nwosu woman who then slammed her front door with a force that caused Mary's brain to rattle in her head.

Mary had been so frazzled by the Nwosu woman's response that she'd spent the following weekend perusing the city's yellow pages for a therapist that was well-versed in the landmine of cultural barriers.

Niall, her soft-spoken Irish therapist, was the perfect man for the job.

'Oh, but you can't take it personal,' he assured her over chamomile. 'The Africans tend to keep to themselves. They don't fraternize with neighbors, you know? See no evil. Hear no evil. That sort of thing,' he added with a flourish.

It had been a bitter pill, but she had swallowed it. Despite how much Mary loved words. The speaking of them. The hacking at them with scissors till they fit the contours of the mouth. The stitching them together so that they formed one long rope that trailed behind her everywhere that she went. She could not fathom what she was supposed to do with the dark, heavy wall of silence wedged between her house and the Nwosus' house.

Ultimately, Mary decided to keep her relationship with the Nwosus civil by drowning their rather violent silence in good old Southern hospitality. She was hopeful that it would make them feel terribly sorry for how they had treated her.

Her hospitality looked like this.

An invitation to a cookout in the humid Texan summer delivered in a taffy pink envelope that smelled of cough drops. *You Are Cordially Invited* in bold gold cursive. Mary, pacing the length of her backyard as she waited for the Nwosus' RSVP in her mailbox, or a glimpse of their faces as they scampered out their house to their jobs in the city. Then radio silence. A vast stretch of more silence. Silence like a slap in the face.

One autumn evening, she spotted the Nwosu woman's ichafu (she'd googled the culturally appropriate name), an odd olive contraption the woman often donned when she stepped out of the house to run errands in the city. Mary ran down her driveway and towards the Nwosus' front yard, a paper bag of carrots and celery sticks pressed to her chest as her slippers pounded against the burning concrete.

'Mrs Nwosu!' she cried out, flapping her arms in the air.

The Nwosu woman turned her back to take flight.

Mary leapt over a shrub, almost losing her balance in the process. She caught herself at the last minute, adjusted her right foot and bridged the gap between herself and the Nwosu woman. She stood in front of the woman's door, her bag of vegetables pressed to her chest as she huffed and panted like a chimney.

'Ah, Mrs Nwosu! I caught you just in time,' she cried, flashing her veneers.

'Oh, eh,' Mrs Nwosu stuttered.

Mary took a hard look at the greys peeking out the woman's ichafu, the brown specks of blood in the whites of the woman's eyes, the yellows of her teeth. She felt sorry for the woman. No doubt, the Nwosu woman did not know where to get a massage or how to find coupons for the neighborhood spas and truly, the unknowns were endless.

Mary pressed four fingers to her forehead. She could feel the wheels of her brain spinning beneath her skin. She resolved to make Mrs Nwosu her pet project, just like she'd made Minnie the hamster her pet project in fifth grade. She would treat the Nwosu woman to the best charcuterie boards. She would teach her to recite the American anthem, to roll her *t*s and soften her *er*s.

'Mrs Green and I attend Pilates classes at Georgie's Pilates. It's a lovely penthouse in the city,' she rambled to a stunned Mrs Nwosu. 'Classes start at 11a.m. on Saturdays and the lady who runs the place is fabulous. Simply fabulous!'

'Pilates, *kwanu*?' Mrs Nwosu croaked, unsure, her eyes glancing nervously at her front door.

'*Kwanu*? Is that a Jamaican, err, Nigerian kind of Pilates? Can't say I'm familiar with it. Georgie's classes are more, you know, contemporary,' Mary said, widening the berth of her smile.

Mrs Nwosu winced. She reached out a hand to open her front door, but Mary blocked her path.

'I think you'd love the classes! After the class, we go to Ralph's. It's a quaint Italian restaurant a block away from the studio. We eat as much cavatelli and drink as much chardonnay as our stomachs permit. They've got the most diverse wine selections in that restaurant. You won't believe it!'

'Er, sorry. Sorry madam,' Mrs Nwosu apologized. She shook her head sideways, placing her right hand on Mary's bony shoulder, and pushing Mary to the side with a force that caused Mary to fall into the surrounding shrubs.

Mary jumped to her feet and dusted brown soot off her DVF wrap dress. Mrs Nwosu was pushing her luck, she thought to herself. She was this close to telling her off and posting her a dry-cleaning invoice for her soiled dress, but she did not give in to temptation. Still, she deserved an apology. She opened her mouth to demand one, but Mrs Nwosu was gone.

Perhaps, if Mary had a smaller, practical heart, that little scene would have signaled the end of her failed friendship with the Nwosu woman. But Mary's heart was as big as Texas. It didn't see color – never! It saw the good in everyone.

It was exactly that big, foolish heart of hers that caused her to throw on her straw hat from the previous year's vacation in Punta Cana, and her monstrous sunshades from a thrift store in the Houston Heights, and her shimmery ULTA lip gloss, and her sundress from Saks, before marching to the Nwosus' front door, a tin foil of brownies in her hands.

The neighbor's door swung open.

Mary raised her eyes to the burly young man standing by the door, ringlets of chest hair peeking out of his fawn singlet.

She ran her dry tongue across her lips. She remembered him from his younger years, a stringy teenage boy with a bobbing Adam's apple, and now he was six feet three inches of pounding muscle, the particular iteration of *big* and *black* that would have had her panties in a twist in the good old days.

She squinted at his chin hair, her fingers lightly strumming her décolletage. If she were a little younger, a touch more daring, she would entertain the prospect of a fling. But a lot of living had happened since Mike handed her the divorce papers and left for Ibiza with Emilia, David's petite Italian tutor. Besides, she still loved Kyle though he caused her a lot of grief.

A slight tremor ran up her arms, then her chest, then her face, as she took tentative steps into the brick house for the very first time. The house was muggy as a Texan summer afternoon. A strange smell filled the air, sharp on the tongue, like rotting bell peppers smoldering in the heat.

Mary gasped.

The living room's walls were a sight to behold. An entire section lined with bronze carvings; their markings intricate enough to cause Mary to wonder if they'd been stolen from the coffers of the British museum. *The Brits had all the best African loot, didn't they?* she thought to herself.

She ran her eyes against the bronze, committing the tribal marks to memory. Her dining room could use one or two African heads, what with Ashley casually commenting on the sparseness of its decor. *Oh Mary, but it's not a bad thing! It's just very Spartan is all!*

Oh, Mary knew a dig when she heard one.

She felt the Nwosu boy's eyes on her. It made her uncomfortable, but in a way that caused her skin to quiver with delight.

'Anyway, your folks home?'

The Nwosu boy took a little too long to respond. Mary smiled tightly. She giggled again. The thin pitch bounced off the chandelier, then fell to her feet.

'Yes. Excuse me for a moment and I'll let them know.'

'Thank you, Nna. Very kind of y–oh, hi there!'

A figure stood behind the Nwosu boy. A bald black female with a shiny face. Mary eyed the girl's greasy forehead. She squinted at the face. It wasn't an ugly face. One might be generous enough to call it pretty. Pretty for a black girl, yes. Not an insult, no. There were different kinds of pretty, is all.

Mary's eyes slid from the girl's brooding eyes to the thick bulb of her nose, before settling on her fleshy lips. She most certainly did not want those lips. No, thank you. But she could appreciate it on the unctuous, oval face. Nothing wrong with that.

'Hi! I'm Mary! It's nice to meet you!' Mary exclaimed, her right palm shooting forward so that the tips of her fingers almost grazed the girl's face.

That was when it happened.

The thing that caused the oatmeal and cranberry raisins in Mary's gut to violently gyrate.

The Nwosu boy jumped between Mary and the strange black female with all the grace of a clumsy ballerina.

'Ma'am, please have a seat,' he commanded, his voice tightly wound around his teeth.

Mary digested the theatrics of it all, each new movement clogging her throat. She gasped for words as her outstretched palm went limp. She could hear Niall in her left ear, cautioning her to keep calm, to do as the Nwosu boy asked. *It's just a cultural nit*, he would assure her with a chuckle, *a silly little cultural mishap*.

She had started to sit down, determined to salvage what was left of her dignity. But she locked eyes with the girl and the discomfort shot up her throat and poured down the sides of her mouth.

Something was wrong about the girl.

Nothing was right.

Not the girl's twisted mouth and its sickening wail. Not the face crumpling to the floor like a bad cake batch. Not the manner in which she charged at Mary – like a prized bull at the rodeo – so that for five terrifying seconds, Mary stood shell-shocked as the girl reached for Mary, her outstretched arms inches away from Mary's flaxen hair.

She tugged at Mary's dress. Mary raised her arms in self-defense. The Nwosu boy grabbed the girl by her thin waist and swept her off her feet.

'Please! Please ma! Help me ma!' the girl sobbed.

Mary wielded the brownies like a shield as she inched away from the Nwosu boy and the manic girl.

'Stay back!' Mary yelled, her heart racing up and down her chest.

All the feelings flashed back. It was Spring Break '98 and she was back in Montego Bay with her sorors. They were walking off the beach and towards their bed and breakfast, their yoga mats wedged between their armpits and the lean of their arms. A gang of locals with clotted faces and oversized hoodies appeared from thin air. They began to tease Mary and her friends, their whispered taunts growing crueler by the second.

Cracker.

Buck Teeth.

You fi wife that?

But it did not stop there. They demanded the girls' purses. Mary stood with her girls, scared out of her wits but brave, always brave, as she waved her mat at the hoodlums, yelling at them to stay back, *stay back or I'll call the cops.*

'I'll call the cops,' she yelled now, again, for all present to hear.

'Ma, please! Please ma! Please, help me, ma!' the strange black girl yelled in Mary's face, scratching the air with broken nails, a crazed expression in her dusky eyes as the young man tried to subdue her.

'Get her away from me! Get her the hell away from me or I'll call the cops on all of you!' Mary screamed as she dashed out the house.

Never again, she thought to herself in bed that night, her face aglow with her anti-aging tinctures.

40

Through the living room's Venetian blinds, Nna watched the neighbor run down the driveway. He could hear the swish of blood in his veins. He could taste the red on his tongue.

Mary would ring up the other neighbors once she returned home.

She would invite them for lunch, recount the details of her short-lived visit to his parents' house over Tex-Mex egg scramble.

If the prospect of Mary's exposé was not so terrifying, Nna would have latched on to the moment's humor – a blonde woman in a large straw hat rushing out the house like she'd witnessed Black Terror firsthand.

He pulled against the doorknob to make sure the front door was locked. He narrowed his eyes at Ikemefuna, stretched out on the marble with her face in her palms. She was breathing hard, forcing air up and down her throat.

'What's the matter, Keme?' he whispered. He was determined to keep his cool.

'Let me out,' she pleaded. 'Let me out, you pig!'

He winced despite himself.

Pig.

'What did you say?'

'Pig,' she repeated.

He stood an inch away, towering over her.

'What?' he pressed, his fingers dusting the tip of his belt buckle.

She eyed his fingers. She looked up at him, her eyes big and haughty.

'Read my lips,' she started slowly. 'PIIIIGGGG!'

His resolve broke. He reached for her neck, but she was faster. She rolled beneath his large swinging arms, caused him to slip on his feet. He started to stand, but she climbed his back, pounded his head with her fists. He felt a lightness in his head, in his chest. He could not shake her off, despite all his trying.

Rushing feet.

A scuffle.

A small yelp.

Someone was yanking her off him. Agbala, her rapa hanging dangerously low. Her slender breasts bouncing against her rib cage.

'What is going on here?' Agbala cried, her voice carrying through the house. 'I said what is all this?'

Ikemefuna would no longer have a bedroom.

'Move into Nna's bedroom,' Agbala said to her the day after the incident with the neighbor. 'There's no reason you should have a room to yourself anymore.'

Ikemefuna's eyes roamed the plain walls as she packed up the few belongings she had brought with her to the

United States. The room was not much to look at, but it had afforded her some privacy. She could lock the door, press her ears to its concrete, feel along its ridges, punch the window, imagine a face in the window of the house next door.

'Don't make me repeat myself,' Agbala snapped.

Ikemefuna stood from her bed. She should never have lost her cool with Nna. But it was getting harder to hold her anger in her body. She could not control the thing. It filled her head with puffs of dust clouds. It overrode her senses.

Since the incident, the Nwosus' had taken to whispering about her.

Has she eaten?

What did she say?

Is she bloated? Bleeding?

And what about her stomach? Any difference?

Ikemefuna tuned out the whispering until it blended into white noise.

There were important things to think about. How were her parents handling her absence? She'd been gone for far longer than the two weeks they'd promised. Why were they not appearing on American News, demanding her release?

Nna barely spoke to her anymore. On the rare occasion that he did, it was with his body, his hands tugging at her arm, drawing her close, too close, so that her windpipe filled with his Tom Ford.

'Who are these people?' he said to her as she lay in his bed on a cloudy evening in the middle of October. He thrust two grainy photographs beneath her nose.

'I recognize your mom,' he huffed. 'Who are the others?'

She squinted at the photographs. She raised each to her face. Her parents, Adina and Dumeje, stared back at her, their plump cheeks glowing through the grain. There was a little boy in both photographs, dark-skinned. His face was inscrutable.

'Where did you find these?' she asked.

'Answer my question.'

She shook her head and returned the photos to him.

'I've never seen these before, but those are my parents. Did you get them from your parents?'

Nna contemplated keeping the truth to himself, but he needed any information he could get.

'I found them in an old cardboard in the toolshed,' Nna started. 'Listen carefully to me, Keme. I've been thinking about our earlier conversations about your mother, and if your allusions are right and your mother is my birth mom, I think I might be the boy in the photograph.'

Ikemefuna placed her palms against her mouth. The weight of Nna's words pressed against her chest as Nna reached for an envelope on his bedside table and handed it to her.

'Look at the envelope. Read what it says.'

Her eyes roamed the block letters.

'My God, Nna.'

Her mind raced. This was the moment she'd been waiting for. Nna was finally seeing the light. She must make sure he stayed on track, even if it meant concocting a story from thin air.

'I wasn't going to mention this before because I didn't want you to think I was making it up …' she started.

'Spit it out.'

'I know for a fact that the boy in the photograph is my brother.'

'I didn't know you had a brother,' Nna said, a puzzled look on his face.

'Forget I mentioned it,' she muttered.

She stole a glance at him. Was she convincing?

'No. Tell me more,' he pressed. 'Why aren't you in the photo?'

'There's not much to tell, Nna'm. My parents had a son before they adopted me and by all accounts, he was the apple of their eyes. Their heir apparent, you know. But I've never seen a photo of him before.'

'What are you saying, Keme? Where is he?'

'Something happened. My parents don't talk about him – at least, not around me.'

Nna clutched his head. He felt like he was racing at full speed and would crash if he didn't slow down. He exhaled sharply. Surely, all of this was just a cruel joke. She had to be in on it somehow. He had to remember she was desperate to return to Lagos, that she would do anything to bargain her way out of his life.

Footsteps pelted the stairs. His parents, Agbala and Eke. They could barge into his bedroom at a moment's notice.

'Teach me to dance Atilogwu,' he said in a bid to change the subject.

Ikemefuna rose to her feet and parted her legs.

'It's all about the arms,' she murmured, her eyes on his arms. 'Follow my lead.'

He tried his best, standing on tiptoes, shimmying back and forth. She allowed herself to enjoy the moment, to forget who she was and what she was doing in Sugar Land, Texas. All she knew was the laughter splitting her throat open.

Then the music quickened in pace and realization came rushing back to her. She was Ikemefuna. Trapped in a house at the end of a street in Sugar Land. Her freedom depended on a man's whims. The alternative was forced motherhood. It was the handmaid's tale, except there was nothing dystopic about *E! News* rattling off celebrity gossip at sunset.

Ikemefuna stepped on Nna's foot midway through a spin. He decided it was not an accident. He pushed her so hard she almost fell. She could feel her consciousness slipping out her mouth as she pushed him back without thought, a fight or flight that triggered their descent into an increasingly dangerous push-pull battle, him toppling over his bed as she tumbled to the floor.

He abandoned his fists for his fingers. Undressed her slowly.

'Wait,' she cried, her palms tightening against his arm. 'Nna'm, you could be my brother.'

He considered her statement for a second, then he shook his head and chuckled. 'That's still to be determined,' he murmured, his lips finding her collarbone. She held her breath, grateful for the decisiveness of his motions, the expediency, like there was no time to waste on kindness.

When he was done, he let her lie beneath the duvet, her nakedness hidden from his sight.

They watched *Jeopardy* in silence. She mimed the correct answers seconds after the contestants. He let her keep those moments to herself, and maybe that was love, or an iteration of love, or a kindness, a mercy, letting a person be, if only for a while.

And then the moment was over, and he changed the station to ESPN without asking her permission, and all she could think of was how comfortable he was with taking things without permission.

The door swung open.

A flood of orange light spilled into Nna's bedroom from the hallway, illuminating the balled socks hanging off the side of a dresser and the rumpled sheets.

Where is she?

We need her.

Not for long.

She folded the excess cloth of her rapa into the space between her breasts and walked towards the light. Agbala and Eke led her down the hallway, past her old bedroom and into the master bedroom with its fish oil smell and kola nuts.

Agbala handed her a tiny plastic tube, the kind a LUTH nurse would shove into her chest whenever she went to the teaching hospital for her annual checkup. Agbala pointed at the door leading into the bathroom. 'Quick quick,' Agbala yelled at Ikemefuna's retreating back, as if she could fast-forward the process.

In the bathroom, Ikemefuna released a thin stream of urine into the tube. She thought of the last few times she'd had sex with Nna. How quick and revolting each session had been. Nothing could have grown out of a grief so big and misshapen, it threatened to swallow her whole.

Agbala dipped a strip into the tube and threw a sharp look at Ikemefuna.

'Now, we wait.'

Ikemefuna felt along her breasts. Light and pillowy, like they'd been in the morning.

She did not want a son with her long lashes and soft skin, or Nna's fleshy lips and berry black thighs. She did not want Agbala and Eke to marvel at his weight and his baby babble.

Eke eyed his pocket watch.

'Now,' he announced, his voice cutting through the silence.

Agbala snatched the strip from the tube.

The seconds piled on top of each other.

Agbala frowned. She reached for her reading glasses and held the strip to the light.

Eke clasped his palms and stared at his pasty feet.

'Positive.'

41

First – a wail, thick as akamu, cut through the rooms of the house.

Then, dead silence.

Then, a second wail, weaker than the first, less gravitas, burst out in short spurts.

Nna sat up in his bed, the ends of his jalabiya bunched against his thighs.

A burglar was his first thought. Burglars were mythical creatures in Sugar Land, fodder for cautionary tales. And yet, there was always the possibility. All it took was one resourceful criminal blending in with the shrubbery hedging the house.

He stood from his sheets, blasts of warm breath forking up his tongue. He reminded himself he was the man of the house. All those years of taekwondo and eba breakfasts prepared him for the moment.

Agbala's wail was close enough. Eke's bark even closer. He inched out of his bedroom and into the hallway. Something flew past his ear. A purse or a body.

Two bodies fell to his feet. Eke. Agbala on top of Eke. Agbala grabbed Eke by his neck, tugged at his cheeks and shrieked with delight. Then she rolled off Eke's torso and landed with a plop on the floor. Her head scarf lay a few feet away from her.

Nna shook his head at his parents' strange celebration. Twenty-eight years and they were still something of an enigma to him. He sometimes struggled to read between their lines, to decode their little rituals, the quick shifts in their moods. He took his inability to understand them personally, turning it over in his head at night, cursing the injustice of being born to parents whose quirks were as foreign to him as teeth tossing.

'She is pregnant, Nna'm,' Agbala announced.

Nna blinked.

Ikemefuna was pregnant.

She was pregnant with his child.

A boy. He could feel it. It felt right, but only for as long as he could stop his thoughts from drifting into the version of reality where she was his sister.

Where was she? It was their moment, hers. Things hadn't been great between them in recent days, but the pregnancy would change everything. It wasn't unfathomable. Didn't new parents often speak about *the baby* like it was a fork in the road? Yes. They celebrated the perspectives it afforded them.

He flew past his parents and into their bedroom. Ikemefuna was still there, curled up on their silk white sheets, her palms on her belly. He watched her belly, its flatness. He'd heard that the early days of a pregnancy were no different from the pre-pregnancy days. It was true; she was still the woman from that first day – small head, and big eyes, and flat midriff.

He crouched beside her, pressed his ear to her belly. Their belly. Yes, this was that kind of pregnancy. He would be that kind of father. He would embrace the ups and downs and sideways of pregnancy. Clench his teeth through every cramp. Cradle his son through the night. He was not a deadbeat in waiting. He was a father, a muse for the family man in car commercials.

'Baby,' he whispered.

She pushed against the sheets, hefted her weight into an upright position. Beneath the unforgiving fluorescent, she looked older than she ever had, her lashes patchy, her face an acne canvas. He grabbed her head and searched her eyes. His lips snapped into a frown. She tried to pull away from him, but his grip was tight, the tips of his nails digging into her earlobes.

'Why are you not smiling?'

He didn't trust her, not in that moment. What was her angle?

'Nna, not now. Please.'

'Answer me,' he insisted. 'What's the matter this time?'

'I don't want to,' she cried. 'Get off me!'

She managed to escape his grip, was turning away from him, curling back into herself.

He folded his arms. It was insulting that Ikemefuna wanted out. Fraudulent, depending on how one looked at it. She'd taken so much from his family already. Shelter, food, a one-way ticket to a first-class American life, his peace of mind, and now she thought herself too good to be his wife. Maybe she would go to great lengths to leave him, including weaving a story about a fictitious brother to turn him against his parents.

He grabbed her by her shoulder. He felt a sharp pain in his ribcage, her elbow, sharp as a scythe. She rammed her elbow into him a second time. He tried to dodge the blow, to push her elbow away. He raised his arm to shield his flank. Somehow it struck her cheek, once, twice, again, the soft punches landing in quick succession, then falling against her shoulder blade, the side of her jaw, the back of her thigh.

A pair of arms pulled him off Ikemefuna. A sigh of relief forked up his throat. Agbala and Eke begged him to keep calm. He could listen to them all day. They were a welcome distraction from the streaky blood congealing on his knuckles.

Agbala blotted the blood on Ikemefuna's lips with folds of paper towel.

'This should be a moment of celebration. Ala has blessed us with a son,' Eke growled from the doorway.

Nna gawked at his fists. 'She doesn't want to have my child,' he muttered. 'She isn't happy.'

Sure, he was raised on Eggo Waffles and corndogs, but he was still a proud Igbo man. He wanted a woman who yearned for him. Who carried her pregnancy like a trophy.

'What business do you have with her happiness?' Agbala asked, pressing more paper towels to the tear in Ikemefuna's lips. 'A woman's happiness is her business, Nna'm. It has nothing to do with you.'

His mother was right. A woman was not a wind-up toy whose mood he got to pick like cloth. Her misery was entirely her own.

'Let us focus on what's important,' Agbala continued. She pointed a finger at Ikemefuna's belly. 'This belly,

Nna'm. This is what we care about. This is what we must protect.'

'We will take turns monitoring her,' Eke added. 'We cannot take our chances, given her recent behavior.'

Nna eyed Ikemefuna's stomach.

Once again, his parents were right. They needed to be right.

They'd gone bearing gifts, billboards of Nna's achievements like the *summa cum laudes,* and the six-figure Big Law job, and the brick-red row house in Fairmount, and the blue passport, and Nna's remarkable knowledge of perfect wine pairings. In exchange, they'd gotten Ikemefuna. They'd tried to make a wife out of her, cleaned her up nicely, taught her the correct use of tenses, the winning yam-to-oil ratio for porridge. They'd paid their dues on time. Finders, keepers, and Ikemefuna was his to keep.

'Eke and I will keep her with us a little longer,' Agbala said, her steely gaze on Nna. 'Emotions are high. You need to spend the night apart.'

Agbala and Nna stepped out of the master bedroom. Eke hung back to care for Ikemefuna. Nna was fine with the arrangement. He didn't trust that he could be around Ikemefuna without a chaperone.

'Nna'm, can I have a word?' Agbala asked as she motioned for him to follow her down the stairs.

'Actually, I've been meaning to talk to you,' he growled at his mother.

'What about? Your attitude over the last few days has been very strange,' Agbala huffed. 'Slamming doors and stomping your feet around this house like you own the place. Is that how we raised you?'

'Can we dissect my attitude tomorrow? I've got something to tell you.'

Agbala appraised her son through her unblinking eyes. She nodded. He gestured at her to wait for him, then rushed into his bedroom and snatched the envelope from his bed.

When he returned, he found Agbala pacing the kitchen.

'Who are these?' he yelled as he pulled out the photos from the envelope and thrust them beneath her nose.

Agbala stared at the photographs for what seemed like an eternity.

'The Azubuikes of course,' she finally said.

'How did we get these photos?'

'What do you want me to say, *eh?*' she snapped. 'I don't remember how we got the photographs. Our neighbors visited us often. It was a long time ago, Nna'm.'

'Read the words on the envelope. *From Mummy and Daddy,*' he pressed. 'Did the Azubuikes send these photos to me? Are *they* my parents?'

Agbala chuckled.

'I blame myself, Nna'm. I should have done a better job of teaching you our culture,' she sighed. 'Igbo elders refer to the young as their children. It's a term of endearment, Nna'm. So yes, maybe the Azubuikes sent the envelope. Who knows?'

Nna ruminated on his mother's words. Through the years, his parents' Igbo acquaintances had given him all sorts of familial titles. *Ojilibeka. Oke Osisi. Ogbu Efi.* If the mood was right, they called him their son. It was possible then, that the Azubuikes were just as effusive. That they looked at him, infantile, and saw their son-in-law.

But wasn't there a difference between a throwaway nickname and a browning envelope from *Mummy and Daddy* stashed away in a toolshed?

'Mom, the woman in the photos looks just like me,' he said.

'And I look just like Mama Ndifreke, your father's older brother's sister-in-law. You don't see me crying about it?' Agbala said without skipping a beat.

Nna opened his mouth, then snapped it shut. Agbala exhaled.

'Nna'm, I'm done entertaining this foolishness. We need that baby.'

'Why do we need the baby?' he sighed, exasperated. 'What does it matter to you?'

'Ala wants you to be a father.'

'Enough of what Ala wants from me, okay? Be honest with me for once, Mom. Can you do that?'

Agbala's eyes rested on the veins thudding against Nna's forehead. 'Nna'm, for your own sake, do not provoke Ala to anger. I have already made her demands clear.'

Nna gritted his teeth.

'Ikemefuna says you and Dad kidnapped her,' he continued, breathless. 'Did Ala ask you to kidnap her too?'

His words hung in the air like dirty laundry.

'Eh, Nna'm? What are you saying?'

Nna waited a few seconds to catch his breath.

'She says that you kidnapped her.' He kept a measured tone. 'That you wouldn't let her leave the house or return to Lagos. That Dad literally ate her passport.'

'What am I hearing with my ears, Nna'm?' she cried, her voice bouncing off the stucco walls. Nna eyed the panicked look on her face, and his heart thawed a little.

'It's okay, Mom. It's gonna be okay. Nothing will happen to you or Dad. I'm going to handle this, okay? I want you to enjoy being grandparents.'

'Kidnapped? All we did was protect this girl. We're sheltering her from America and its trouble. Is that now a crime? *Chai!*' Agbala squealed. She sniveled. 'We will lose our house, Nna'm. She'll turn us over to the authorities. They'd believe her.'

Agbala paused to stare hard at the ceiling. She seemed deep in thought.

'We will wait for her to deliver the baby before we put her to rest,' she said, her voice suddenly devoid of emotion.

'Put her to rest?'

'Must I spell it out, *eh?* Can you not use your critical thinking?' she hissed.

'Spell it out, Mom,' Nna replied drily.

'I hate to say that word. It tastes somehow …' she screwed her face up, 'disgusting in my mouth.'

'Mom—'

'Fine. No need to say anything more.'

Nna blinked. He took a step back, away from Agbala.

'Her parents are your good friends, Mom. How can you even consider doing such a thing?'

'The Azubuikes are many things. And so is your wife.' Agbala said, her face darkening.

'Are you hearing how crazy you sound?' Nna whispered. He looked around frantically, his eyes widening with a mix of shock and fear. He was used to his mother's outlandish statements, but this was different, insane.

'None of this is our choice,' Agbala pressed. She threw an anxious look at the top of the stairs. 'Ala tells me that this Ikemefuna will be nothing but trouble if we don't take care of things *fast fast*. You must remember that we are just Ala's vessels.'

Nna regarded Agbala, the shadows beneath her eyes. They stood in silence, mother and son. The day's events weighed heavily on his shoulders. Try as he may, he couldn't shake off the feeling that his parents were hiding important details of his life from him. And yet, they were all he'd ever known. For as long as he could remember, it was him and them against the world. They'd left their life in Lagos behind and toiled on foreign soil. Eke, a cab driver by day and a computer engineering student by night. Agbala braiding 4C hair from dawn to dusk, tucking dollars in her brassiere. Section 8 housing to a down payment for a Sugar Land house. Now, they embodied the American Dream. They deserved to reap their fruits. He must remember he was all they had in this country and it was his duty to protect them from everyone, including themselves.

42

In the morning, Nna watched Ikemefuna run through an Atilogwu routine by the kitchen windowsill. He replayed his last conversation with his mother as he rehearsed his apology to Ikemefuna. Surely, his mother had been out of her mind. He half-expected his mother to jog down the stairs that morning, a bright, contrite smile on her face, and ask him to forget about the previous night's conversation.

'Are Igbo girls naturally built like coke bottles or are you the exception to the rule?' he mewled at Ikemefuna, a cheeky smile on his lips.

Ikemefuna kept mute.

His smile faltered. He rose from the netted counter stool and walked towards her. An image of her dead body on the parquet flashed in his mind.

'Baby,' he started, throwing his arms around her waist, and planting a kiss on her earlobe. 'I'm sorry for last night.'

She froze in place, her arms hanging stiffly by her side.

'Last night should never have happened. I'm not that guy, Keme. It won't happen again and that's a promise,' he murmured, his face nuzzling her neck.

She slumped, unresponsive. He turned her face towards him.

'What's it going to take, Keme? A dozen roses? A shopping spree at the Galleria?'

'Fine,' she sighed, staring at the ceiling.

Agbala rushed into the kitchen, interrupting the moment. She waved her cellphone in the air.

'Mom can this wait?' he groaned, his eyes on Ikemefuna's hips.

'No. We need to make this phone call,' Agbala insisted. 'You don't impregnate a woman without sharing the good news with her parents.'

Nna caught his breath. The photographs he had been scrutinizing for weeks were etched in his mind, and their subjects: Adina and Dumeje.

Eke entered the kitchen, his chest bare, his belly hump spilling over his belt buckle. 'Coffee, anyone?' he muttered in his sleepy voice, a chewing stick hanging down his mouth.

Agbala fumbled with her cellphone. Nna stifled a smile. His mother wasn't the nervous type, but she seemed overwhelmed by the mechanics of the call. He massaged her shoulders as she dialed a number from memory, her cheeks squeezed inwards in concentration.

The phone began to ring on speaker.

'Maybe they are still sleeping,' Eke murmured, his voice bright and hopeful. 'This phone call can wait a little, can't it? We can give it some time.'

Agbala started to nod, her finger hovering above the end icon, when someone answered. 'Hello?'

The thin sharpness of Dumeje's voice sounded like pencil on parchment. Nna remembered Dumeje's voice from long ago afternoons in the living room of the Southwest Houston apartment, a receiver pressed to his ear.

'Dumeje. It is me,' Eke enunciated slowly, as though something important would get lost in the line. 'How are you, my dear friend?'

'I'm fine, my friend! Very fine indeed. Wait a minute. Let me call Adina. *Adina!*'

Shuffling feet, urgent whispers, more static.

'*Ewo*. Eke!' the feline voice purred into the receiver. 'Longest time! How are you?'

Nna's eyes fluttered shut, surprised by how quickly his body took to Adina. The tightness in his chest. The sudden lump in his belly.

'I am fine,' Eke replied. 'Very fine, indeed. In fact, I am here with Agbala, Ikemefuna, and Nna.'

'*Ewo!* Nna'm, my son!' Adina exclaimed, her words tumid with emotion. 'How is my darling boy?'

'I—' Nna stuttered. He raised his eyes from the cloudy screen to Eke, then to Agbala, a lump forming in his throat. He cleared his throat. 'I'm fine, ma'am. And you?'

'My son, I'm fine o. You sound so old. Like a big man. An *Americana* for that matter.'

'Keep quiet! What do you know?' Dumeje yelled at Adina, his thin voice slicing through the static. 'Nna my son. Don't mind the woman. She doesn't know anything about anything. You're not old. You're a fine, young gentleman, you hear me?'

'Thanks sir.'

'Dumeje and Adina, my old friends,' Agbala started. 'At long last, we have good news for you.'

'Go on, woman!' Dumeje exclaimed. 'Don't keep me waiting in my old age. Or do you want me to drop dead from a heart attack before you say what must be said?'

'Patience is a virtue, my old friend,' Agbala hissed, a flash of anger galloping across her face. 'Your girl is pregnant with our boy's first child. A boy for that matter. Oh, yes! Ala revealed him to me in a dream.'

Adina and Dumeje dissolved into a chorus of barks, the one singing praises into the static as the other wept with wild abandon.

Chukwunna!

Ewo!

'You have been so patient my friends,' Agbala pressed on. 'Book your flight to Houston as soon as possible. Nna is waiting for you.'

'My son,' Dumeje yelled. 'I cannot wait to see you again in the flesh.'

Nna registered Dumeje's words. He raised a brow at Agbala and Eke.

'Same here, sir,' he responded slowly. 'Your daughter is a great girl. You did a great job with her. She's here too, if you'd like to speak with her.'

The skin of his throat bristled as the static filled the room.

If Dumeje heard Nna's offer, he ignored it. 'I raised her well for you, you know? I said to myself, my son deserves the best of the best. He does not need one of those *yeye* girls who lack home training,' he exclaimed.

'My son,' Adina whispered. 'Please be kind to her.'

Suddenly, the lump in Nna's throat splintered, its rubble shooting up into his mouth, his heart pounding in his ears.

'What do you mean?' he yelled after the distant voice. 'Ma'am, can you hear me? I said what do you mean by *my son?*'

Eke swiped to grab the phone out his hand, knocking it to the floor instead. The four of them watched as it clattered to the floor, disbanding into whorls of limbs as each dove to the floor to pick the phone.

Ikemefuna's fingers grazed the phone. 'Mommy! Help me! Please!' she screamed.

Eke snatched the phone from her grasp and ended the call.

'My God!' Agbala cried as she rose to her feet. 'What is wrong with all of you?'

'They called me their son,' Nna yelled back. 'They said I was their son.'

'And so?'

'Is there something I should know? Tell me! Now.'

'How many times must we teach you about your Igbo roots?' Agbala sighed. She stooped to pick her hairnet from the yam tuber leaning against the cooker. 'In our culture, when you marry a woman, you marry into her family. Your in-laws become your second parents. I've explained this to you, Nna'm.'

He shook his head sideways. No. He wasn't buying Agbala's explanation. Not this time.

'Why did you snatch the phone from me? Why won't you let Adina respond?' he pressed.

Agbala regarded him.

'Why would I?' she asked finally, her voice a bitter hiss. 'You think I'd watch you make a fool of yourself in front of our in-laws?'

Nna pressed his head to the kitchen's stucco wall. A memory formed behind his eyes. The hazy image of a tottering plastic cradle in a carpeted room. Mosquitoes descending on his exposed skin like enemy combatants. A young woman crouching inches from his face, cooing at him, her gap tooth shooting out the flap of her gums.

The Sugar Land kitchen came into focus. He felt the heat of Agbala's glare on his face. Her lips parted into a rictus grin, teeth shining beneath a soft fluorescent glare.

He blinked.

He squinted at her teeth.

Where did the gap go?

43

That night, Nna edged closer to Ikemefuna till he breathed the cheap tang of the flavored bar soap on her skin. He wanted to wake her up from sleep and make her revisit the things she'd said about his parents. He would confess that he'd been scared to confront her accusations because he wasn't ready for the truth.

Truths were rigid and unwieldy. Once allowed to enter, they changed lives and crushed spirits. The search for the truth drove men crazy, caused them to question everything. He would talk to her about the fight. She was family so he could be honest. He would confess that he'd liked the heat of her elbow on his flank, the way it sanctified his rage, made it into something righteous, spurred him to react.

Beneath his comforter, his fists were compact, cool to the touch. They were the fists of a gentleman. He had the receipts to prove it – a montage of him picking out long-stemmed roses at a farmer's market in Brooklyn; lovingly cupping the tear-stained face of Bunmi, then Zainab; holding doors open as passers-by mouthed earnest thank yous; massaging away the knots on needy backs; restraining drunk men from lunging at female bartenders. The list was endless.

He reached for the journal on his bedside table. Pulled out the photographs from the toolshed – Adina with her vacuous eyes and shamefaced grin. Dumeje's spidery arms curving against her waistline.

Nna brought the photographs to his face.

There it was. The gap in Adina's teeth. Just like the gap in his.

He ran his thumb against the flat sheen.

Adina was the gap-toothed woman from his vaporous Lagos memory. He was sure of it.

He had to do something. But what? Confronting Agbala and Eke was pointless. It would get him nowhere. They would feed him their spiel about his roots. About neighbors turned in-laws turned family. As if that explained the vicious thumping in his gut.

Ikemefuna shifted away from him, a soft sigh escaping her lips. He stared at her arched back. He still couldn't believe that Agbala had suggested they kill her, like she was a buffalo in an African Safari and they were American tourists.

He could pull the plug on the madness, fly to Lagos with Ikemefuna. He could meet the Azubuikes in the flesh, couldn't he? And kill two birds with one stone – get to the truth about the Azubuikes and win brownie points with Ikemefuna.

He made fast calculations as the idea of a Lagos trip crystallized in his head. Bode had an older brother who worked at the consulate in Atlanta. He would get a visa for himself, a replacement passport for Ikemefuna.

He sat up in his bed, suddenly unable to sleep, imagining how his parents would react to it all. Though it didn't really matter. By the time they found out, he and Ikemefuna would be gone.

44

November 2019

Ikemefuna was eight weeks into her pregnancy when she first noticed the shift in the air.

A tenderness that altered Agbala, Eke and Nna's body language as they tiptoed around her.

Something was off.

Her body – newly foreign and increasingly combative – frightened her. A sudden heaviness in her breasts, its excess fat spilling out the sides of her bra. Its morning sickness and its sensitivity to smells. A mood that changed directions with the wind. A sharp sense of smell that picked up everything, from the noxious boxers at the foot of Nna's bed to the expired milk at the back of the fridge. Bouts of exhaustion that stretched for days.

'Ma, I think I need to see a doctor,' she pleaded with Agbala as they scrubbed beans for moi moi by the kitchen sink. 'I don't feel too well.'

Agbala's eyes slid from Ikemefuna's face to the belly beneath the girl's oversized tee.

'What for?' she asked. 'You are barely even showing.'

'Ma, I feel weak. I'm worried about my health . . .' She trailed off, considered her words carefully. 'I'm worried for the baby.'

Agbala tugged her cheeks and flashed a smile.

'It's normal to feel tired when you're pregnant my dear,' Agbala confided as she took the basin of beans from Ikemefuna. 'Now, why don't you go lie down while I finish up the rest of the cooking?'

Since the pregnancy, bowls of yams – roasted, boiled, or fried to a sunbaked brown – had begun to appear. 'Eat,' Agbala would command, her yowl soft and slippery like undercooked egg.

And an onslaught of kindness. A foot rub. A head massage. Veins pushing against knuckles as palms kneaded Vaseline into Ikemefuna's back. Nna moving upholstery, and sneakers, and carpets, and loose floor tiles out of her way as she made her way around the house. Nna following her everywhere like a house fly. Sleeping when she slept and waking up when she woke up. Lingering outside the bathroom when she was trying to take a shit.

At the same time, she began noticing Agbala's unannounced absences, only showing up to breakfast and dinner, her hair disheveled, her eyes yellowed from exhaustion. That she murmured vague sinister phrases beneath her breath like *Ala sends her greetings*.

The omnipresence of belly rubs. Buy one get one free. Buy none get one free. Each rub, an overfamiliar acquaintance who stayed too long. A constant friction on the surface of her skin. Three pairs of rough brown palms molding her body into temporary shapes, feeling along the perimeters for a pulse.

Ikemefuna hated her new normal. The strange new body with its unborn guest. Her obligation to push it out her womb and love it with all her heart.

More than anything, she longed for Nkemdili's gentle pressure on her calves and the woman's soothing encouragements like *ndo* and *it is well*.

She often thought of the phone call with her parents – that short, strange spell, their voices filling up the kitchen as they took turns to dote on Nna. She had sought their reassurance and their rage. In return, they'd exchanged pleasantries with her abductors.

Why had they not asked about her? Did they not care about her well-being?

After that phone call, her knees had buckled beneath her and she'd fallen to the kitchen floor. She'd refused to stand up until Agbala and Eke grabbed her by her limbs and pulled her to her feet. She'd toppled over once they released her arms, the stark reality of her truth crashing down on her, causing her to gulp for air.

No one was coming to her rescue.

Not even her parents.

Still, she latched on to the promise of Nna's rebellion. She'd watched him lash out at his parents after the phone call to her parents. Clearly, he still had his suspicions that his parents were hiding the full extent of their relationship to the Azubuikes. She hoped his doubts would translate into action. But she would not rely on Nna alone. She must take matters into her hands.

On some nights, she pretended to sleep until Nna's snores filled the room. When they did, she slid out of his bed, crept out of the bedroom, down the wrought-iron stairs, past the foyer. She pressed the stucco walls of the living room, pushed against the shuttered kitchen windows, knocked on the dining room's hardwood, her eyes sweeping the house for a fighting chance, hoping to find an open door or keys left unattended. Nothing.

But sometimes, she returned to bed not entirely empty-handed.

Sachets of rat poison.

A slender knife with a carved wood handle wrapped in a head scarf and tucked away beneath Nna's mattress.

45

On a chilly evening in November, Ashley sat on a folded chair in her best friend, Mary's backyard, nibbling overcooked fried chicken and pretending to love it. As she braced herself for the next bite, something caught her eye in the top window of the house next door. Someone had raised the blinds to reveal the insides of a bedroom. From a mirror leaning against the bedroom wall, she spotted a man and woman lying side by side on sheets. They were straight out the pages of *Vogue*, a centerfold of tousled afro, lean brown chests, darkening eyes, twisted limbs, and lace panties. Their hunger for each other clearly insatiable.

Ashley sighed wistfully. She barely remembered erotic love, the whispered supplications and sticky cum. It had been so long since anyone pried her open with deft fingers. So long since she felt a quickening in her chest.

The woman dropped upon the man, her breasts sandwiched against his chest as she stroked his chin. The man slapped his palms against the sheets and yelled into his clenched fists. Ashley clutched her cheeks and sighed. She could feel the sting of embarrassment start to rise to its surface. She pretended to look away as the woman approached the window.

Ashley squinted at the woman's midriff. Was that a belly bump? Yes. Ashley stiffened, her cheeks turning a fiery red. The closest thing she had to a child were two dozen frozen eggs at a fertility center in downtown Houston. She rose from the chair and barged into the house. She'd done enough people watching for one day.

Inside the bedroom, Ikemefuna leaned closer to Nna.

'Nna'm, are you sure you don't want to audition for this show?' she asked, pointing at the *Who Wants to be a Millionaire?* on the screen. 'This one that you know all the answers to the questions that they are asking.'

He planted a wet kiss on the bulb of her nose.

'I'll audition if you promise to sit in the front row and cheer me on,' he murmured into her neck.

He reached for the remote control. She slipped a palm beneath the mattress and pulled out the head scarf with the knife she'd snuck out the kitchen the day before. She tucked it behind her, swallowed. She raised her head to Nna. He was fiddling with the volume buttons on the remote, a moony smile on his face.

He started to reach for her waist. She rolled away from him.

'Not again, please. I am feeling queasy.'

She stilled her body for an argument, or worse, his fists. She still remembered the day she'd learned she was pregnant. They had pushed against each other, his punches meeting their target. They'd reminded her of her parents in the kitchen of the Lagos flat, in their bedroom, behind their bathroom door, her father reaching for a pound of her mother's flesh.

He pulled her closer. He ran his palms along her neck, then the crenellations of her spine. She hoped that his hands would not brush against the head scarf. He tugged her cheeks a touch too hard. She could bear a little pain, so she let him. He stroked her neck and belly. She giggled, unsure about the sounds coming out her mouth, the tenseness of her body.

'How is he doing?' Nna murmured, planting a kiss on Ikemefuna's neck.

'Pay attention. He just made it past the $100,000 mark.'

'Not the contestant, stupid. I'm talking about my son.'

Ikemefuna pulled away. His tone reminded her of the days before the pregnancy. Of his palms tightening against her waist and his fingers digging into her skin.

But he reached for her again. He felt around the darkness for the roundness of her belly. He found it, pressed its perimeters, gently at first, the movements of his fingers building into a crescendo, his eyes darkening as Ikemefuna winced at his hands contracting against her warm flesh.

'He's a calm one,' she murmured into the dark.

'That's my boy.'

On the screen, Chris Harrison shook his head at the bright-eyed Hispanic contestant. *Seals is the wrong answer. Sea turtles lay their eggs in a nest they dig in the sand.*

'You're going to leave me, aren't you?'

Nna's question pierced the dark air. The weight of his arm pressed down on her shoulder.

'I'm not leaving you, Nna.'

God. He was so needy.

'Good. It'd be silly of you to try.'

She kept her arms by her side as he planted kisses on her forehead.

'I talked to my parents earlier today,' he continued, his lips hovering above her belly.

'Yes.'

'I told them I'd take you to dinner. There's an Italian restaurant in Westheimer. All the rigatoni alla vodka you can get. You will love it.'

'Do they serve it spicy?'

'Eh. Not Nigerian-level spicy.'

'I don't want it if it doesn't light up my tongue.'

'God. You're so Nigerian,' he laughed.

She searched her brain for a quirky response. Nneka liked to flirt with questions, so maybe …

'Am I?' she cooed.

'I love it.'

'And when will you whisk me away to Philadelphia?' she whispered softly. She imagined herself in an airport. Another body in a sea of bodies.

'You're a persistent little thing, aren't you?'

'You haven't met enough Igbo girls,' she replied with a chuckle.

'Mmh. What does it matter? What matters is that I'm with one now,' he said, pulling her into a tight embrace and planting another kiss on her saliva-coated forehead, then her nose, then just above her lips. Drawing her top lip into a kiss, then her collarbone.

'You're right,' she murmured into his ears as his palms grazed the head scarf. She gulped. 'All that matters is that you met this Igbo girl.'

He reached for the glass of water he always kept by his bedside table. She grabbed the head scarf and slid it beneath the bed. She could hear the scratch of its blade on the freshly waxed floors as it sailed away from her fingers.

'What was that?' he asked, eyeing her.

'What?' she croaked, blinking at him.

Nna shrugged.

'I thought I heard something.'

She threw her head back and laughed with her throat, like Nneka would do when she wanted to seduce Obinna.

Nene, you should see me now, she thought dryly. *I'm making you proud.*

They rolled around the sheets, their skin projecting the images on the TV screen. Outside the window, the cedar leaves scratched against the house. Ashley air-danced to the crunch of fried chicken. David and his buddies from swim practice pressed their faces to his bedroom window, their foggy breaths painting concentric circles on the glass – *If we're lucky, she'll stand next to the window this time. Just wait for it.*

Nna untangled his limbs from Ikemefuna. He peered at her small, round face.

'Nnaemeka Jnr,' he said.

'Sorry?'

'Our son. I want him to have my name.'

He placed his palm on her belly for the tenth time that night, gazed into her eyes.

'You know, that's my uncle's name too. My father's older brother,' she said, her eyebrows crinkled in concentration. 'You will love my uncle if you meet him.'

'Will I?'

'Yes. I'm sure you will, Nna'm.' She reached for more words. 'He recently moved from Aba to Lagos.'

'Is that so?'

'You'll get on with him like a house on fire.' She kissed his elbow. 'Maybe ...' her tone measured; her palms clasped. '… we could fly to Lagos before the year runs out. You will meet my parents, my best friend Nneka and her boyfriend Obinna.'

'Mmmh.'

She smiled. Progress. She snuggled closer to Nna, running her fingers through his chest hairs. He'd told her it turned him on.

'And you can finally get some answers for yourself instead of relying on your parents' lies.'

'Excuse me?'

'Come on, Nna. We've gone over this already. We both know they are hiding something from you. The phone call to my parents said as much.'

'Word of advice, Keme? Don't speak about my parents like that if you're trying to sway my opinion in your favor.'

'Nna, all I'm saying is that a trip like this would—'

'I don't want to hear it.'

'I'm just trying to help—'

Nna jerked forward. He sank his teeth into her lips to shut her up, biting until he tasted the warm gush of sweet metal, felt it streak his teeth.

She pressed his neck, his carotid artery. He couldn't breathe. He savored the growing tension in his chest. He released her lips from the grip of his teeth, spat out the bits of skin that stayed behind. He gulped the air and grinned at her. She screamed so loud, it tumbled down the stairs, beneath the front door, and into the neighbor's backyard.

Nna flung off his sheets and jumped out of bed. Ikemefuna pressed a wad of tissue to her bleeding lips.

'You're trying to leave me, aren't you?' he yelled. 'That's why you're so desperate to return to Lagos.'

'No,' she whimpered.

He punched a wall and cursed out loud. It was impossible to know who or what to believe. His parents with their vague answers and shifty eyes, or Ikemefuna with all of her visibly cunning antics.

All he knew for certain was that he was going to Lagos to meet the Azubuikes. He'd already contacted Bode about a Nigerian passport for Ikemefuna and a visa for himself.

Bode had confirmed that his brother Gbenga could procure both, but the wait time to receive the passport and visa was close to six months. Bode offered a quick fix – a $1,000-bribe to expedite the processing times. He'd cursed Bode's entire lineage as he Venmoed it to him.

The door to Nna's bedroom flew open. Agbala rushed in in her satin bonnet, a mug of Rooibos pressed to her chest.

'Mom,' he started, that word perching uncomfortably on his tongue. 'All she cares about is returning to Lagos.'

'Enough,' Agbala cried, enveloping a sniveling Ikemefuna in her arms.

Eke rushed into the bedroom. He forced Nna to sit down, to count to – *ten, nine, eight, seven, six, inhale, exhale,* till Nna's heavy breathing puttered to a stop.

'I'm trying, Dad. She makes it so hard,' Nna sighed, his fingers distractedly rubbing the sore spot on his neck.

'It's okay,' Eke assured him. 'You hear me? It's okay.'

'She knows how to get under my skin.'

Agbala led Ikemefuna into the master bedroom and sat her on the bed. She studied Ikemefuna's bleeding lips. Tomorrow, she would press iodine in the wound.

'It will hurt for a while,' Agbala murmured as she pressed a wet cloth against the red. 'Three days, maybe a week. And then fresh skin will cover the scabs, and it will be as good as new. But you have to be more careful.'

Agbala studied Ikemefuna's face – her eyes red with tears, her snot-filled nose, her puce-colored lips, and the wrinkles that shot out the sides of her mouth like whiskers. She pressed Ikemefuna to her chest.

'You're too young to be this sad,' she said. 'By now, you should know how Nna gets sometimes. He can be short-tempered. Quick to anger.' She wet her finger with saliva and scrubbed the dry blood coloring the sides of Ikemefuna's cheeks. 'Find ways to be patient with him. Don't press his buttons. Touch them lightly. You understand?'

Ikemefuna nodded. It seemed unfair that she should have to adjust to Nna's anger. As if she too was not short-tempered. Quick to anger. As if her rage must make room for his instead of meeting it, blow to blow, till the fermenting anger consumed them both.

'Now, no more crying. Clean your eyes. Put a smile on your face and go and apologize to your husband.'

46

Agbala watched her daughter-in-law through a muslin veil of peppery steam. The dexterity in the flick of Ikemefuna's fingers as she laid fork first, then knife, on either side of each dish. Agbala cupped her mouth in her palms, pretended to yawn, but in truth, she was smiling. A full flash of teeth.

The girl's pregnancy was nearing the end of its first trimester, which meant that she only had six months left of living to do. Agbala sucked her inner cheeks. It was unfortunate that the girl had to die, given that Agbala was starting to warm up to her. She could feel it in her heart. Not that it mattered either way, but it was nice to not be in combat mode all the time. To unclench one's jaw and fists. To exhale a little. Blessings to Ala for the pregnancy. It was making all the difference.

Ikemefuna placed a 2017 Pinot Noir at the center of the dinner table. It felt strange to think, but Ikemefuna reminded Agbala of a younger version of herself. She was growing to appreciate the girl's resolve, her strong-headedness, her quiet strength, the way she kept Agbala, Eke and Nna on their toes. She'd been exactly like Ikemefuna at that age, staring past her older sisters and dancing to the beat of her own drum.

Clearly, Ikemefuna was not Adina's daughter. She was made of something tougher, steelier, with a thirst for blood, the acrid flavor of revenge. It terrified Agbala. And yet, it made her fond of the girl.

'Enough,' she nudged Ikemefuna who had begun to wipe down the dinner table with a wad of Kleenex. 'Sit down. You've done enough.'

Nna clambered down the stairs. He wore a dress shirt and a pair of boxers. 'Conference calls,' he said with a sigh in response to her arched brow.

When did he grow so big? It seemed like it was just yesterday when she and Eke arrived at the George Bush airport with a precocious Nna in tow. He'd slept in the clasp of her arms as his pooled saliva gathered in the inner curve of her elbow. And now, here he stood, all man and muscle, and how could her heart not burst out of its chest?

She'd not always believed she would make a great mother. In her youth, motherhood was a stick used to clobber young women. Mothers. They were perpetually tired zombies with watery milk gushing out of their nipples. Their life cycle was trading briefcases for feeding bottles. Adding inches to their gut from snacking on cornstarch. She wanted no part of it.

Then she grew older, and age gave her a seasoned mind and hips as wide as a highway. She did the required reading, learned of powerful women like Funmi Ransome-Kuti. Women who were as much mothers as they were martyrs, women who pressed their waffling babies to their bosoms with one hand and led nations with the other, and why couldn't she too have it all?

She wanted it all.

Nna was her answered prayer.

An overnight delivery from Ala herself.

She'd rolled up her sleeves and done the hard work of fattening him into a young man. Slipping extra servings of ugba in his abacha. And now he was a juicy tenderloin, primed and prepped for fatherhood.

She held on to her cloth napkin with its splotches of stew as Nna planted a kiss on Ikemefuna's forehead. He caught her eye. She smiled at him with her full teeth.

A month had gone by since he began to ask questions, flashing those pictures from the toolshed. She would be the first to admit keeping the photographs there was poor judgment on her part. She should have set them on fire all those years ago. And then that cursed phone call with the Azubuikes.

She raised her eyes to Nna's face. He was pulling out a chair and asking about the Falu red vase that was once on the coffee table in the upper-level living room. The one Ikemefuna hurled at her neck while he was away.

'Oh, that one,' she hummed. 'Ikemefuna broke it by mistake. Isn't that so, Ikemefuna?'

She turned to stare at Ikemefuna, but she was gone.

47

Nna sat in the air-conditioned dining room of his parents'
house, his elbows pressed to the glass top of the chintzy dinner
table Eke had unveiled the previous year. He tried to dismiss
his apprehension about the sour-tasting yams. Agbala prided
herself on her ability to comb the aisles of Mama Anselem,
the biggest African food store in Southwest Houston, for the
sturdiest yams. She refused to commit to a tuber until she'd
held it up to the store's bright light, pressed it to her nose,
and felt along its ridges with her pinky for decay.

Nna took a third bite of a yam. It had to be a rotten batch.
Agbala previously mentioned that Ezichi, the middle-aged
Igbo woman who ran Mama Anselem and was often found
sashaying down its aisles of palm oil and netted sponges,
now sourced her yams from a remote village in Aba instead
of her Iowa wholesaler. It was likely that the yams had begun
to go bad during the lengthy journey from South-East Nigeria
to Ezichi's yam-flour-coated wood shelves in Southwest
Houston.

But by the third yam – hard as stone, its bitterness so bold
it caused Nna to spit, his fork bounced against his dish before
clattering to the hardwood.

'Sorry about that,' he muttered, mostly to himself. He surveyed his parents faces for the same discontent he imagined his face reflected – pursed lips, raised brows, a thin splash of sweat above an upper lip. But Agbala wore a blank face, her eyes on Ikemefuna's empty seat. Eke ran a napkin through his goatee. His wife was somewhere upstairs, having excused herself to the bathroom.

'I'll be just a minute,' Nna announced to the table. He pushed back his chair and rose to his feet. He stumbled out the dining room and into the kitchen, a heaviness descending on his forehead.

He fell against the granite countertops.

He reached for the hard stucco walls, a plastic bucket, garri basins, and yam tubers as the world around him turned a dusty mauve.

He tried to fight the heaviness, to latch on to anything in the dusk. The outline of a ladle. An empty egg crate. He stumbled forward, then backwards. He sank to the parquet.

He could taste the gurgle at the back of his throat.

Like almonds gone bad.

Or worse.

Much worse.

Lead.

Poison.

Footsteps.

Something or someone was approaching the kitchen.

Ikemefuna?

Surely not.

Agbala stumbled into the kitchen a few moments later. She bumped into the cooker. Against the walls, and plastic buckets, and garri basins, and yam tubers, her hip bones shifting in and out of place with each stagger. Her eyes were heavy with a dangerous dizziness as she stumbled forward, determined to find her bearing.

Agbala heaved, the soft pink of her tongue sticking out her mouth like the tongue of a bonobo in heat.

'Nna'm, I don't feel well,' she croaked.

'She poisoned us,' Nna muttered, feeling through the darkness for the bony outline of Agbala's arms. 'She must have added something to the yams.'

'She wouldn't dare,' Agbala insisted, hobbling to the shelf beneath the kitchen sink where she'd stored a small grey jute, no larger than an arm, with her stash of rat poison. She'd discovered two fat rats running around the garage in the summer and had wasted no time buying the poison from the Kroger a half mile away. At the time, she'd thought the poison a good investment thanks to its high potency and long shelf life. Now, she leaned against the kitchen sink, sweat dripping down her browbone as she counted the sachets.

On her third count she screamed. The kitchen windows trembled in their frames.

No.

It could not be.

It could not possibly be.

She was missing five.

She never missed anything. Not with the second pair of eyes at the back of her head.

Except she was missing something. She really was. Five full sachets of poison, gone missing. Poof.

'*Arueme!*' she cried, barnacling towards the dining room with what remained of her strength.

Nna stumbled out the kitchen and into the dining room where Eke lay beneath the dinner table, clotted lines of mucus spilling down his lips. Agbala shuffled past him and crouched beside Eke. Eke released a weak cry. Seeing his father was alive, Nna left his parents and hobbled up the stairs, into the hallway. He leaned by the banister, his breath fizzing in his throat as his heart pounded against its cage. Ikemefuna could be anywhere. He could be walking towards his death. He took a deep breath and stilled his nerves. He gathered what remained of his strength and made for Ikemefuna's room. Cautiously, he pushed open the door to her room: Empty, save for the soldier ants circling a mound of boiled rice on a dresser.

He barged into Agbala and Eke's bedroom, its air thick with multivitamins and soursop. Empty too. He dragged his way on to his bedroom. Tom Ford and rumpled sheets. He saw Ikemefuna's back stir, watched her dash behind his headboard. He heard a rustling behind a tin of shoe polish. Saw the hem of her rapa. He lunged at her, but was too slow to duck beneath the knife in her hands. Her eyes were dark and determined, her lips a mean slit of concentration. He fell to the floor. She towered over him now, poking at his torso with the edge of the knife till fresh blood tumbled down the waterfall of his thighs.

'Key! Give me! Give me, now!' she growled.

Nna dug through his pockets.

'Where is it?' Ikemefuna yelled as she flashed the knife at the stretch of skin between his eyes. 'Tell me now or I will—'

Thwack.

A wet thud.

Ikemefuna's head snapped forward. She fell to the hardwood floor.

Nna crawled away from her limp body. The thin heel of a rubbery green akpola shoe lay next to her. He stared up at the form in the doorway.

His mother. All five feet and four inches of her.

'She will stay this way for a while. I think I struck her with just enough force to knock her out cold,' Agbala heaved weakly, her lids struggling to stay open.

Nna and Agbala observed Ikemefuna's still body.

'She tried to kill us,' he croaked, staring in disbelief at the tiny woman on the ground.

'She is growing wings, Nna'm,' Agbala murmured as she hobbled towards him, a bottle of water in her right hand. 'And I fear that very soon, we won't be able to clip them.'

Agbala and Nna stood in silence, their eyes on the figure at their feet.

'And Dad?'

'He will live.'

'What on earth, Mom! She almost killed Dad?'

'No need to panic. I'm boiling a potion. Dongoyaro, ose oji—'

'What the hell is that?'

'Oh, don't you worry about it. It's a homemade health potion. Ala owns the recipes. I simply follow her instructions.'

Nna sighed. He was too weak to question his mother.

'Mom.'

'Yes?'

'Thank you for saving my life.'

'You're welcome my son.'

'I don't know what to do anymore.'

He stared at the marbled mound of Ikemefuna's belly peeking out the bottom of her tie-dye blouse.

Agbala pressed him to her chest and wrapped her arms around him. She'd shown she would put him first, even at her weakest, and was that not the greatest proof of a mother's love?

He could abandon the Lagos trip, come clean to her right there and then. Apologize to her for daring to believe the girl who'd just tried to kill him.

'Nna'm, she will not leave this house with your son.'

He shook his head, unconvinced.

'Time flies. Before you know it, you will carry your son in your arms.'

'I will carry my son in my arms,' he repeated.

'And she will be dead,' Agbala muttered, staring at Ikemefuna's still form.

Nna groaned.

'Moooooom. Enough of that nonsense.'

'Oh yes,' Agbala cooed, her face breaking into a gnarly smile. 'I have some snakeweed I'll add to her yam pepper soup. Not that *yeye* rat poison that anyone with a sharp nose can easily sniff out. My second-cousin Chidimma who lives in Dallas plucks snakeweed from her village in Nnewi each time she visits Nigeria. She uses it to treat her son's anxiety, but the right dose will cause a man to die in his sleep.'

'Come on, Mom,' he sighed. 'Drop it. Keme is clearly suffering from some sort of mental illness. What she needs is treatment.'

'Listen to me, Nna'm. It is a natural plant. Just like kale and spinach. Even if oyibo people run their oyibo tests on her, they won't find anything out of the ordinary.'

'You can't be so sure.'

'Nna'm, I'm sure.'

They stood in uncomfortable silence.

'Anyway, let me check on Eke,' Agbala said, turning to leave the bedroom.

'Mom?'

'Yes?'

Nna held his mother's eyes. The details of the Lagos trip slid up his throat. It teetered at the tip of his tongue. A visa and a passport in the works. Nonrefundable one-way tickets. The suitcases he had started to fill.

'Thank you. For everything.'

48

Agbala went to great lengths to protect herself from minor inconveniences. In 1984, she married a quiet man with a weak chin because it meant that she would never have to submit to a man for as long as she lived. In 1994, she moved across continents to distance herself from her neighbor Adina's watching eyes each time she strolled the neighborhood with her son in tow. And years later, she would use her husband Eke as a buffer against inconveniences – encouraging him to play middleman on the rare occasion she needed to send seasonal greetings to Adina. *Happy New Year!* he would stammer into the cellphone. *Nna is alive and well!*

She leaned against the bathroom door and tried to ignore Eke's revolting snores. She'd feared for his life as she forced thick Dongoyaro down his throat that evening, until, finally – after what seemed like an eternity – his eyelids flew open. Now, she practiced her lines in her head as she scrolled through her contacts for Adina's number. Agbala was out of options. She would make the call to Adina herself. She would keep it short and as sweet as she could, all things considered.

'Hello?'

Adina's voice filled the bathroom.

'Er, hello,' she stuttered.

'Why are you calling me? Is everything alright?' Adina whispered.

Agbala sat down on the edge of her bathtub. It was dawn in Lagos. She pictured Adina in bed with Dumeje, her anxious eyes glued to his sleeping form as she cradled her phone to her ears.

'Yes. I mean, no,' Agbala started. 'There was an incident today.'

'Incident? What do you mean by that?'

'The girl tried to kill us all.'

'My god.'

'Indeed.'

'How so?'

'Rat poison. She added it to our lunch. If not for the Dongoyaro in my refrigerator, we would all be dead by now.'

'How is he?'

'Who?'

'You know who I'm talking about,' Adina whispered harshly. 'We've been worried sick since the last call.'

Agbala bit her bottom lip. She didn't care for the woman's tone.

'He's alive and well. That's all you need to know,' Agbala offered coldly. 'I of course spoke to Ala about today's incident. Ala refuses – and I must add that I agree with Ala – but she refuses to spare Ikemefuna at my family's expense. Ala is thirsty for the girl's blood, and she is running out of patience. Soon, I may let Ala take what's owed her.'

'But you can't do that,' Adina cried. 'How can you do that?'

'Adina, please. I'm just the messenger.'

'You liar,' Adina cried. 'You wicked li—'

Agbala hung up and rose to her feet.

Her breath shot out her mouth in quick spurts. She leaned against the bathroom's tiles, her heart pounding against her chest. That mosquito of a woman knew how to press her buttons. Eke was always telling her to make an effort with the woman. She'd thought giving the woman a heads-up about her daughter's impending death was a nice enough start, but alas.

Agbala returned to her bedroom and lay beside Eke's trembling frame. She tried to sleep, but Adina's biting voice rang in her head. She closed her eyes to rid her head of it.

No, shutting off Adina's voice was not good enough. She needed to right the woman's wrong.

Agbala lay in silence as the seconds mounted.

Then a knowing smile stretched across her lips.

She asked Ala to cause Adina great loss. The kind to drive a woman to the shores of madness.

It was what the ungrateful woman deserved.

49

Ikemefuna's labored breathing woke her up – swathes of air rolling in and out of her lungs like moss. She let it slow, then quicken, held it between her teeth, pressed her tongue to it – all to convince herself that the breath still belonged to her.

She had found herself where Agbala left her, spread across the chenille blanket in her old bedroom. She blinked away the dried blood crusts in the corners of her eyes, caught glimpses of herself in the mirror swinging off a nail on the wall. The purplish sphere spreading across her arms. Her twisted limbs and swollen lids.

Last night was not her first attempt to kill Agbala and Eke.

She'd been trying to kill them since her first night in America, lying on her scratchy bed, a sense of doom pressing against her sternum.

She'd insisted on cooking their lunch the next day. Fried yams and egg sauce.

She was careful with the poison, pinching it between her thumb and index finger, sprinkling it in Agbala and Eke's broths and stews.

The first time, Eke complained of a stomach bug. Agbala barely blinked. The next time, she increased the dosage. Two pinches in the pap. Three pinches in the moi moi. Eke had spent hours in the bathroom. Agbala brewed bitter leaf to calm her rumbling stomach. The third time, Eke chewed Panadol tablets. Agbala threw up next to the mantelpiece in the living room. And all the while, Agbala blamed the African food store for selling them expired produce, insisting that Ala had revealed that fact to her in a dream.

This time, she'd tried to kill Nna too. Before she met him, she'd hoped he was different from his parents. But he was just like them. Violent and impulsive. The poison was supposed to work. She'd emptied three sachets of the greige powder in the mackerel sauce, dusted it against the yams, her fingers steady, her breathing calm.

She listened intently as her breath puttered out of her throat like blasts from a faulty Yamaha generator. She committed a formula to memory – *inhale, exhale, repeat.*

Her gut told her Agbala, Eke, and Nna wanted to kill her. She'd watched enough Nollywood to feel the hunch. In those movies, the women were merely birthing bodies. Childbirth happened to them and the men discarded their wives' postpartum bodies for firmer ones. Or they sacrificed their wives' bodies to ritualists in exchange for blood money. They would likely wait till the baby was born. She couldn't imagine them risking its precious life to get rid of her.

She peered out of the window. The day was blinding in its newness. A cluster of blackbirds congregated on the windowsill as sunlight spilled its gold ink across the sky. She still remembered the fraying red rapa she had folded and placed at the foot of her box springs on the morning of her trip to Houston. Nkemdili grinning from ear to ear, reminding her to remember her in America. Her last meal in Lagos, a mug of farm fresh yoghurt and three greasy puff puffs.

The new day brought new laughter. Soft, at first. Delicate, like gossamer. The shuffling of feet from somewhere outside the room. She could trace the dark shapes through the peephole – a pair of faded blue jeans, whites of eyes, a strict dash of moustache.

Very soon.

Haven't we waited long enough.

She shut her eyes. She smelled the egusi on the hardwood, bits of browning spinach sticking out the epoxy. She burrowed into the mattress, her back to the water stains on the ceiling. When she opened her eyes, Nna stood at the open door, a wary expression on his face.

'Do you have a minute?'

She sat up in bed. He sat next to her. He examined her face, his face inches away from hers.

'My lovely wife,' he murmured. 'When exactly did you decide to kill me?'

She gathered her words.

'Nna'm, I think your parents are planning to kill me,' she said. 'I see the way they look at me, the disgust in their faces. It's like they are waiting for the right time to strike.'

Nna shook his head.

'I was just trying to strike first.'

'And you think it's wise to tell me this?'

She shrugged. 'I have nothing to lose. Nothing I say would make a difference.'

'You're crazy, Keme,' he muttered. 'I won't dishonor my parents by entertaining this conversation.'

They sat in silence, Ikemefuna with her eyes on her thighs as Nna's right foot tapped the hardwood.

'Keme, I hope you know that I'm in a tough position. First, you come into my life claiming to be my wife,' he continued. 'Next, you morph into my parents' victim. Then your mother's old photos start to show up everywhere and it turns out that I look like your mother. What the hell is going on, Keme?'

'Maybe our parents exchanged us at birth?' Ikemefuna offered brightly.

'Not possible. You weren't born when I left Lagos.'

'Or your parents abducted you from my parents?'

'Watch your words,' Nna spat, his fists tensing. 'Let's imagine for a second that your mother is my biological mother. What kind of tortured soul approves of her son marrying her daughter?'

'An abused woman,' she whispered, her eyes catching Nna's eyes. 'Nna'm, if you're serious about getting answers, book that flight to Lagos.'

Nna looked away from Ikemefuna and at the bedroom's windowsill where a blackbird with a rusty plumage was nibbling a beetle.

50

By the end of the first trimester, Ikemefuna's stomach cramps had increased in pain and frequency. Agbala often offered to massage Ikemefuna's abdomen. She applied gentle pressure on Ikemefuna's hipbone, her ribs, her flank. Eke massaged Ikemefuna's swollen ankles with his tiger balm. 'No more chores for you,' he said through rows of cinder-block teeth. 'Sit in one place, for the baby's sake.'

Nna was different too. Save for the odd moments Ikemefuna caught him staring at her with a wildness in his eyes, he remained on his best behavior, swinging his ropy body to Wizkid and throwing air kisses at her belly.

Nna was the one who brought up Lagos.

It came up without prodding on her part.

It was just before sunrise. He'd woken her up for sex and she'd given him his fill. She stared at his limpid eyes and pursed lips.

'What are you saying?' she asked. She wanted to be sure she'd heard right.

'Look, I've been doing some reflecting and I think I'm ready to visit Lagos,' he said. 'I want to ask for your hand in marriage the right way, like a true son of the soil,' he added with a flourish. 'Don't you want me approaching your father's doorstep with tubers of yam and palm wine?'

'That would be nice,' she said with a grin, though she didn't believe him.

He narrowed his eyes at her.

'I thought you'd be more excited.'

'I am, Nna'm,' she said. She planted her elbows in the mattress and propped her head up with her cupped palms. 'But why the sudden change of heart?'

'What does it matter?' he asked, and there was an intensity to his tone. 'I got you a passport. It should get here today. I've been tracking delivery.'

'No way.'

'Yes way. I pulled some strings at the consulate. You'd be surprised what $1,000 can get you when it's dangled in front of overworked Nigerian civil servants.'

'Can you give it to me when it gets here?'

He tilted his head to observe her, a frown on his face.

'Do you not believe me?'

She sighed.

'I didn't mean to offend you, Nna'm. My curiosity got the best of me.'

'Then don't worry about your passport. I'll keep it safe.'

He wouldn't show her the passport because there wasn't one, she thought bitterly.

'And tickets?' she asked.

'I've taken care of that too. Start packing, Keme. We're leaving soon.'

'How soon?'

'I can't give you specifics just yet. But be ready.'

'Do your parents know about this?'

He shook his head sideways. A vein ticked against his temple.

'Let's keep it that way,' he added. 'They don't need to know everything.'

'But what if they find out? What do we say if they see us packing?' she pressed, her alarm bells whirring.

'Like I said, my parents don't need to know everything.'

Ikemefuna snapped her mouth shut. The last thing she needed was an aggravated Nna. She desperately wanted to believe him, but it was hard to believe she could survive Houston long enough to return to Lagos. To the city's concentrated blasts of humid air and its swarm of roaming feet. She tried to imagine her feet traversing its earth – from the stone and asphalt of the Lekki-Ikoyi link bridge to the grit sand of Iyana Ipaja. But her mind drew a blank.

Still, she began to secretly pack that evening. She gathered the bits of her scattered around the Sugar Land house. A red scrunchie. Three basketball shorts. A foundation vial two shades off. A pair of faded Levis beneath a couch. When she was done, she could taste the rubbery airplane peas on her tongue. *Seatbelts please*, she mimed to her reflection in Nna's bathroom mirror.

'What are you thinking?' Nna asked her the next morning. He sat at the kitchen counter, sucking on a grapefruit. She peeled the scaly skin off a second, readying it for his teeth.

'Nothing Nna'm. I'm—' She hesitated, mulling her words over. 'I'm just happy. You're doing the right thing.'

She hoped she sounded convincing, that there was no lump in her throat, or that if there was one, he did not see it. He pulled her to his lap.

'Yeah?' he queried, his voice low and teasing. His palms slid to her thighs. 'I make you happy, huh? How happy? Show me.'

At night, in bed, Ikemefuna could still feel Nna inside her, between her legs, tossing and turning in her womb. She worried that even if she managed to return to Lagos with its heat, and its hawkers, and its tin-roof houses, and its keke maruwas, the city would not fix the pain in her new round body. That she would be forced to carry the pain with her for the rest of her life.

51

Nna did not love Ikemefuna.

The absence of his old love hit him as he stared at her sleeping head on his chest and wiped the thin stream of saliva running down the side of her cheek. Where, once, he might have felt a gentle tug in his chest, there was nothing, only a dull, pounding headache and a cramp in his shoulders from lying stiffly on his back. He shrugged his right arm slightly and stared in satisfaction as Ikemefuna's head rolled off his chest and onto the sheets.

The morning was making its way into the sky with warm streaks of peach and purple. Lexus wheels were beginning to tear down Sugar Land on their way to jobs in the city. Soon, Ikemefuna would yawn and a cloud of stale air would spring from her lips. She would scrub off the dirt in the ridges of her eyes, flash a smile at him and turn her face away.

He would smile back at her. He would pull her into his arms. He would nuzzle her neck with his jaw and peck her forehead. Women loved forehead kisses. They swore it was more meaningful than full lip kisses. More honest. A peephole to a man's heart. He would give her as many forehead kisses as she wanted because like it or not, she was the mother of his unborn son.

The reality of her pregnancy hit him all over again. He was going to be a father, a person to be emulated and revered. His son deserved the very best – piano lessons and international vacations and parents who served blueberry pancakes on the weekend. He would be gentler with Ikemefuna. He would dredge up the remnants of his love for her for the sake of their boy.

The pregnancy was in its second trimester. He'd read somewhere that the bump would be more prominent, so the other day he'd felt along her belly for a bump. In response, she nudged his palm off her and tried to cloak her quiet rage in a smile mask. As if her body was not pulsing with the rage.

'Lie down,' he had asked, and she had allowed her shoulders to fall against his sheets.

He untied the rapa and let it fall to her sides. He ran his palms against its smooth exterior as she stared at the ceiling in silence. He increased the pressure of his palms on her belly so his son could feel his touch.

Ikemefuna's shoulders stirred. She yawned, blinked open her eyes and smiled at Nna before turning her head away.

Her passport and his visa had arrived in a discreet brown envelope that morning. He'd rushed to his bedroom with the envelope before his parents could accost him in the living room. He'd torn the envelope open.

There it was: her passport and his visa.

He'd changed their flights to the very next morning.

The pregnancy was in its second trimester. Time was of the essence.

He hosed down the RAV4 and spent two hours sorting through his closet for Lagos-appropriate clothes, rolling each tank into a cylinder and sticking it in his suitcase. Ikemefuna said the men in Lagos wore wife-beaters and knickers. *It is the weather*, she said. *The sun never leaves the sky.*

Ikemefuna hid the suitcase in his closet when she heard approaching feet. The packing done, they lay on the hardwood of his bedroom with their palms behind their heads.

'What are you feeling?' she asked.

'I'm half and half. Anxious and excited,' he said. 'It's my first time returning to Lagos. I don't know what to expect.'

'Don't be anxious, Nna'm. I'll be your Lagos guide,' she said. 'And your job is fine with the break, yes?'

'I got a scolding from my practice group coordinator for the short notice.' He grimaced. 'Thankfully, my friend Bode is covering for me on my current deals.'

'Mmmh.'

They lay in the silence. Nna thought of the phone call with the Azubuikes, Dumeje's awe and Adina's quiet joy. They'd sounded exactly like his parents, their English marinated in thick Igbo stock. He'd fallen in and out of love with their daughter, proposed to her, gotten her pregnant, and now, they were getting ready to board a flight to a city he barely remembered because he needed to know why he resembled her mother.

He chuckled to himself as Ikemefuna's face brushed against his arm. Their story was one for the books.

52

Nna spent the evening with his parents – knowing that in a few hours, he would be en route to Lagos with Ikemefuna. Between Agbala's amphibious eyes and Eke's compulsive pacing of both floors of the house, he needed to stay alert.

For as long as he could remember, his parents had demanded full disclosure. They welcomed the mundane details of his life with open arms. He would tell his father the exact number of composite resin fillings in his mouth after a dental exam. He would walk his mother through his row house via Skype, point out the faulty outlet in the guest bathroom. Hiding the Lagos trip from them required a great deal of effort.

Later that night, Nna sat on the tufted comforter spread across their bed. The house three blocks away was growing red bell peppers, he announced. He'd spotted a stalk the other day. His parents squinted at him. He cleared his throat. Was it just him or did the new Earl Grey taste different? Perhaps, it was time to switch back to the previous brand?

When he stood to leave the master bedroom, he felt his parents' eyes on him.

'Nna'm, is there a problem?' his mother called from her bed.

He smiled brightly, became a sun.

'No, Mom. Of course not,' he said. 'I just feel a bit tired.'

She took a sip of the warm brew in her cup.

'Okay o. You seem a bit tense, that's all.'

'We're leaving for the airport tonight,' he announced to Ikemefuna when he returned to his bedroom.

She paused the commercial on the TV screen and sat up in bed.

'We'll head out once they fall asleep. Our flight isn't until 7 a.m. so we have some time.'

'How do we know they're sleeping?' she asked, sweeping her palm against the grain of his bedside table.

'I'll listen,' Nna said, tapping his nose with a smile.

Eke was a fast sleeper. His snores fell in short rapid gusts. Agbala took her time with sleep. She gave in at the thirty-minute mark, her low-pitched snores blending into the background.

Nna tiptoed down the stairs with his luggage on his shoulder. He waited anxiously for Ikemefuna. She was slower on her feet. Finally, she showed up, her small feet lightly tapping the stairs as she jogged down its incline.

'You left your phone in the bedroom,' she whispered. 'Here you go.' She slipped the phone in the pocket of his joggers.

He pushed open the front door, inhaled the earthy rain smell on the concrete. They slid the luggage in the trunk of the RAV4, jumped into their seats.

'Ready?' he asked.

She nodded.

Nna pulled out of the driveway of the Sugar Land house and drove until it was a specter of brown in the rear-view mirror. He stared at the small of Ikemefuna's back as she pressed her head to the plexiglass. He squeezed her palm. She glanced at him. He thought that he saw a thing in her eyes just as it widened to make room for the break of her lips, and the crack of her smile, and the glint of her teeth. But he was not sure of it. A man was never sure of these things.

53

Ikemefuna had waited until Nna was outside the house, washing the RAV4 in his jean shorts, to dig through his belongings for his cellphone. He must have forgotten it somewhere since there was no bulge in his jean pockets. It turned up beneath a pillow. She fumbled along its sides for a button, held it down till the phone whirred to life. She had scrolled past the weather app and the notepad, her appetite growing as she drew closer to Adina's broken English, deep-fried in a thick Nsukka dialect. She could almost smell the pomade in her mother's threaded hair.

'Hello.'

A heady mix of emotions rushed to her brain. The long blur of months spent wishing for her mother's voice.

'Mommy, it's me. Ikemefuna,' she whispered into the smudged screen, her eyes on the bedroom door.

'You. You're still alive?' Adina spat out, her terror palpable. 'You are not dead?'

Footsteps.

More footsteps.

The footsteps came from inside the Sugar Land house. Or they came from the other end of the line. Or there were no footsteps, just a bad network cracking beneath the weight of forced breath.

She started to rush out the door when she caught sight of a dark shape beneath the bed. She stooped to pick it. She could feel the knife's smooth handle beneath the head scarf. She clasped the bundled scarf in one hand and flew out of the bedroom, down the stairs, and through the front door of the Sugar Land house.

There was a pounding in Ikemefuna's ears.

It took her a moment to realize it was coming from her chest.

54

'Fela or Miles Davis?'

'Fela,' Ikemefuna yelled above the din of trumpets blaring through the Toyota's speakers.

Nna threw a cheeky smile at Ikemefuna, and she caught it with her teeth. He had been driving for all of thirty minutes, tearing past rows of cedar trees, their branches shaking loosely in the morning breeze. He wound down the Toyota's windows. Trusses of air brushed through Nna's cropped afro.

Ikemefuna dropped the head scarf on the floor of the passenger seat and stuck her face out of the window. She needed to escape Nna. He was the most unpredictable Nwosu – unable to fully commit to either the hero or villain role. She wondered about the extent of the damage if she crawled to the edge of the ledge and thrust her body through the thin space above the glass.

She pictured the moment in her head, her body in the air. Her forehead smashing into concrete. The whites of her eyes stained a fresh mauve, like burst raspberries. Her knees cracked beyond repair. Her splintered arms waving at oncoming traffic. Rows of tires crunching through her ribs till she was one with the tar. She retreated into the car, turned her focus to Nna's hands, latched to the steering wheel.

Ikemefuna cooed her appreciation as Fela's trumpets spilled out of the Toyota. She thought about the previous Christmas, Adina's thighs sandwiched against Nkemdili's in a packed event center in Victoria Island. Both women had attended the opening of *Fela and the Kalakuta Queens*. Had cheered loudly as Ikemefuna made her way to the stage to sing along with the rest of Fela's wives. Had wiggled their hips, the one's shoulders bumping against the other as their lips curved into giddy smiles.

She had just begun to smile when Nna's deep-throated growl of Fela's lyrics pulled her back to the moment. She giggled softly, tucking the clasp of her arm in Nna's arm like she'd seen her mother do when her father allowed her mother to sit in the front passenger seat of his van.

'You must take me to Fela's shrine when we're in Lagos,' Nna yelled above 'Water No Get Enemy'. 'I want to see all of it.'

'It's a date,' she yelled back.

The nausea spread a thin mesh on her forehead. She'd imagined a new chapter of her life. She and Nna in their new forever. They would jog up and down the Lekki-Ikoyi link bridge, drive up and down the Third Mainland bridge, pause by kiosks to ask sleepy-eyed mallams for directions to the New Afrika shrine.

None of that mattered, because her suspicions were right. Her mother's reaction on that phone call confirmed that he planned to kill her.

'How are you feeling?' Nna asked.

'Content.'

She liked *Content*. It was simple. Not open to misinterpretation.

The sky's obsidian black stretched out for miles. A green signage alluded to the airport being a half mile ahead. The thin mesh of her nausea was now a thick dough. It pressed against her cranium. She shut her eyes and dug her palms into the cloth of her seat as the Fela in the air pounded in her chest.

'Shit. We need to stop for gas,' Nna said.

She opened her eyes in time to catch him veering off the highway.

Where did the music go?

It was there only a second ago. She was sure of it. It had left behind a giant hole in the air that was slowly filling with Ikemefuna's faltering heartbeat, the scratch of Nna's palms on the steering wheel, the slow whir of the air-conditioning, the steady thud of her nausea.

She looked down at her left arm and noticed that it was no longer locked in Nna's. Somewhere between her practiced breathing, it had returned to her side. She stroked the papery skin of her thumb against Nna's wrist as he made a sharp turn down a dark alley.

She had grown to expect her mother's gentle touch in the aftermath of her father's violence. Adina would pick out her prettiest dress and clasp her faux pearls around her neck and dust fine particles of mineral powder against her bruised eye and sit beside Dumeje, a plasticine smile on her sallow face. Then in an easy-to-miss leap of a limb, she would rest a palm on Dumeje's wrist and let her thumb run short, circular motions along his wrist.

Ikemefuna blinked away the imagery of her parents and focused on her thumb and the short, circular motion it was running along Nna's wrist. The headlights from a passing car pierced through the windscreen of the RAV4, illuminating the stress lines on Nna's forehead.

Ikemefuna clenched her fists.

Nna parked the car in what seemed like an empty parking lot.

She tried to latch on to something in the scenery. Everything was pitch black. From beside her, she heard a rustling. Nna was struggling to untangle himself from something. The seatbelt.

She had never learned to drive. Dumeje had told her it was not a woman's place to drive. Adina had nodded her acquiescence, and that was the end of that. But she knew enough about vehicles to know that seatbelts were important.

She reached for Nna's wrist, felt the darkness for the thing. She started to ask him if there was a problem. He leaned towards her. Her heart leaped as he reached for the scarf on the floor of her seat.

The knife. It was in the scarf. She snatched the knife from the floor and thrust it forward. He leaned away from her.

'Careful now,' he purred, a mocking laugh bubbling out his mouth. He lurched forward, swiped at the knife, but missed. 'Give me that. I noticed it sticking out your scarf when you got in the car. You can't take a knife through airport security.'

'I spoke with my mom. I know what you're trying to do,' she cried, brandishing the knife at him. 'Get away from me or I'll kill you!'

'Keme, listen to me. I'm not trying to hurt you. Quit being so paranoid,' Nna said. He tried to keep the swell of panic in his chest from filtering into his voice. He eyed the dashboard. There was enough time to make the flight. 'Just hand over the knife. We could get in trouble with airport security if you take that to the—'

Aaaargh!

Nna yelped. Her kick had met its target, squashed his jaw into a thick paste of blood and dentine. It caught him by surprise. He bleated into the night, scrambling to peel himself off her skin.

He grabbed the hem of her dress as she reached for the lock. Airplane-appropriate had been the intention. Easy access to the restroom and ease of sleep. Breathable. But she had not thought of the ease of his fingers ripping it off her skin, the air of the car filling with the zip-zap of cheap fabric as she tried to push him off.

Ikemefuna's world dissolved into swirls of luminous grey as she swiped the knife in every direction. So much had happened since she arrived in America with her twin cornrows, her Ghana-must-go bags, her dopey grin and good intentions. She was still afraid of America and its terrors – drug lords, college kids in cropped tank tops high on Percocet, trigger-happy cops, that one dead serial killer from the C&I channel, resurrected. But they paled in comparison to the man beside her. So human – from the Tom Ford in her throat to his breath fogging up the glass.

Run jare.

Nothing and nowhere was safe. Not the Sugar Land house or the second-floor flat on Number 25 Uyime road. Not neighbors who stood on doorsteps with brownies or peeped through bedroom blinds. Not her mother's quick-fire Igbo or the suffocating embrace of a lover.

Her mother's voice rang in her head. Adina had assumed she was dead.

She caught snatches of the present moment. Nna tugging at her arm, yelling at her to hand over the knife. The force of her elbow connecting with his forehead. Her clenched palm pulling the doorknob. Nna's fists swinging at her as she tumbled out of her seat and onto the tar.

He leaned forward, grabbed her by her panties. She tore the flimsy thing off her body with the knife and ran from the car.

What was that?

The fading neon of a gas station storefront. A puff of cigarette smoke like cotton candy. The tinkle of bells and the steady throb of music. Something urban.

She ran into the station, her breasts slapping her ribcage as her feet pounded the concrete slabs. Her naked body rushing head-first into that store, her eyes blinking away the harsh lights illuminating Kleenex and paper plates and insecticides and Twix and spilled coffee on countertops and a drowsy clerk fiddling with the knob of a radio, his oversized Kurt Cobain tee swinging from his scraggy body.

'Help me,' she croaked. 'Please.'

55

William Hall Jnr fiddled with the radio knob and pressed his right ear to the dust-coated plastic. The frequency's strength increased each time he lifted the radio. His fingers were cramped from trying, albeit unsuccessfully, to hold it at a ninety-degree angle. He set the radio on the counter and rolled his eyes as he dialed past stations playing trap music, a particularly trendy subgenre of hip hop that was even more ingratiating than the prototype.

It was all everyone listened to these days, including his stepfather Jonathan, a WASP who wore the same plaid shirt and rumpled Levis every day and referred to black folks as *The Blacks*.

Will spent ten minutes trying to get the radio to work. He grudgingly settled for Migos. Migos, he decided, was better than the store's thrum of convenience. The squish of nacho chips in plastic. The bump of a Pepsi can against a Monster can. The clatter of ice into a bucket beneath a dispenser.

Will's eyes darted to the wall clock above the aisle with the red plastic cups. 3:03 a.m. Which was exactly four hours and fifty-seven minutes till his shift was over, or till

Linda marched into the store, her bad leg trailing behind her, or till he sat through Linda's tirade on anything and everything before mumbling a weary *hello*.

Linda would ignore his feigned attempt at friendship. She would say *this place smells like shit*. Or she would say *you look like hell*. Or she would say *I bet you didn't sell shit all morning*. Or she would say *can you at least try to pretend to care*. Or, sometimes, when she'd downed a few too many tequila shots, she would say *I wish Mr O would just fire you*. Will would stand behind the counter, a teasing grin on his gaunt face, because he knew that it drove Linda mad to see him smile.

Will tried not to think of Linda. There were better ways to kill time, like scrolling through his burner Instagram account and leaving comments beneath Jess Brinkley's photos. Like that one with the pout, and the bra top, and the imprint of nipples, and the barely-there cheerleader skirt.

U make me so hot. I wish u were here ryt now.

He would leave more messages via her DMs. Those ones, more graphic than their predecessors, loose-tongued and deviant, peppered with obscene requests that were never granted. And yet, Jess liked the attention. He knew it. He could feel her eyes on him through the cracks in his phone screen. He could see her glossy smile. It was why she never blocked him. Never chided him for his level of descriptiveness. Hell, she once *liked* a comment of his, only to unlike it a second later, but not quickly enough to keep the proof of her hunger for him from popping up on his screen.

Jess liked your comment.

Of course she did.

Will leaned against the counter, his left elbow wiping off the sticky sphere of soda a customer left behind. Jess had updated her Instagram feed with two new pictures. The first, a crop top showcasing her tan midriff. Washed, high-waist denim shorts. The second, a peach slip dress bedazzled with her nipple imprints. He started to zoom in on the peach dress, his breathing jagged, when the store's front door burst open with a force that caused Will to drop his phone.

His beady eyes shot to the door. He bit down on his tongue to temper the nerves that ran wild each time the door swung open in the early morning hours, and someone dragged their bedraggled body through the aisles in search of soggy hot dogs or bad coffee.

There was no one at the door. He started to think he'd imagined the swinging door. Perhaps, his overactive imagination—

'Help me, please.'

There was someone in the store. Breathing his air. Staring at him. Speaking to him. He lowered his gaze from the flashing neon to her wild eyes. The hairs at the back of his neck tingled. She was not so much a person as she was a bald black face with red eyes and bruised cheeks. With busted lips and a row of bloodied teeth.

She was naked, yes. Worlds apart from Jess-The-Tease with her crop tops and nipple imprints. Everything was stripped bare for his consumption – big, swollen breasts; round, exposed belly, and where was the fun in that? The mystery? The intrigue? All he had was his disgust. He rubbed his eyes and squinted. What was that in her hands? A knife. She was flashing a knife at him.

He reached for the nearest object, his eyes glued to the blowsy woman who was beginning to advance on him, her cracked lips curled into an ugly plea like a zombie in a low-budget movie. He hurled the metal cash register at her. He watched it connect with her chest. He sighed with relief as she toppled over and fell to the floor.

911. What's your emergency?

Uhh, Will speaking. I work at the Valero on Crown street. The cops better get their asses here right now. I need them here right fucking now!

The front door swung open. Again. What on earth? It was like he was in one of those thrillers where bad shit happened to gas station attendants like him. Clanging bells. The swoosh of air. Will's heart in his mouth. A black man – built like LeBron James – blood dripping down the sides of his mouth.

'Hey man,' Will started. He reached for his phone and aimed it at the man like a gun. 'We are closed.'

'I don't want anything,' the man started, walking towards the writhing, naked woman. 'My sister. She's unstable. She ran away from our house.'

He threw Will a knowing look.

'Ah, man,' Will said, his wariness melting into compassion. No, not quite like LeBron. He was a carbon copy of Dean Thompson, a popular linebacker at Will's high school. Same broad shoulders and tree-bark skin. 'Sorry 'bout that. She rattled me, man. I thought it was a robbery. We've seen a lot of those in these parts of late.'

Will wrung his palms beneath the counter. He had just thrown a register at the man's sister and what if the man tried to retaliate in some form? Where were the cops when he needed them?

From behind the safe bridge of the counter, he watched the man pick the naked woman from the ground. He watched the woman thrash against the man's skin, landing a series of blows along his spine. The man sized Will up, deciding on his next line of action.

'Look man, I already called the cops,' Will yelled in his deepest intonation. 'I don't want to cause you no trouble, okay? So how about you take your sis and go? You can still beat the cops if you leave right now.'

The man nodded as he walked out and marched across the parking lot, accompanied by the tinkling of the store bells. Will stepped out from behind the counter to pick the register from the floor. With the register wedged between his forearm and his flank, he watched the man's retreating figure through the store's glass. He thought he saw the scuffle between the man and the woman grow increasingly heated. He thought he heard a yell, but he was not sure. He had turned up the radio's volume so that the trap music blasting through the store drowned out everything else.

Will bopped his head to Migos. Trap music, he thought to himself, was surprisingly soothing.

56

Officer Clermont gulped his leftover Starbucks coffee, his beer belly reverberating in tandem with the loose skin of his throat. He squeezed the Styrofoam into a golf-sized ball and aimed it at the waste basket next to his office door. He scratched an itch on his neck and sighed at the pus and skin crust in his finger beds. He really should stop by St Jude's for a checkup. Make good use of that Aetna.

But before hours of mindlessly drifting between hospital waiting rooms and restrooms, a tube of dark yellow urine in one hand, there were interview notes, forensic files, and police reports that ran the gamut from tipsy college urchins committing petty traffic violations to an armed robbery at the neighborhood Chase bank.

The thin stack to the left of his desk caught his eye. The events of the early morning incident replayed themselves in his head.

He'd gotten the call just as he kicked off his boots to lie on the bed he'd once shared with Hannah, his ex-wife. It had happened outside the Valero a mile away from the George Bush airport. The one with the Tostitos and corndogs that drew throngs of weary bodies on their way home from Atlanta or Amsterdam. Officer Clermont himself was something of a repeat customer at the Valero. Three days ago, he'd pushed open its rusty door for a piss break and a pack of Orbit gum.

He reached for his paper folder. He flipped through pages from the crime scene, parsing through his interview notes.

He stared at the ceiling and tried to collect his thoughts. Someone had tried to flee the scene, claimed self-defense.

Officer Clermont pictured the victim's busted bottom lip and bloodied teeth when he shut his eyes. The stab wounds scattered across the torso. It made him sick to his stomach to think about it.

He'd moved on quickly from the victim, unable to stomach all that blood. An hour-long interview with the solemn Nigerian couple who were in a state of shock, incapable of forming coherent sentences. They'd given him the basics, a skeletal outline for his notepad. They'd welcomed the girl to their home with open arms. Cooked for her. Given her free rein of their house. But something, they said, was wrong with her heart. Because she'd repaid their kindness with her threats and her poison. They said it was a miracle that they themselves were still alive.

The couple's neighbor – a willowy blonde named Mary – mostly corroborated their statements. She sat across from Officer Clermont, her eyes red at the rims. She spun a longwinded tale about the primary subject of the investigation, pausing every now and again to wet her bright pink lips with a flick of the tongue.

Yes, she knew the boy.

They lived across from each other for years.

He was mostly mute, stayed indoors, kept to himself.

Imposing too. *Have you seen those muscles?*

Something aggressive about him she couldn't quite put a finger on.

Yes, she knew the girl.

Quite well, indeed.

Yes, quite well, although she'd only ever met her once. Once was a lifetime sometimes, you know?

Yes, the girl was violent.

Had lunged at poor Mary at their first meet-and-greet, so violent that Mary was forced to run out of the house with her flip flops wedged under her arm. A fact her son, a pimpled adolescent who accompanied her to the station corroborated.

The whey-faced store clerk who smelled of cigarette smoke and damp boxers gave his two cents.

Something looked wrong 'bout them. I can't say for sure, but I could tell they were trouble.

Finally, Officer Clermont thought about his own barely coherent conversation with the unclothed black girl and her thick African accent. The girl had tried to flee the crime scene. When apprehended, she whispered something about self-defense, her English so broken in the middle and blunted at the ends that he struggled to follow its threads. What little he understood were as follows: the dead man in the Valero parking lot with a knife sticking out his chest colluded with his parents to kidnap her. Then held her captive in their house. Then he impregnated her against her will and tried to kill her.

Officer Clermont could still see the black girl's busted bottom lip and bloodied teeth as she huffed about how she had pleaded with *evribodi* (was that a person?) to come to her aid, but *evribodi* had turned their collective backs on her. *Evribodi* had taught her that she was the only one who would fight for herself. And scream for herself. And wrest the knife from the dead man's grasp for herself. And stick it in his heart for herself.

Officer Clermont rubbed his temple with his thumbs. He wondered about the killer's upbringing. He had watched his teenage daughter Gabby turn to sour fruit. He had learned that the only way to keep a youngin' in check was to watch her like a hawk. So he'd fought for joint custody of Gabby and built a fort around her.

It was called being a good parent.

Something the killer's parents knew nothing about.

57

Adina Azubuike was not a particularly emotional woman.

When she got the news of her parents' death in a bus accident on the night of her wedding, she patted her eyelids with a tablecloth. She swallowed two tablets of Panadol. She slipped into the bunk bed she shared with her sister, Adaugo. There, she massaged the heaviness in her breasts and slept away the headache that had wrapped her cranium in a tight embrace.

And when eight years later, she caught Dumeje between the legs of Nkemdili, her thirteen-year-old maid who arrived in Lagos from Aba the day before, Adina patted her eyelids with an ichafu. She swallowed two tablets of Panadol. She slipped into the king size bed she shared with her husband. There, she massaged the heaviness in her breasts and slept away the headache that had wrapped her cranium in a tight embrace.

She knew how to grind pain between her teeth and digest it in large gulps of water, its peaty taste barely leaving a stain on her tongue. To plaster a smile to her lips and stretch it till it reached her earlobes. To wrap her body in thick wool and shut out the world for long hours on end, only opening her eyes to go about her business, her pain a foreign body at the bottom of her womb.

So when Agbala rang Adina up in the early hours of a Tuesday morning, Adina clamped her teeth together before she pressed her ears to her phone. Adina listened soundlessly as Agbala screamed into her ears from all those miles away (was it a hundred? a thousand? hundreds of thousands?). Adina reached for her almost empty bottle of Panadol and the glass of water she kept on the stool by her bed.

Adina stared at the other end of the bed, the half that should have been carrying Dumeje's body. Dumeje had not returned from the fuel station the previous night, a reoc-curring theme on nights he craved new skin. Younger skin. Softer skin. Warmer skin. Tighter skin. More fertile skin. Without effort, she pictured Dumeje booking Room 05 at Flavors, his favorite brothel in Ikeja. The one with the zinc roof and spirogyra-plastered walls. The one that doled out generous discounts to repeat customers. The one with the phone number Adina knew by heart.

As Adina listened to Agbala's thundering voice, she considered slipping into Nkemdili's room and sitting at the edge of the other woman's bed so there would be a second body in the room to bear the width of her pain. Over the years, her relationship with Nkemdili had grown in new and surprising ways, so that her strong disdain for the thirteen-year-old house girl morphed into a stirring pity for the eighteen-year-old adolescent, a fierce protectiveness over the twenty-one-year-old woman, and a shared kinship with the thirty-four-year-old lady. One borne out of creating space in their respective wombs for Dumeje's fists, cum and kids.

Adina bunched the hem of her night dress above her knees and tried to slip out of her bed, but the growing volume of Agbala's tears wrapped itself around her knees and kept them glued to the bed as she waited for Agbala's shrieks to subside.

Surrounded by the darkness of her matrimonial bedroom and the heaviness in her legs, Adina's mind flashed to that afternoon all those years ago when she made the rash decision to share the story of her broken womb with Agbala.

She could still hear Agbala's foot, impatiently tip-tapping against the backyard's concrete as she recounted each one of her miscarriages through sniveling tears. It was only yesterday that she and Dumeje had slipped out of their bedroom in their house clothes, down that airless stairway and into the backyard they shared with the Nwosus.

Adina ended the call and placed her phone on her bedside table. She sighed. All that yelling was starting to give her a headache. Adina opened her bottle of Panadol, slipped six tablets into her palm, and threw the tablets into her mouth. In bed, she raised the wooly blanket over her head till she was completely buried in it. In the comforting darkness, she returned to that fateful night in Agbala's backyard, her shoulder brushing against Dumeje's as she waited for Ala to reveal her fate.

'Ala has spoken,' Agbala announced, staring into a calabash of twigs. 'Listen with your eyes, and your ears, and your nose, and your mouth.'

From her vantage point on the pebbled ground of their communal backyard, Adina watched Dumeje pick the wax from his ears with his index fingers and wipe it on Adina's thighs, his eyes distractedly roaming from Agbala's face to the woman's calabash.

'You have found favor in Ala's eyes,' Agbala announced, and Adina wondered if the tremor she heard in Agbala's voice was merely the Lagos wind pushing and pulling against the hibiscus tree growing out a side of the gutter in the backyard. 'Ala has heard your cries for a son, and she is prepared to grant your request.'

Dumeje released a hoarse yelp. It was nothing like Adina had ever heard, its tenor long, pitiful, and puttering to a standstill as he locked eyes with her. Her intestines formed a tight braid. She was not prepared to make room for another lump-sized serving of Dumeje in her womb. To bring it into the hostile world of the second-floor flat on Number 25 Uyime road. To force her heart to love the thing. She was not prepared for fresh blood, sticky like toffee pudding, running down her inner thighs.

Agbala released the guillotine, her voice sharp and cutting.

'He will not be yours. At least not immediately. Ala says Eke and I must raise the boy on Ala's behalf,' Agbala announced, her voice firm. 'Ala is a possessive mother, you know. She likes to raise her sons before releasing them to their earth parents.'

Dumeje started to protest but Agbala shot him a withering look and raised a palm.

'Now, before you start to grumble, listen to me with your ears. It will work like this. Eke and I will care for your son until Ala is ready to release him to you.'

Dumeje's arm tightened around Adina's shoulder as though she, and not Agbala, was the bearer of the news.

'Truth be told, Ala is being generous by giving you one of her sons. She wants you to know that her son will come at a high cost,' Agbala continued. 'Financially, mentally, physically, and spiritually. He will be a beast of a man. Handsome and hungry. Demanding. Charging through everything in his path. He will take and take till you are depleted of all life. But a son is always a blessing. You must never forget that.'

Adina stole a glance at Dumeje. He shook his head sideways. Agbala's words subdued him, ground his tongue into pate. He sighed into the night, a pained expression on his washed face.

'You said Ala will release him to us when she is ready,' Adina whispered, her eyes on her bare toes. 'What can we do to show her we are worthy?' She gulped. 'How do we show her we are ready to be his parents?'

Agbala raised her head to the sky and chewed on her inner cheeks. Adina observed the woman, her trembling throat, the impatient jerk of her left foot. She wondered if she should have been less trusting of Agbala and her so-called relationship with Ala. Perhaps, she should have insisted on speaking with the other women Agbala had assisted with childbirth. Hadn't she heard that Lagos was brimming with false prophets who promised desperate women the world in exchange for a pound of their flesh?

'You are in luck. You have found favor in Ala's sight, so she does not ask for much. She simply wants you to find her son a worthy girl when he comes of age. A virgin that is easy on the eye.'

Agbala paused for objection. Hearing none, she continued.

'When the time is right, I will send for the girl. I will introduce her to the boy as his wife. She will give herself to him completely, until she is pregnant with a male child of her own. In the moments after she births her son, Ala will take the boy from her and release your son to you.'

Adina's head swam with all that new information. She could barely keep track of the logistics of it all. Her son would live with Agbala. Adina would raise a girl for him. When he is old enough, he would have a son with the girl and Ala would take the infant in exchange for her grown son. It was a simple transaction on paper. And yet, so much could go wrong.

'And would we co-parent our own son? I have a friend in Aba. He's divorced from his old girl, but he gets to see his son once a week,' Dumeje croaked, his face aghast.

'You will not co-parent the boy. Eke and I will be the only parents he knows,' Agbala confirmed, her eyes solemn. 'But when the time is right, your son will return to you. It is not our place to question Ala.'

Dumeje released a stuttering cry.

'And the girl?' Adina whispered. 'Where do we find her?'

Agbala blinked.

'Heh?'

'The girl we will raise for our son. How would we find her?'

'Ahh her,' Agbala said, waving a dismissive palm. 'Don't concern yourself with her for now. When the time is right, Ala will bring her to you.'

And what happens to her after she gives birth to her son?' Adina pressed.

'Why do you concern yourself with her?' Agbala hissed. 'She will die of natural causes shortly after childbirth. Ala will see to it.'

Adina grabbed fistfuls of elephant grass to calm her inflamed chest. She tried to wriggle her toes, but a shooting pain radiated up her thighs before settling in.

'Does she have to die?' she whispered.

'No,' Agbala said, a small smile forming on her lips. 'But it's easier that way.'

Dumeje ran his palms against his kneecaps and whistled into the night.

'We are ready,' he said.

58

The darkness in the sky had begun to make room for day-break.

Daybreak came in streaks of spectral blue and neon pink. With the rhythm of Nkemdili's feet shuffling around the flat. Adina burrowed into her bedsheets. Nkemdili was no doubt dusting chairs and center tables and dragging the bristles of a broom against the staircase. Soon, she would knock on the door to the master bedroom to ask Adina for a list of meals that had to be cooked, or the estimated time of Dumeje's arrival, or *will he return at all?*

Adina burrowed deeper into her sheets, as though burrowing deeper into her sheets would block out the morning and all its demands. Like the weighty responsibility of breaking the news of Nna's death to Dumeje. Like the sting of Dumeje's fists after he had visited all the bars in all the crevices of Lagos Island, and sampled all of the long islands, his eyes distant, his teeth bared. Like Nkemdili and her big bones, and shifty eyes, and wrinkled hands, flinging her body between Adina and Dumeje to soften the sting of his blows.

Adina folded into herself, became a neat square at the edge of her matrimonial bed.

Dumeje had begun to prepare for his trip to Houston, ironing, and re-ironing his Isiagu. Sifting through maps of Texas on Google. Murmuring *Nnaemeka* in his sleep.

He was hungry to discover his son like the boy was uncharted territory, to draw an X in all the places they were alike. Adina had begun to echo his excitement, laughing when he laughed, and clasping her palms when he clasped his palms, and ignoring the fact that her joy rang false, sat foreign on her skin. *Yes, Nna has your voice*, she reassured him. *Yes, Nna has your laughter*.

But whenever Dumeje looked away from her or stepped out of the second-floor flat on Number 25 Uyime road, she dropped her pretense like hot coal and collapsed against the living-room tiles or Nkemdili's large, warm arms.

She spent her nights worrying that Nna having his father's voice meant that he had his father's fists. That like his father, Nna was quick to anger. That his punches fell against skin in quick, balletic motions that offered no room for rest. Feared too, that she would go to that Houston, and arrive on Agbala's doorsteps, and meet Nna, the son she pressed to her bosom in the thick of a Lagos Harmattan before Agbala took him from her arms. That she would look into his eyes and see a stranger, or worse – his father.

Then on the phone with Ikemefuna, she had tried to study the rise and dips of Ikemefuna's voice as Agbala, and Eke, and Nna, and Dumeje celebrated Ikemefuna's swollen belly. Had tried to call out to the girl. To ask her a litany of questions, like *how are you*, and *are you being strong?* But no matter how thoroughly she searched for the thing, she could not find her voice.

So yes. She sat quietly on that phone call and pressed her ears to the air for the rise and fall of Ikemefuna's breath to convince herself that Ikemefuna was still alive. Once, she heard a cough like a bleat, or like a whisper that lacked body, and the weight in her chest lightened. The girl was still alive.

Then there was the second phone call. That one that came in the early hours of the previous morning. She, half asleep and half stuck in a nightmare. Pulled into the present by the American number flashing across her screen.

'Hello.'

She had known, even before Ikemefuna responded, that it was her. They call it a mother's intuition.

'Mama, it's me. Ikemefuna,' Ikemefuna whispered, and Adina winced at the panic in the girl's voice.

She had not known what to say. *Sorry* seemed inadequate. *What do you want?* – abrupt. After her last call with Agbala, it was clear that Agbala was thirsting for blood. It was a wonder that the girl was still alive.

Small talk had never been her strong suit. She'd always found it ungainly, too heavy, her limbs sticking out in odd directions as her tongue fumbled around her mouth for the right retort to inquiries about the weather or the state of her life. She played with the hem of her skirts when the silence stretched between statements, her heaving chest desperate to offload the less chaste details of her life to the nearest acquaintance, like the back that hurt from the last time she tumbled down the stairs, or the urine that had begun to burn since Dumeje last slept with her.

'You. You are still alive?' she spat out. 'You are not dead?'

She hated how she sounded. Rough and scratchy like sandpaper as her breathing fell against her collarbone in large, troubled swathes.

Ikemefuna started to respond when she hung up the phone, slid beneath her duvet, and shut her eyes, listening to her heart pound against her eardrums. Like it was the only thing itching to run. Like she too did not dream of marathons.

Then this morning happened, Adina in her silk hair bonnet and chaplet, Agbala's voice ringing in her ears, her brain.

'Our boy is dead *o*,' Agbala screeched, her cries cutting through Adina's eardrums. 'Our Nnaemeka is dead!'

Adina tightened the wool blanket around her shoulders and patted her lids with her handkerchief.

'Are you hearing me? *Nnaemeka is dead!*' she repeated. 'The devil-girl killed him! We tried to keep him safe but the devil-girl killed him. *Ewoooo!*'

Adina let the words sink in.

Ikemefuna killed Nna.

Ikemefuna who did as she was told. Ikemefuna who would not hurt a fly. Ikemefuna who feared her own shadow.

Where was the sense in that?

Adina slipped beneath her duvet, blocking out the loudness of the day. There must be a misunderstanding. A mistake of sorts in the details of the incident. Perhaps, someone else had killed her son and was trying to pin it on the girl. Or, she thought, her throat jammed with wet hope, he was not dead at all. Just maimed, or better yet, unharmed. A case of mistaken identity.

It was only a matter of time before the oyibo criminal justice system straightened out the wrinkles, what with its attention to details, DNA evidence, and state-of-the-art everything.

Then a different thought, more powerful, wafted into her mind.

Memories of a prepubescent Ikemefuna, marching through the metal door of the flat hours after Adina abandoned her at Akande market. Of Ikemefuna and her brazen anger, flinging her body at Dumeje, matching him blow for blow as Adina cowered beneath the dinner table. Of Ikemefuna, listening intently as Adina assured her that the women in America were different, their tolerance nonexistent.

Had she built her son's killer brick by brick, then smuggled her to him, a Trojan-horse? Did she spent decades of her life grooming Ikemefuna to kill Nna?

Adina reached for more Panadol. She pictured Dumeje receiving the news of Nna's death, and she swallowed. She shut her eyes and stroked her throat, imagining volts of blinding pain shooting through Dumeje's heart.

A loose smile settled on her lips.

She started to drift into sleep when she heard the sound of metal scraping concrete. Of footsteps sprinting up a flight of stairs. Of wood, likely the dinner table in the living room, clattering to the floor.

Where is that witch?

Where is she?

ISN'T SHE TIRED OF EATING MY SONS?

Adina shut her eyes, stilled her pockmarked skin for Dumeje's fists, and mouthed a quick prayer to the Christian God.

59

Nkemdili, a big-boned woman who had served as the Azubuikes' house girl for over two decades, dragged a chair to the balcony of the Azubuikes' flat to observe the goings-on on Uyime road. From the balcony of her oga and madam's house, Nkemdili watched the neighborhood boys roll a deflated tire in muck. The mallams return from ablution with their multi-colored plastic kettles. The little girls with wood beads at the tips of their didi gathering in a corner to play suwe, their little feet hopping around the squares they had drawn in the sand with the pointy edges of their fathers' koboko.

Nkemdili had the flat to herself. Her madam, Adina, was admitted to the hospital after the man's last beating, a lashing that had been so long and so thorough that not even Nkemdili falling against the man to absorb the shock of his blows could keep Adina from clinging to the fringes of life by a hair. Adina's yelps had been so loud that the neighbors who usually increased the volumes of their stereos to drown out the Azubuikes' wahala had banged on the flat's metal front door and begged Dumeje to *leave the poor woman alone.*

But if there was anything Nkemdili had learnt from her years with the Azubuikes, it was that there was no stopping Dumeje. Not until the object of his violence had stopped shrieking and sprinting and lay flat on the floor and played dead.

Dumeje's fists liked moving targets.

Nkemdili knew this because she was a moving target.

It was a fact that Dumeje had discovered when she was thirteen and sleeping in the storage room in the flat with its packs of toilet paper, and malt crates, and Bournvita tins, and rickety towers of tinned tomatoes.

His fists had stumbled across her in her first week in that house. His aimless feet had marched into the storage room in search of Lipton but instead, found her breasts. She had stirred from her shallow sleep, stuttered a *Sir* at the stocky man towering above her bed frame, her shifty eyes clouded with fear as he pulled her to his thighs and raised up her cheap polyester.

She had felt him swell as she struggled to free herself from his clammy embrace. Then his breaths had grown more jagged, and his fists had tightened against her hips as she yelled into the darkness and tried to jump out of bed.

She soon realized that the yelling was useless.

Adina could not save her from the man because Adina could not save herself from the man. The neighbors could not save her from the man because they were content with dunking their cabin biscuits in lukewarm tea as they speculated about the grunts that slid down the stairs and slipped out the narrow slit beneath the metal entrance door of the flat.

And so with time, Nkemdili taught herself to play dead because Dumeje loved a moving target. Playing dead was how Nkemdili made room in her womb for a baby, watching in amazement as her belly swelled into the shape of a tiny pawpaw, then a soccer ball, then a full-sized blom blom. When the time came for her to push the child out of her body, she did so between a carton of Indomie and a box of old camphor-scented clothes in that storage room that doubled as her sanctuary.

She hoped that having the man's child would win her more kindness in the house, but the birth of the girl was a curse, truly. Whatever little kindness Dumeje reserved for her disappeared with the birth of that girl, his eyes narrowing with exasperation each time the girl cried for Nkemdili's breasts. And Adina? She avoided Nkemdili even more fiercely than she previously did, unable to stomach the sight of the baby girl, who was for all intents and purposes, an emblem of her husband's infidelity.

Nkemdili did not want the girl even more than Adina and Dumeje did not want the girl. She was only fourteen and had hoped she would enjoy her youth before she was forced to bear the brunt of motherhood. And so on one fateful afternoon, after Adina sent her to Alausa to buy raffia baskets from a one-eyed weaver from Maiduguri, she stuffed the crying girl into a polythene and took a detour on her journey back to the flat, hanging on to the roof of a danfo heading to Makoko. There, she left the crying girl by the Lagos lagoon and hoped that her death would be swift.

Her daughter refused to die. Or how else could Nkemdili explain the fact that upon her return to the flat, the very same girl she had left in Makoko was in Adina's arms, her tiny mouth tugging at Adina's blackened nipple?

Through the years, Nkemdili had watched the daughter she left for dead grow into a fierce young woman. Had done what little she could for the girl. Slipping boiled yams into her porridge beans whenever Adina turned her face away. Flinging her big bones between Dumeje and the wood door of the girl's room whenever he smelled of whiskey. Scrubbing the soot off the girl's feet when Adina left the girl in Akande market and the girl had to find her way back to the flat. And on the morning of the girl's departure to America, Nkemdili had pressed her daughter to her chest and begged the girl to remember her in America.

A mournful cry rose into the air from the ground below. One of the little girls playing suwe had tried to hop over her square and in the process, she had fallen flat on her face.

Nkemdili swatted away a house fly on the balcony's ledge and patted the moisture gathering in the hollow between her breasts. Indeed, she had begged Ikemefuna to remember her in America. But what she really meant to say was that the girl should not forget who she was in America.

She was Ikemefuna Azubuike.

The daughter of Dumeje Azubuike and Nkemdili Okafor.

It did not matter what lay ahead of Ikemefuna in America. What mattered was that Ikemefuna had proven, time and again, that she would find her way home.

60

'Water?' the blonde detective sitting across the table from Ikemefuna asked her as she stood from her metal chair.

'Yes, please,' Ikemefuna croaked at the woman. 'Thanks, Anna.'

She massaged her throat. It was parched from all the speaking she had done in the last twenty-four hours. She leaned into the rigid metal and scanned the room. It was an interrogation room, just like the ones in raw footage from her C&I shows. Its emptiness seemed staged. Grey windowless walls. Two mismatched metal chairs. A desk wedged between the chairs.

'I'll be right back,' the blonde detective (*you can call me Anna*) mouthed, a faint smile on her lips.

Ikemefuna watched Anna's retreating figure. A bout of exhaustion washed over her face. She must keep her eyes open. Closing them meant seeing Nna's widened eyes fading to a nothingness. The spattered blood on her thighs. The snug handcuffs digging into her skin. *You have the right to remain silent. Anything you say can and will be used against you in a court of law.* The pong of urine on scrubbed walls. Plastic trays of trinkets on a conveyor belt, just like the security checkpoint at an airport. *Say cheese.* A flash.

'Hello, Miss Azubuike.'

She raised her eyes from the desk. She recognized the balding man with droopy lids. He'd been one of the first officers on the scene. He'd asked her a dozen questions as she stared at the warm blood pooling at his feet.

She sighed. Where was earnest Anna? She missed the small comfort of their first-name basis.

He pulled the metal chair.

'How are you holding up, Miss Azubuike?' he asked. He placed a recorder on the table with little fanfare.

'Where is Anna?'

'Officer Skjolaas will be back soon. In the meantime, I have a few questions I'd like to go over with you.'

Ikemefuna pressed her face to her palms.

'I've told you everything already. Why must I repeat myself?'

'When did you first learn you'd be returning to Lagos with Mr Nwosu?'

'Do my parents know I'm here? Has anyone been in touch with them?'

'Miss Azubuike, you may have a hard time believing this, but I want to help you,' the officer said. His eyebags aged him a ton. He looked like he hadn't slept in months. 'I can't help you if you don't answer my questions.'

She willed herself to believe him.

'I don't remember the exact date. Three days ago, or so.'

'Did he share any details about the trip with you? Did he arrange for accommodation in Lagos?'

She searched her mind for the details. Nna pressing her skin to his chest, whispering the plan in her ear. Her stiff back and cautious joy.

'He didn't say much. Just that he wanted to return to Lagos to meet my parents.'

'I see.'

'He didn't want his parents to know about the trip. I think he suspected they were hiding important details about his childhood in Lagos.'

'What kind of details?'

Ikemefuna mulled over the question. She decided the truth would complicate things for her.

'I'm not sure. He never discussed the details with me.'

'Did anything out of the ordinary happen after he mentioned the trip to you?'

'Nothing really, officer. Except . . .' She shuddered. 'I don't think he truly planned to take me to Lagos. I think he only said so to get me out of the house in the middle of the night.'

'Why is that?'

'His sudden desire to visit Lagos didn't make sense to me. He'd lashed out at me earlier for suggesting we visit Lagos.' She stared at the door. Where was Anna and her water? 'I wanted to believe the change of heart so badly. Then on the night of our departure, I placed a call to my mother.'

'You previously mentioned you no longer had a cellphone,' the officer noted, his eyes narrowing at Ikemefuna.

'Listen to me—' The panic swelled in her chest. 'I didn't have a cellphone, but Nna forgot his cellphone in his bedroom just before we left for the airport. I only had a small window, so I called my mother.'

The officer nodded. Ikemefuna exhaled.

'My mother picked my call. She seemed off, officer. It was like she was scared to speak to me. She said she was surprised I was still alive.'

'Are you saying your mother—'

'Yes officer. I am saying my mother expected the Nwosus to kill me.'

'Yet despite your suspicions, you got in a car with Mr Nwosu?'

'I was running out of options,' she cried. 'I was tired of waiting for something to happen to me in that house. I alerted a neighbor, but she didn't believe me. I tried escaping from a restaurant, but the diners thought I was a problem child, so they restrained me. I just wanted to get out of that house,' she sobbed.

The officer waited for her tears to subside. He did not offer her a tissue.

'I hoped that he'd stop somewhere so I could make a run for it.'

'Did anything eventful happen during the drive?'

'Nothing, until we got to the gas station.' She paused.

'What happened when you got to the station?'

'Well, he tried to kill me.'

Officer Clermont took notes on his note pad furiously.

'He tried to kill you?' he repeated. 'Tell me more. What exactly did he do?'

She took a deep breath.

'He had a knife, officer. It was on the floor of his car seat. He reached for it. He ripped off my clothes to keep me from escaping, but I was able to run out the car before he could kill me.'

'Did you fight back?'

'I hit him. I think a few of my punches landed.'

Officer Clermont nodded.

'I knew that station was my last chance to make it out alive. So, I ran into the store and asked the store clerk for help, but he panicked and threw the register at me. My next memory was of Nna, slinging me over his shoulder and heading back to his car.'

The officer nodded. His tired eyes betrayed no emotion.

'The farther we walked from the station, the more I could feel my life slipping out my reach,' she continued. 'I fought him like my life depended on it because it did. I managed to wrestle the knife from Nna.' She gulped. 'He was going to strike me with it. He'd started to turn towards me, so I grabbed it from him, and I pierced him with it. It was either me or him and I didn't want to die.'

Officer Clermont studied Ikemefuna's face. Her solemn eyes and pointy chin. He motioned for her to continue, but she had resumed the sobbing. This time, with tears.

'What do you think, Anna?' he asked outside the interrogation room. He was back in the room next door where his partner Anna Skjolaas was observing the interrogation from a tiny monitor mounted to the wall.

'Well, she's a lot more articulate now,' Anna said, her eyes glued to the screen.

'All that adrenaline's starting to wear off,' Officer Clermont noted.

'This one's a doozy,' Anna said. 'You met the victim's parents already. Thoughts?'

'Nutjobs,' he replied. He eyed the bottle of water on the stool next to Anna. 'They're into some sort of West African religion. It's possible they kidnapped her as a part of their religious rites.'

Anna shrugged. She opened the bottle of water and took a large sip.

'Cases like these with an ethnoreligious angle are some of the hardest to close,' she said. 'All that woo-woo stuff blurs the line between what counts as consensual and what is a crime. Arranged marriages happen all the time, Bob. She could just be a disgruntled bride who grew bored and decided to spice things up with murder.'

Officer Clermont scoffed.

'One more thing – she claims the victim had the knife up until they left the store and she grabbed it from him in the heat of their scuffle. But the store clerk and the CCTV footage suggest she already had the knife when she ran into the store,' he noted. 'We've sent the knife to the lab for fingerprints.'

Anna inched closer to the monitor. She watched the diminutive girl shift in her seat. The girl raised her eyes from the table and stared straight at the hidden camera on the wall above the doorpost.

'I don't trust her,' Anna said, her back to the screen. 'Let's get a judge to grant us a search warrant for the victim's house in Sugar Land. We'll turn that place upside down till we find our smoking gun.'

Officer Clermont sighed. He'd hoped for a quiet weekend. He was supposed to take Gabby to the dentist for a cleaning.

'Look alive, Bob,' Anna said with a smirk. 'We've got work to do.'

Acknowledgments

It takes a village to write a novel. I am grateful for my village.

To God, the author of my life. Thank you for writing this chapter into existence.

To my parents, Nchekwube Okechukwu Nworah and Calista Obiageli Nworah. Thank you for raising a proud Igbo woman. For the high expectations and the daily reminders that my dreams are valid. Your encouragement fuels my life.

To my siblings, Nchekwube Princewill Nworah, Chika Veraldine Nworah, and Dubem Henry Nworah. Thank you for checking on *House Woman's* progress. For wanting to read the early drafts despite my firm refusal. I saved the final version for you because you deserve the very best.

To my extraordinary literary agent, Sharon Pelletier. Thank you for being my trusted advocate and guide.

To my editorial A-Team: Olivia Taylor Smith, Ore Agbaje Williams, Chris Heiser, Carla Josephson, and the Unnamed Press and Borough Press teams. Thank you for reading multiple drafts of *House Woman*, combing through its paragraphs for fault lines, asking tough questions, and ushering me to the finish line.

To *House Woman*'s first readers and devoted cheerleaders: Esther Edoho and Oluchi Agbasi. It warms my heart to know that *House Woman* would always have a home on your bookshelves.

To the Queens College girls who read my unfinished stories and advised me to become a published author. To my Temple Law peers who cheered me on. To girlfriends from near and far: Teni, Nonye, Anu, Arwa, Davina, Funmi, Ada, April, Osazenoriuwa, Farida, Liz, Chisom, Allie, Leggy, Doshima, Fatima, Paige, Frances, Scarlett, Amarachi, Fola, Shania, Brianna, Aiman, Dera, Mayowa, and Tola, to name a few. Thank you for the good, good loving.

To Deba Ede Imafidon. Thank you for preordering more copies of *House Woman* than you would ever read.

To Ukamaka Olisakwe, Nwanne'm. Thank you for the sturdiness of your support.

To Professor Robin Davidson, my creative writing professor at the University of Houston-Downtown. Thank you for the afternoon in your office when you held my gaze and told me I could be an author.

To the authors who read *House Woman* and sang its praises. I am humbled by your kind words.

To my sweet friend, Mansour Al-Hawasy. I miss you dearly. I hope I made you proud.